IRON CIRCLE

JUSTIN JOSCHKO

Month9Books

Trade Paperback ISBN:978-1-948671-35-4
ePub ISBN: 978-1-948671-54-5
Mobipocket ISBN: 978-1-948671-55-2

Published by Month9Books, Raleigh, NC 27609
Cover Designed by Danielle Doolittle
Map illustration by Zachary Schoenbaum

Month9Books

To Baby #3

AMERICA-THAT-WAS

Prairie
Republic

The Middle
Wastes

Republic of
California

Fallowfield •

Visalia
★

Juarez •

Far
Sea

Mejica

La Republique
Du Quebec

La Reine
Noyee ★

Jericho
★

Free State
of Niagara

Vineland
★

New
Canaan

Outer
Baronies

• K City

The New
Confederacy

New
Atlanta
★

Delta
Sea

Galileian
Ocean

IRON
CIRCLE

Part I: Gone South

1: The Pueblo

"Psst! Selena. I see something."

The words filtered down to the murky waters between wakefulness and sleep where Selena had been floating for some time. She surfaced reluctantly, unsealing the sticky film that coated her eyelids. Wan, midmorning sunlight slanted across a haze-heavy sky, cutting through the wagon's slats and casting a grid of dim shadows over her legs. She rose from the flatbed and worked the kinks from her shoulders.

Simon gnawed his lower lip. His fair skin looked especially pale in the hazy light, which seemed to leach color from the landscape even as it illuminated it. He pointed in the direction the wagon was headed. Selena followed his finger to the horizon, where a strip of crenelated reddish-brown rose from the parched yellow-grey of the surrounding earth.

"Your brother has keen eyes," said Marcus from his place on the wagon's perch. They'd had a coachman at one point, but he grew wary of traveling so far south, and it soon became more economical to purchase their own wagon and horses. "The *pueblo* lays a few miles distant yet. We will reach it soon."

Selena rubbed her face, preparing a reply and discarding it as irrelevant. Her brother's eyes were anything but keen. She vividly recalled putting on his glasses in a moment of curiosity, only to see the world dissolve into whorls of borderless color. But she came from Jericho, capital of New Canaan and one of the last true megalopolises of a continent raised by famine and war. And while much technology was lost in the Last War some hundred years before, the New Canaanites still retained machines—and the knowledge to use them—long since vanished from the continent's crumbling middle, and lenses on the coast far surpassed the crude twists of scavenged glass and bent wire known in the heartland. Thinking on this brought along the unpleasant realization that there were things about her life in Jericho she actually missed—a fact she usually managed to club into submission before it could fully rear its unwelcome head. Better to remember the angel ears and trustless glances, the Templars with their truncheons and carbine smiles, the constant flicker of fear that killed with the special cruelty of slow heat, under which hope boiled away like water in a cook pot until the dry metal blackened from the flames. Memories like these made it easier to accept that the home she'd always known was gone forever, that her future, if she had one, lay on the west coast, in the Republic of California, where the final defiant flames of democracy guttered like a windblown candle but had not yet been extinguished.

"Let me guess," said Selena. "Another half-hour barter stop before we move south again?"

"Perhaps quick as that, though it may take longer. I must find my *fiador* and pay my debt. Once this is absolved, we make for the west."

Selena sat up at the news. Heading south had been the only way around the mountains, but as their bulky crenelations receded, the westward paths had begun to tug at her chest, insisting—rightly— that every mile's detour cost her precious time. "And your, whatever you call it—"

"*Fiador*. How you say, bondsman."

"Right. He lives here? I thought you were from Juarez."

"Just so. But Juarez lies many days south, and I have no wish to return. Thorin has men to collect his debts outside the city. It is more efficient this way."

Selena nodded at this fortunate bit of news. Her fingers circled the stub of ragged tissue that had once been her right ear. Scabs clung to the tender flesh, and the whole right side of her head retained an angry reddish glow, but the wound was healing cleanly and the howl of torn skin had been replaced by a maddening but promising itchiness, which tempted her to scratch and scolded her with a stab of pain whenever she gave in. Simon spotted her fidgeting and she pulled her hand away. His expression stung her with its naked sympathy.

"Is it still bad?" he asked.

"Getting better, it's been a lot worse." She shrugged off his concern like a rain-soaked jacket, ignoring the wounded look he gave her.

The *pueblo* crouched to the right of the southward road, a huddle of adobe and salvaged timber. Flecks of sand and grit barbed the wind, lending even gentle breezes a sharp, desiccating quality. Selena squinted against the midday sun and watched for signs of trouble. Things grew wilder in the south. The yellow locust, for all its faults, at least served to hem its dwindling communities together. Bandits who took to its endless swaths of sickly fronds would find no travelers to pillage and few villages to raid. Here, the earth's very barrenness lent it a perverse sort of fecundity, as the locust never came to ravage its meager bounty.

Horses and cattle grazed by the roadside, their haunches thin from anemic forage. Women in serapes of rough-spun fibers rustled through rows of sparse corn, gathering ears in wicker baskets hung around their necks. The rows were wide-set and marred by gaps where the weaker plants had withered. Each living stalk rose from a hillock of soil darker than the surrounding earth, bulwarked by a mound of whatever fertilizer the farmers could scrape together. Fallowfield's farmers had struggled to produce a truly healthy yield, besieged as they were by legions of yellow locust, but their fields seemed a veritable Eden compared to the scraggly acres on display here.

The *pueblo* was little more than a horseshoe of sun-bleached adobe lining a single wend of clay-capped road pockmarked by the hooves of passing cattle. A few merchants hocked bits of scavenge—ragged tarps, tools chipped and rusted to virtual uselessness, hole-riddled linens, dolls with warped and melted faces—from kiosks of salvaged plywood.

Despite these pre-War trappings, the town itself was clearly a new build. The bones of the cities from before the Last War were nowhere in evidence. The merchants' wares likely came from some nearby ruin, an eschar of twisted steel and crumbling concrete too rotten to foster life. They'd passed a number of these on the way south, cities felled by some mighty conflagration that continued to haunt the soil, spitting sickness upon travelers foolish enough to venture inside. The destruction set upon these places was uglier and more absolute than in the Middle Wastes, where cities merely choked as the yellow locust tightened its noose around their necks inch by merciless inch.

Superstition held that the blight that felled the cities clung to the smallest hunks of its debris, and any who carried its plunder would soon succumb to a shivering, anemic death. Selena doubted this was strictly true—the merchants were still alive, after all—but she'd learned that large-scale salvage from the cities was uncommon, and many passers-by eyed the merchants' wares as if they were strange and sickly creatures prone to bite.

Marcus drove the wagon to a dusty plaza, where a wind-powered pump drew gasps of watery air from an exhausted aquifer and into a tarnished stone basin, where it condensed into sparse but drinkable liquid. He unhitched their horse and led it to a dry trough, which he filled with a few splashes of water from their depleted canteen. The horse lowered its head to the splintery basin and lapped at the water. Marcus stroked its mane until it finished drinking and led it to a patch of fenced-in earth functioning as an open-air stable.

Selena chewed the corner of her thumbnail. Below her, Simon

squatted in the corner of the wagon, sketching quick portraits of passersby in the dust with his index finger. The pictures were as minimalist as the medium demanded, little more than two or three squiggling lines, but their suggestion of depth and texture was impressive. She nudged him with her foot.

"I'm gonna go with Marcus when he pays off his debt. I want you to stay in the wagon and keep an eye on our stuff."

Simon glanced skeptically to the front of the wagon, where their dwindling supplies formed a meager pile. "What stuff?"

Selena frowned. "Food and water aren't nothing, Simon. You'd think a month in the Wastes'd teach you that much."

Her fingers drifted to their familiar spot against her thigh and traced the comforting ridges of the data stick in her pocket. She thought of the look on her father's face when he'd given it to her, the calm façade plastered ineffectually over a chasm of fear. It contained key information on a terrible new weapon devised by New Canaan's Diocese of Plague, and Selena's job was to get it to the Republic of California. War between the two states was imminent, and without the sliver of plastic in Selena's pocket, the Republic would fall, and New Canaan would be free to spread its tyranny all the way to the shores of the Far Sea. But even worse, in a strange way, was that her parents' deaths, public and horrible, would be for nothing. They had sacrificed everything they had to ensure the Republic survived. If Selena failed in her quest, she would be failing them as well.

These thoughts churned through her mind, tightening her grip on the data stick. The weight of a continent teetered on its tiny plastic fulcrum, and she felt a flutter of nausea at the thought of how easily it could tip to one side or another. With a twinge of unease, she removed it and slipped it into Simon's palm. Parting with it caused another pang in her belly, but she might get patted down, and such an object would raise uncomfortable questions.

"Keep this on you at all times. Not in the bag. Somewhere a pickpocket couldn't nab it."

"What do you expect me to do if someone tries to take it?"

In answer, Selena reached in her bag and pulled out a pistol. Its slim chrome barrel flashed in the sun like a shark's incisor. She set the gun at Simon's feet. Simon made no move to touch it. It was the same gun Simon had used to save Selena's life, and mortally wound Fallowfield's power-mad Mayor. *Ex-mayor*, thought Selena, schadenfreude glinting like a piece of gaudy costume jewelery.

"There's no bullets left," Simon said, his voice a near-whisper.

"You know that," Selena said, sliding the gun closer to his feet. "They don't."

Sighing, Simon picked up the gun as if handling a large and potentially poisonous insect. He tucked it gingerly in the pocket of his sweater and rumpled the fabric to hide its conspicuous bulge.

Returning to her bag, Selena weighed her own options. They had three guns to their name: Simon's pistol, a sleek automatic given to her by Fallowfield's farmers for her assault on Manor Hill, and a wide-bore revolver she'd plucked from the dead hands of Bernard Templeton, The Mayor's chief enforcer. *Ex-chief enforcer*, smirked that petty, irrepressible voice.

Her pistol had three bullets left in its clip, the revolver two. None of the calibers matched, which made for an agonizing bit of arithmetic. Should she leave them all with Simon? Take the empty one? She was the better shot, and would be wading into unknown waters during the exchange—but she'd also have Marcus with her, who experience showed was better than any gun. She hefted the automatic and chewed her lips with indecision. Frankly, the thought of Simon with a loaded gun worried her more than the thought of him being attacked without one. He might have taken out The Mayor with a pistol, but he was the first to admit that had been more luck than anything, and his obvious anxiety around guns compounded their danger.

In the end, she tucked the automatic into the back of her pants, draped her rough-spun serape overtop of it, and tossed the bag to Simon.

"The one in your pocket's for show. Only go for the revolver if you really have to. Use both hands and aim for the belly. It'll kick like hell, so hold on tight."

"What if I miss?"

Selena considered the question.

"Don't," she suggested and leapt from the wagon.

2: Not So Wise to Trust Small Men

Selena found Marcus in the paddock, dickering in *Mejise* with a bent-backed hostler over the price of feed and tending. The hostler spat in the dirt and smiled at Marcus's entreaty, revealing a half-set of crooked brown teeth. A grey beard, matted with dirt and some kind of topical oil, hung in ropey strands from his chin. He stroked it lazily. Marcus held up a ten Standard note and tore it neatly in half. He handed one of the pieces to the hostler, who spat again through his crumbling teeth, this time with derision, balled the paper in one palm and stuffed it into the pocket of his overalls. Marcus tucked the other half into a pouch beneath his serape and walked away.

"What was that about?"

Marcus threw his hand up in dismissal. "Feh. Just business. He would like to swindle us, this hostler. We shall see if he gets his other half."

"You're about to hand over ten thousand Standard to some crony in a *pueblo*," said Selena, dropping her voice as she named the astronomical figure. "Are you that worried about spending a ten note?"

Marcus sucked his teeth. He treated her to a paternal smile she found particularly infuriating. "We are far from your New Canaan, 'Lena. It is not so wise to trust small men when the bigger men do not stand so close."

Selena rolled her eyes. "Fine. Let's just get you paid up and get out of here."

Her pace quickened, Marcus's languid stroll dragging like a weight on her heels. Winter seemed to advance every instant, the air chilling by imperceptible degrees as the coming snows marched south. If the weather fell hard enough to hold the passes in the foothills, they'd be stuck until spring, their only option to venture farther south and swing round the coast—a lengthy venture she doubted they'd have time for.

They passed the storefront facades of the *pueblo's* lone street, where the road narrowed to a tangle of alleys and covered pathways. Shadows stood shoulder high, segmented by bursts of sunlight. Selena followed Marcus until the path widened into a hidden courtyard where a few men with hollow cheeks and bruised circles under their eyes tossed dice at a clay wall, and a gaunt woman in a dress of moth-chewed lace plied her trade by a broken fountain.

Marcus approached a doorway flanked by burly men in austere black attire. One had a rifle slung over his shoulder, its barrel serrated with rust; the other held a length of pipe loosely between thumb and forefinger. Its sleek length distended at the tip, where a large bolt had been worked into the bore to form a makeshift cudgel. They stood with arms crossed, biceps bulging with swirls of tattoo ink. The gun in Selena's waistband chafed the small of her back. She wondered if bringing it had been a mistake—it certainly wouldn't make for a good impression if she were patted down. But the men at the door merely nodded to Marcus and seemed to pay her no mind at all.

"That was easy," Selena said when the men were out of earshot. "I thought those guys'd be trouble."

"They are not so worried about who comes in," replied Marcus. "More so who comes out."

The first thing Selena noticed was the silence, which was as uncomfortable as it was imperfect. The room gasped with the sort of hushed somberness that snatched at every little sound, magnifying sniffs and coughs and miniscule shifts of posture. Joints cracked, fabric rasped against skin, chairs scraped the tiled floor like swords on bone.

Shadows hung thick from stone pillars. Sunlight slanted through a few narrow windows, but most of the light came from corn oil lanterns dangling from the ceiling by iron chains. Greasy flames hissed and spat from crude wicks. Stone tables bisected the room, at the far side of which sat men in chambray shirts noticeably unrumpled by labor. They were the clothes of businessmen, clean and neatly pressed. Larger men stood farther back, their vestments rougher and more noticeably worn.

Across from the well-dressed men sat peasants of far humbler stock, men and women stunted by toil, their skin cracked and leathery from years in the sun. They hunched at their seats, eyes downcast, and laid their offerings on the table. Juarezian *pesos* and New Canaan Standard mingled with Republic dollars from beyond the mountains and sprinkles of rarer currencies from distant enclaves and city-states. Some shored up their payments with coins from fallen empires or bits of rare metal—chips of gold or silver, pewter goblets, coils of copper wire. Others offered bushels of corn or bottles of cloudy liquor. One motioned to a live chicken tucked under one arm, his free hand stroking the creature's twitching haunches.

The moneylenders studied the proffered wares impassively, counting money into piles or biting coins or holding bits of scavenge up to the light for inspection. When they'd assessed the payment to their satisfaction, they dabbed sleek metal pens into bowls of ink and jotted down itemized lists of the offerings and a total value, checking against amounts owing in a leather-bound ledger. They wrote the final balance twice and slid the papers to the peasants for co-signature. Some scribbled their names in shaking hands, but most drew symbols or made a simple X on the page. The moneylenders tore the sheets in half, handing one back to the peasant and tucking the other into the back of the ledger. One of the burly men would clear the desk while the peasants shuffled away, writs clutched to their chests.

The whole thing proceeded with an orderly bureaucracy that surprised Selena, tinged as she was with the urbanite's prejudice toward the backwoods. She found herself comparing the process with the registries and reportages of Jericho, admiring the efficiencies of her homeland and repulsed by that admiration. Any kind thought about New Canaan emerged from her like pus from a boil, squeezed out with a mixture of relief at its expungement and revulsion that something so vile could have come from inside of her in the first place.

Marcus watched the desks until the center one became free. He approached without invitation and sat across from a thin, bookish man with a bulging forehead and pointy chin. A mustache, its black hairs threaded with bits of grey, sprouted from his upper lip, slickened into two points with styling wax. A flinty, astringent smell rose from his ink-stained hands, unpleasant in its cleanliness. He looked up from his ledger and smiled—a gesture Selena inferred from the deepening wrinkles of his cheeks, for his lips hid beneath the fronds of his mustache.

"Marcus Ramirez," he said. "It's been some time. Three months, if I'm not mistaken." He flipped deftly through his ledger and ran his finger along a column of names etched on its dry pages, clicking his tongue as he worked. "Yes, three months and two days. There will be penalties for your lateness, Marcus."

"Levee as you like, Hector," Marcus replied. "I will make no complaints, for today I feel generous."

Hector's cheeks twitched. Teeth flashed beneath the curtain of his whiskers. "As you like. Do you wish to put down for all three months, or buy back some principal?"

"Not some. All."

Marcus raised the sack he'd dangled nonchalantly at his side and plopped it on the table. The neck came loose, spilling a thin stream of Standard over its bulging belly.

Hector's face grew pale and lineless. He pawed through the bag, making no effort to count it but merely assuring himself that the payload was not some clever bit of trickery. With pursed lips, he gathered up the stray bills, tucked them back in the bag, and pushed it back toward Marcus.

"I can't be guarantor for this, Marcus."

"What are you guaranteeing? The money is there. All of it. The interest too. You need only bring it to Thorin with my compliments."

Hector rapped his fingers on the edge of the table. His mustache twitched from side to side. He shook his head minutely, as if in answer to a question only he could hear. "You should not have done this. It isn't Thorin's wish to be paid back all at once."

Marcus smiled, though Selena spotted an artifice to its angles, as if it were a painting touched up for show. "If Thorin so dislikes my money, he need not take it at all. I would not hold such a slight against him."

"You can ask him yourself."

"Are you not his bondsman, Hector? It is for you to speak with his voice in such matters."

"Not such as these."

Marcus huffed. "Well, if Thorin demands these words from my lips, he shall have them. I will, in this case, need a stay of interest for my travels. Three months should do it."

"Juarez is not so far as this."

"Perhaps, but I have other business that is, how you say, most pressing."

Hector's voice hardened. "No business of yours is more pressing than Thorin's. You are in his debt, and will come and go at his pleasure."

"Thorin has no right to command my movements. I do not wear his brand."

"No, but you wear his debt. It was your intention to shed it outside the bonds of your agreement. By this trespass, he summons you. And you shall obey."

The last wisp of a smile vanished from Marcus's face. "I am not *marcado*, Hector. You do not have the right to keep me in bondage, debtor or no. So says *la paz inquieta*."

Hector shrugged. "We shall see."

He made a small, almost casual gesture with one hand. A trio of burly men emerged from the shadows. The first shouldered a rifle while the second drew a pistol from a leather holster. The third, large and unarmed, merely cracked his knuckles.

Hector made a brief chopping motion with one hand. "No closer. He is quick."

The rifleman's eyes flicked from Marcus to Selena.

"*Y la chica?*"

Hector glanced at Selena as if he'd just noticed her. His long face looked drawn and weary.

"*Traela.*"

Marcus stiffened. "She owes no debt to Thorin. Leave her out of this."

"If you wanted her out of it, you should not have brought her into it."

Throughout the exchange, Selena took in the layout of the room, charting lines of escape or attack. Her conclusions weren't encouraging. She counted nine men on Hector's side, excluding the two just outside the door, plus half a dozen debtors who she highly doubted would raise a hand in her defense. If anything, they might attack in concert with Hector's men, in hopes of currying a little favor. Her eyes moved from man to man, judging capabilities, aggression, likely first moves. The man with the pistol seemed cocky. The bore of his gun sneered in Marcus's direction. The rifleman was more studious, his posture rigid. He kept the rifle pinned between her and Marcus, and a quick pivot of his waist could put either in his sights. The doorway stood thirty feet behind her, a distance that would give either man plenty of time to aim and fire.

Her pistol pressed imploringly at the small of her back. She might gain a second or two by surprise, but she was no gunslinger, and Hector had more men than she had bullets. Even with Marcus on her side, neither fight nor flight seemed a wise course of action. She cursed Hector for his bureaucrat's deceit, Marcus for his fool's bravado—and herself, too, for leaving Simon alone.

Marcus seemed to reach a similar conclusion. His hands worked into fists, long clever fingers bulging with limber muscle. When he next spoke, it was through gritted teeth. "You are making me break a promise, Hector. I will not forget this."

Hector shook his head sadly. "No. I do not suppose you will."

3: Ugly Dreams

The sun thrust down from its noonday perch like the molten head of a branding iron. The cold would creep back soon enough, dragging its shivering misery in tow, but at the moment, Simon almost missed it. He wiped sweat from his forehead and dried his fingers on the seat of his pants. Dust clung to his clammy palms. He cleaned them as best he could and resumed drawing figures in the dirt with his index finger.

Patterns encroached on patterns in a palimpsest of scuffs and etchings, scored smooth by the motion of his fingers. His fingertips left only the barest impressions in the fleeting dust. He wished he had some paper—even a pencil would've been something. He thought of his art supplies, the fresh canvases and horsehair brushes piled in the annex of The Mayor's besieged manor, and sighed.

Traffic on the *pueblo's* main road thickened as the sun reached its zenith. Peasants filtered back from the morning's harvest to seek shelter from the heat of the day. A man with bulbous knuckles and a nose like a malformed root vegetable hauled a cart of corn ears from the fields. Its wheels were oblong and crudely carved from slabs of wood, and their uneven revolutions gave the wagon a lurching, drunken look. Simon felt a spasm of fear as the cart bearer glanced his way, a sharp tang that soured into shame as the peasant carried on, indifferent to the boy's presence. It was pretty pathetic, being scared of a sick old man who could barely lug his meager pickings to market, but that didn't stop Simon recoiling from every passing shoulder that brushed against the wagon, or casual glance tossed his way. Fallowfield had left him shaken and jittery and filled his nights with ugly dreams of death and fire and white teeth grinning madly beneath soulless silver eyes.

A flurry of townsfolk burst from a nearby alley, followed by a procession of large men moving with stiff, purposeful strides. Heading the line was a stoop-necked man with a wide, black mustache. Behind him, mostly obscured by the broad shoulders of his retinue, flickered a familiar pattern of red and black. Simon looked closer and caught a fleeting glimpse of Marcus's face, followed quickly by Selena's.

Simon's breath clotted in his throat. He watched helplessly as the grim parade marched into the neighboring paddock, where they entered a barn and disappeared.

Indecision pinned him in place. Should he follow them? Maybe this was simply part of the repayment process. They could be going to a bank, or getting a witness, or something. A final glance at the procession made this doubtful—people don't get frogmarched like that to a business transaction, surrounded by a bunch of armed overseers. He clutched the wagon's guardrails and squeezed until his fingernails sunk into the wood.

4: A Cornered and Dangerous Animal

The barn was brighter than Selena expected. Thick columns of sunlight pierced the roof, chunks of which had been ripped away by wind and time. A sour tang of manure hung about the straw, though the air was too dry to be truly pungent. It felt stale more than anything, brittle and flavorless as two-day-old bread.

Hector led Selena and Marcus to the far end of the stables, past rows of skinny horses. Their ribs stood out in pronounced corrugations on their chests. Stable hands brushed them down or filled their troughs with cloudy water, pointedly ignoring the procession as they filtered into the backmost stalls.

The animals here were healthier, firm muscle under glossy coats. Three of Hector's attendants began readying the horses while another two approached Selena and Marcus. The first—barrel-chested, a lumpy face distended slightly at the chin and forehead, as if yielding to firm pressure against its cheekbones—pointed a revolver squarely at Marcus's chest. The second held out a hand, palm up. He was wirier than the others, with overlong arms and bow legs that kinked strangely at the knees. A seemingly random assortment of metal piercings glinted in queer constellations on his face—three copper rings through his ear, a spike-tipped stud in his nose, a band of ersatz gold through his cheek.

"Alright, kids. What goodies you got for me? Knives? Knuckle dusters? Hand 'em over." His fingers twiddled.

Selena's eyes skimmed over the room, sifting for escape or leverage. The nearest exit was a small square window set too high up to vault through, the next an open door thirty feet down a straightaway. Sighing, she took out her pistol and presented it to the wiry man, butt first. His eyebrows rose in silent surprise. He took the gun and passed it to his comrade, then reached out once more.

"That's all I've got," said Selena.

"We'll see," the man replied. He patted her down, slapping briskly at her shoulders and slowing at her hips, where his index finger explored the perimeter of her waistband. His hand lingered at her crotch, groping for a weapon that was obviously non-existent. She smelled the rankness of his breath, felt his respiration quicken as it buffeted her cheek. She bit her lip and said nothing, teeth settling in familiar grooves worn from past indignities silently endured.

Eventually, he had his fill and turned to Marcus. He reached out more cautiously this time, as if beckoning to a cornered and dangerous animal.

"I'm gonna need your toadsticker, Marcus."

Marcus's lower lip curled. The whites of his narrowing eyes disappeared into twin portals of darkness.

"You joke, surely."

"No joke," said the barrel-chested man with the gun. "Hand it over."

Marcus withdrew a slender rectangle of glittering chrome cushioned with pads of black crosshatched leather. His thumb caressed a trigger, and an eight-inch blade sprung from the handle.

Hector's men took a step back. The barrel-chested man thrust his pistol out with both hands. Silence clung to every surface, an immense static electricity ready at the slightest nudge to unleash its fatal voltage. Marcus's dark eyes met the other men's one by one, his face smoothed out to a blankness more sinister than rage. The barrel-chested man's finger tightened on the trigger.

Marcus's wrist swiveled and the blade snapped shut. He shouldered the wiry man aside and presented the knife to Hector.

"You will treat this with care," he said.

"Of course, *ese.*"

With that, the venom seemed to drain from Marcus. He slouched back beside Selena, his shoulders slightly hunched, his gaze downcast. He worried the hem of his serape, massaging the roughspun fabric through his fingers.

"If you think pride will keep me from Delgado and Evangelista, you are mistaken. The trinity court will hear of this."

By the tone of Marcus's voice, Selena could tell this statement was meant to hold weight. Yet Hector merely shrugged. "You can tell them what you like. But I don't think you will get much of an answer."

5: Rock Bottom

Occasionally, when duty had brought his parents to inspect the fishing villages along the coast of New Canaan, Simon would be allowed to accompany them. He relished these trips, rare as they were: the hum of the mag-train on its slender track, more felt than heard; the salty tang of the ocean air, a stark contrast to the stink of factory runoff and algae blooms that greased the waters on Jericho's wharves; the contented sigh of space between their tiny houses and along their cobbled roads, smooth vistas where no angel ear could hide in hopes of catching an unpatriotic admission from a hapless Shepherd.

He would spend these mornings strolling along the rocky beaches, searching tidal pools for crabs, tossing pebbles into the sea, or spotting spires piercing the water's surface in the distance, steel tombstones memorializing the drowned cities long since swallowed by the rising sea. On warm days he would even splash about in the water, paddling along the shoreline with his stolid breaststrokes or leaping over the waves as they crashed, pretending they were enemies he would smite with his falling elbows.

Once a riptide caught him, and he found himself dragged into open water too deep to touch bottom. He wasn't in real danger—it was a mild current that lasted only twenty yards, and he was a competent swimmer—but for a moment the frigid waters seemed to congeal in a rime around his heart. His fear at that moment was not of drowning, but of the unseen fathoms that lay beneath him, in which it seemed anything might lurk. The ocean floor—perhaps five feet below the reach of his toes—opened like a set of monstrous jaws, belching forth unspeakable creatures from the hadal depths of his subconscious.

The memory rose to his mind, perfectly crystallized, as he climbed down from the wagon and followed Selena into the paddock. He felt the same portentous dread at approaching the precipice of an unknown and unknowable realm, as if toeing the crumbling edge of some vast cliff, below which yawned a darkness so deep it was tangible. Fallowfield had been strange, but the people had still been, in a way, his people. Many had come from New Canaan once, and the language they spoke was his own.

Peasants eyed him with curiosity, exchanging remarks in their alien language. One came up to him and said something in the southwestern tongue. He knew it for a question by the cadence, but beyond that, he had no idea.

"I'm sorry, I don't… I'm not from here."

He ran off, the peasant still jabbering behind him. *Maybe I'm not allowed in here,* he thought. *Maybe it's against the law.* He pushed on anyway, reasoning that without Selena and Marcus to protect him, he was in as much trouble as he could imagine already.

Selena and Marcus emerged from the barn, surrounded as before by their overseers. Simon ducked down beneath a pile of straw, feeling faintly ludicrous to the peasants on his side of the paddock, who could see him clearly. The men led his sister to a black carriage with barred windows and a stout oak door. They ushered her and Marcus inside, closed the door, and slid an iron band across the doorway. It clacked home with the sound of a judge's gavel.

Simon reached for his pistol, recalling as it settled against his palm that it was unloaded. He'd left the revolver in the wagon with the rest of their things. Apart from the empty pistol and the data stick, he had nothing but the clothes on his back. *Way to be prepared, genius.* He considered bluffing, even rehearsed a few tough-guy lines in his head—each spoken with a gruff, whiskey-tempered gravitas his actual vocal cords could never hope to emulate—before the carriage rolled off with Selena and Marcus inside. A curtain of dust dragged behind them.

A dozen impulses pulled Simon in every direction at once. While he struggled, some deep-buried instinct kept him from crying out to her. This was very bad, but surely drawing attention to himself could only make things worse, so he stood and watched in mute agony as the carriage disappeared along the southerly road.

When the carriage had faded from view, Simon's paralysis left along with it. He scurried from the paddock, fleeing with only the vaguest intent of location or purpose. He ran simply to run, to be gone from the present before its jaws snapped shut around him. He was alone in a strange country with no map and little currency, helpless as a castaway adrift on a bit of wreckage, subject to the absent mercy of the sun and the sea.

He climbed back in the wagon and the rock bottom to which his battered heart had plummeted gave out, plunging him, however impossibly, to lower depths.

The bags were gone.

6: The Uneasy Peace

The darkness didn't surprise Selena, but the noise did. Iron-shod rims crunched and scraped over hardpan while an ungreased axle whined in its socket. Every nick and bump in the road pummeled the carriage's suspension and set its bones to groaning. The stink of rust and congealed oil rose from the floorboards, and light filtered through horizontal slits too narrow to be properly called windows, their slim apertures further blocked by grids of spun wire. Selena and Marcus sat opposite one another on benches suspended from the wall by diagonal lengths of chain. Her hands worked open and shut, by turns making fists and unmaking them in recognition of their futility.

"Well, this sucks," she said.

Marcus accepted the statement with a grim nod. "I am sorry for this, 'Lena. I will set things right."

"You might want to get started on that."

"I am afraid there is little I can do until we reach Juarez. Hector has overstepped, but a *fiador* is law beyond city limits. Delgado and Evangalista can hold him to task, but they are miles away."

"Who are they?"

"Heads of the *pandillas*. Delgado leads *Los Hombres Sencillos*, Evangelista *Las Dagas Negro*. Together, they are two of *La Trinidad*. Thorin is the third."

"So what can the other guys do about it?"

"Even debtors have rights in Juarez. Thorin can recall a debt and require payment in person, but he cannot restrict my movements."

"That Hector guy seems to think otherwise."

Marcus smiled without humor. "Men of the borders can sometimes forget the laws of their homeland. The trinity court will hear my case. Thorin's judge will dismiss it, but the others will see justice done."

"But won't Thorin just do what he wants anyway?"

"Perhaps in some things, but not in this. The moneylender's honor is the bedrock of the city. The other judges will hold firm, and to ignore their judgment would be to invite bloodshed. Such is how rests *la paz inquieta*—the uneasy peace."

Selena's tailbone began to ache from the vibration of the bench. She shifted her weight to one side until the pressure abated. "I don't know how much I'd trust a peace that's got 'uneasy' right in the name."

"All peace is uneasy, Lena. It is better when both parties admit it, yes?"

"Depends. It didn't seem to do much good with Hector."

Marcus smoothed a wrinkle from his serape. "Hector is a bondsman. Such men have much power, but their lives are often short. There is no room for error. I expect he means for me to deliver my full payment to Thorin myself. That way if money should go missing, no blame can be laid at his feet."

"You could have told me that before I went in with you, you know."

Marcus studied his feet. Shame sat strangely on his face, as if wedged into a place where it didn't quite fit. "I did not anticipate this. Perhaps I should have. For that, I am sorry." He looked up, the ever-burning ember of humor in his eyes snuffed out. "When the matter is settled, I shall get you west. This I promise."

Part of her wanted to spit the comment back in his face. She didn't doubt Marcus would make good on his word—her short but eventful tenure as his protégé showed her that the man, despite his faults, had a warped but solid core of integrity—but a man's word mattered little if he lacked the capacity to carry it out. Even if he managed to resolve the situation promptly, the detour had cost them precious time.

Swallowing her anger, she nodded once to Marcus and settled her head against the wall of the carriage. Her thoughts turned from her own predicament to Simon's. The poor kid was on his own again, and this time he didn't have a single person who even spoke his language. Her stomach clenched at the thought of how he might be feeling. Would he think she'd abandoned him?

Of course not, she thought. *He knows I'd never do that.*

Does he? Countered a sly voice somewhere in the deep folds of her mind. *You've done it before, haven't you?*

She thought of that night in Fallowfield, the shots from Bernard's gun slashing through the rapeseed overhead. *I didn't have a choice then. Plus, I came back, didn't I?*

Yes, she'd come back. But she'd also known where to find him when she did. There was no Manor Hill this time where she could trust to find him waiting. He was alone in a tiny *pueblo* with nothing but a few days' supplies to his name. And it was her fault.

With these unhappy thoughts swirling through her mind, she closed her eyes and did her best to make the minutes pass.

7: Dust and Penury

Simon knew the plan was doomed from the moment he passed through the store's crumbling archway. He could see it in the sneer on the shopkeeper's face, in his reflexive grasp for a cudgel near his forearm, in the empty spaces along his shelves where food and supplies should be. He pushed on anyway, driven by the momentum of his initial resolve, which had required several minutes of deep breaths to muster and couldn't be easily dissipated.

A stink of dust and penury choked the stale air. Ignoring it as best he could, Simon smiled and raised a hand in greeting. The shopkeeper's heavy black eyebrows drew into an irritated point in the center of his forehead. Simon went to speak, but a sticky film glued his tongue to the roof of his mouth. He yanked it free with a clammy smack and swished a paltry dose of saliva about his mouth. The words came on his second effort.

"Hi. Um, I'm wondering if you could help me." He spoke slowly, over-enunciating each syllable in the vague hope it would make him more comprehensible.

The shopkeeper continued to scowl but said nothing. Simon put even money on whether or not the man could understand him—and if he did, long odds on him liking what he heard. Still, there seemed little for it but to continue. *At least he hasn't clubbed me yet.*

"It's just that I'm traveling west, and all my stuff's been stolen. I can get by without a lot of it, but I'll need some food and water for the trip. I don't have any money, but I could trade you if you like."

Simon reached in his sweater and pulled out the pistol. He held it loosely by the butt and made sure to point the barrel at the floor, but he may as well have shoved it in the shopkeeper's face for how he reacted. The vengeful point of his eyebrows crumbled to a nervous heap. His ruddy skin paled, putting the flecks of old acne scars in stark relief. His hands scurried away from the cudgel and shot upward, palms presented imploringly outward. Very slowly, he dropped one hand to a small drawer behind the counter and began removing fistfuls of coins and paper currency.

"No, wait," Simon cried, raising his own hands. "That's not what I meant. I want to trade. Trade."

The man set two handfuls on the counter and pushed them toward Simon, motioning at the pile with a shooing gesture. Simon nudged it back with his free hand. In response, the man angrily added another fistful of coins to the pile. Simon squeaked, a sound of mingled frustration and fear.

"I don't want to take your money. I just want some food and

something to carry water. Food. Water." He pointed as he spoke each word, first to a small bushel of mealy apples, then to a tin canteen. "If you give me those, I'll give you the gun. It's good, it works and everything. It just needs ammunition. Deal?"

The shopkeeper's eyes flicked to the cudgel and back. Simon swallowed. The man obviously had no idea what he'd intended with the exchange. If he put the gun down now, the guy would probably take it as Simon losing heart and surrendering. He might wind up getting his brains bashed in, or being frogmarched to some *pueblo* court where he would plead his case in a language no one else in town spoke.

Doing his best to suppress his guilt, Simon found a burlap sack on the shelf and began stuffing it with whatever foods he could eat without preparation: apples, apricots, a few pears with nicked skins, mushy apricots, some dried wriggles of indeterminate meat, and a slab of cheese flecked with mold. He hefted the bag several times, replacing bits where he felt he'd taken too much and adding back when he felt he didn't have enough. Eventually the second-guessing grew unbearable, and he forced himself to accept what he had, adding only the canteen.

The shopkeeper watched the whole exchange, enraged and bemused with equal measure.

Simon gave him a last apologetic look and backed out of the store. He stood outside the doorway for a panicked moment, waiting for the shopkeeper to shout out thief in his strange, sibilant tongue. The word didn't come. Perhaps that shopkeeper feared retribution if he alerted the authorities too soon, or perhaps he thought his cries would be greeted with indifference. Either way, Simon couldn't afford to speculate. He shoved the pistol in his pocket and made his way to the *pueblo's* main road, glancing as inconspicuously as possible over one shoulder with every fifth step.

8: A Jangling of Nails and Knives

Selena was unsure whether she was awake or asleep. Tedium had fused the two into a misshapen whole, a state of semi-somnolence that lay before her like a featureless grey slate. Days and hours grew murky. Time beat instead in the shifting tempo at which her keepers brought her food and water, or changed the rancid bucket she and Marcus used as a chamber pot. She was thus unsure whether Marcus's hand on her shoulder shook her awake, or whether he simply drew her attention from a haze of hibernation.

"We are close, 'Lena. Come."

He brought her to the window and pointed to a sign rising from the sand and scrub grass that had marked their surroundings since leaving the *pueblo*. It stood on a posted of rusty iron, a wooden plank on which some palsied calligrapher had painted the words *Ciudad Nuevo Juarez* in shaky red letters. Selena spoke little of the southwestern tongue, but she'd gleaned enough from her travels with

Marcus to piece together its meaning.

"If this is New Juarez, where's Old Juarez?"

"Some miles east and south, on the far side of the river. It burned in the Last War."

Beyond the sign, the ground rose and flattened into a plateau, where the road grew irregular slabs of flat stone and fed into a sprawling urban center. The place was big—the largest inhabited city she'd seen since leaving New Canaan. Like Fallowfield, it was a new city, its ground untroubled by relics from before the Last War, but where Fallowfield favored the ordered, bucolic simplicity of a farming community with its intersecting thoroughfares and gridded sub-streets, *Nuevo Juarez* sprawled like a thicket on a hillside. Adobe structures piled one atop another. Streets ran in kinks and curves, and alleys diverged at strange angles from the main roads, which swelled at varying intervals into cobbled plazas filled with market stalls. Narrow boardwalks lined the bigger thoroughfares, their dusty planks warbling with the clamber of crowds. Carts and wagons trundled along the streets, carrying loads of produce or mounds of clay or workers bundled tight as cords of wood.

The vendors and merchants dressed in garbs of quiet prosperity, simple cotton shirts free of rips or wear, silk kerchiefs or wide-brimmed hats offering a bit of utilitarian ornamentation.

The workers—those who hauled loads and drove wagons and mucked out stalls for livestock—were a haggard and sun-browned bunch, their bare arms blistered and blotchy and mapped with scars. Their chests and faces bloomed with tattooed symbols. The designs were crude, drawn by hands that were untrained or indifferent despite their focus on a few common motifs: a black triangle, tapering down to a fine point; a single drop of fluid, tinted red; and above all a green star. Selena saw the latter ten times on a short stretch of road. In a few cases, it looked clunky or misshapen, as if superimposed onto a previous image poorly excised.

A fierce-looking man with a shaved head and iron studs in both nostrils bore the most arresting design: a corona of sleek red lines fanning outward from the nexus of his left eye. Arced lines connected each spoke at consistent latitudes, giving the design the appearance of a spider's web.

The carriage slowed its pace and lurched to a halt. A heavy bolt slid home, and the door swung open. Light toppled into the room. Selena squinted against its ruthless brightness. Hands grabbed her wrists and hauled her to her feet. Her fighter's instincts longed to lash out with a right cross, but her muscles were cramped and rusty enough for her better angels—or her more sensible ones, at least—to wrest back control. She went willingly where the hands led her, her head downcast until an awning blunted the sunlight's razor keenness.

The hands—belonging, she now saw, to two of Hector's men—led her through a pointed archway into a dim room with a marble floor, its exact dimensions masked by sultry drapes that hung from its high-domed ceiling. The midday heat vanished, replaced by a crisp, dry air scented with wisps of odd spices. Sticks of aromatic reeds unfurled strands of pale smoke, which mingled with thicker plumes from a fat cigarette dangling from the lips of the room's central occupant.

He sat atop a dais of dried clay painted gold, his chair a piece of pre-War salvage upholstered in various silken fabrics and adorned with jewels. He wore a velvet robe with a flared collar and silver hem, epaulets pluming chin-high from its crimpled shoulders. Rings glittered on every finger, and necklaces hung thick enough to form a sort of gaudy chainmail from collar to navel. He looked like an ignorant peasant boy's idea of a king—an image capped, figuratively and literally, by the crown of polished black metal balanced on his head. Selena glanced at Marcus, wondering how best to react to this absurd man, but his face betrayed none of the sly humor she'd expected. She saw only hate there, buried under a slather of fear.

The strange king eyed Marcus with a smile. "Marcus Ramirez. It's been a long time. How nice of you to venture south."

"It was not my plan, but I am glad it pleases you, *senador* Thorin."

"*Senador* no longer. I am *Jefe* Thorin. I have a new role now, as you can see." He motioned to his throne.

"It suits you," said Marcus.

If Thorin noticed the implicit slight, he gave no sign. "Hector tells me you wish to make a payment against your debt to me."

"Just so. I have acquired every *centavo* I owe you, even to the expected interest. It was in Hector's hands, last I saw it."

"And I delivered it as promised," said Hector. He nodded stiffly to a sack near Thorin's feet.

Thorin motioned to one of his attendants, a wispy boy of fourteen or so with a green star tattooed on one cheek. The boy stepped forward, hand outstretched. Thorin snubbed out his cigarette into the boy's cupped palm. The embers sizzled against his skin. The boy closed his eyes but seemed otherwise indifferent to any discomfort. His smoke extinguished, Thorin hefted the bag onto his lap and surveyed its contents.

"It's in Standard?"

"Yes. Every penny, as they say."

"Something wrong with the *peso*?"

Marcus shrugged. "Standard travels farther, yes? It has never been a problem before."

"Nor is it now. Your payment is accepted. It is not, however, sufficient."

Marcus's mouth shrank into a narrow black line. "If you count it, you will see—"

"I *have* counted it, Marcus. It is a large sum, to be sure. It makes me wonder where a *barrendero* like you scraped together such a fortune. But your debt was to be paid over many years, not in a big lump." He dropped the bag onto the dais and kicked it. "Our schedule was agreed upon on both sides. There are penalties for broken oaths, Marcus."

"For late payment, yes. But who would begrudge being paid back early?"

Thorin flashed his crooked teeth. "I would."

"You cannot refuse to relinquish a debt, *Jefe*." Marcus spoke the word like a curse. "The trinity court will hear of it."

Thorin's laughter hit Selena's ears like ice water. There wasn't a molecule of friendliness in it and only the sourest sort of joy. It was a sound that couldn't be handled without inflicting injury, a jangling of nails and knives.

"Very well. By all means, plead your case."

Thorin clapped his hands. A few moments later a gaunt man in ragged, grease-stained clothing shuffled from behind a velvet curtain. His skin had the loose saggy look of muscle gone slack. Stubble covered his chin in patches of black and grey, and a green star blazed on his right cheek, the skin around it inflamed. He looked at Marcus with eyes drowning in pouches of purple flesh. Marcus held his gaze, jaw slightly agape.

"Manuel?"

The servant gave no sign of recognition. He stood before Thorin with shoulders slumped, his head hanging forward like the bulb of a wilting flower. "Yes, *Jefe?*"

"Fetch Delgado and Evangelista, would you? *Senor* Ramirez wishes to plead his case before the trinity court."

"Yes, *Jefe.*"

He pushed aside one of the drapes to reveal an oak cabinet standing on ornately carved legs—more pre-War scavenge—from which he drew two large jars. He carried them under his withered arms, hugging the smooth glass tight to his chest. Another servant, moving with well-rehearsed ease, set out a pedestal retrieved from behind another bit of drapery. Manuel placed the jars on the pedestal, positioning them at just the right angle to catch a sliver of sunlight and illuminate their contents.

Each jar held a human head floating in some kind of preservative brine—though floating was inapt, as the heads barely fit their containers and had been wedged inside, their faces pressed against the glass. The tight confines gave them a smeared, grotesque look, cheeks collapsing into eye sockets and noses pressed into warty stumps. Selena couldn't discern much of anything about the men from the remains, though Marcus seemed to recognize them without trouble. His complexion, already diminished by days without sunlight, took on the ghostly near-translucence of a cave fish.

Thorin clearly relished this bit of theatre. He stood and took his place beside the pedestal, hands clasped behind his back. "The trinity court is in session, *Senor* Ramirez. Please state your case."

"But ... you cannot ..."

"Times have changed. The triumvirate is no more. The *Hombres* and *Dagas* are all *Hijos* now. Most were happy to join and have assumed positions of honor. Those who did not, like Manuel here... well, they saw the light soon enough, eh?"

He slapped Manuel on the back. The blow was jocular and glancing, but Manuel nearly buckled under its force.

"Your claim is discarded, Marcus. The court is dead. Delgado is dead. Evangelista is dead. There is only me. And you are my dog. When I say bark, you bark. When I say bite, you bite. If you disobey ... well, bad dogs must be put down, no? Though one must not blame the pup alone. The fault often lies with the bitch."

The last bit of flexion seemed to abandon Marcus's joints. He stood as if bound at every inch to a thin steel column. Only his fingers moved, beset by a trembling Selena thought impossible of his steady hands.

Thorin's attention turned to Selena.

"And what to do with this one?"

His eyes crept up and down. Displeasure puckered his lips.

"God's bleeding asshole, woman. Where are your tits? And those shoulders. You're built like a boy."

"Some men like that, *Jefe*," said one of Thorin's attendants, a round-faced man with a scraggle of beard dangling from his chin.

Thorin spat. "Deviants. It's a sad thing when men hold such unhappy appetites. Still, for every man, a taste. Take her."

A guard moved to grab Selena by the shoulder. She broke two of his fingers and flipped him over her back, hurling him into the second man as he charged. His forehead drove square into the second man's gut and they went down in a groaning pile. The fight took her, keening her ears and hewing back the periphery of her vision until the whole room flooded in. At the far edge of her attention, she saw Marcus smile.

It took six more men to subdue her. They pummeled her to submission, splitting the skin above one eye and igniting fresh flames of agony along the ravaged fringes of her wounded ear. A few giggled as they dragged her to Thorin, though they were the nervous giggles of men who skirted death by inches. On each side of her, a man held one of her arms in both of his own, while a third kinked his elbow around her neck. The others stood a few feet back, ready to rush in if necessary, though the fight had left Selena for now. She had a knack for choosing her moments, and this wasn't one of them. She glared at Thorin. Inside her, an infant fear began to wail. She smothered it in its crib.

This show of defiance seemed to amuse Thorin. He laughed and clapped his hands, his rings clacking together like silverware at the start of a rich and bloody feast. "This girl is more a man than you, Manuel! The first to stick her will come away with a stump. No, the Circle's a better place for her. Bring her to Todd and see if he's interested."

Thorin's men came for her again. This time they were prepared. She felt something sharp slide into her arm just below her shoulder. Coldness spread through her body. The room grew dark, the floor slanted abruptly to the right, and a ragged black hole swallowed her up.

9: Scavengers

To think just a few days before, Simon had caught himself missing the cold.

It was with him now, a handsy admirer running its fingers along every inch of exposed skin, panting gusts of rime-flecked wind into his ears, tugging on him with its relentless, smothering embrace. This was no frigid blast of New Canaan winter—the temperature hung well above freezing, while the sparse foliage of the roadside shrubs and the small birds flitting about their branches clung doggedly to autumn. A good jacket and woolen cap would have been plenty. But Simon had neither, only the chambray shirt and cotton pants he'd worn the day he fled The Mayor's manor, plus a crude shawl they'd bartered for on the road. The outfit left him fighting a war of attrition with the weather, and the weather had him hopelessly outgunned. It picked off his body heat degree by exhausted degree, left his face chapped and peeling, filled his bones with ground ice.

As his outside chilled, his insides burned. His empty belly sizzled like a kettle boiled dry, its brittle metal warping under hunger's relentless heat. The canteen dangled from his belt loop, a useless appendage tapping out a ragged march beat on his thigh. He'd drunk its last dregs that morning; the food he'd finished two days before. The provisions he'd taken from the *pueblo* shop, so seemingly bounteous at the outset, had been laughably meager in practice. He'd never realized how much food a person ate in a day. It didn't seem like much when parceled into meals and snacks, but it went fast.

Never before had he felt such hunger, such thirst, such utter exhaustion. Even on his long trek through the Middle Wastes, when Fallowfield had risen from the desert of yellow locust and saved them, he'd never gone a day without at least some small bit of sustenance. Supplies had been meager, dwindling as they went into little more than a handful of mealy fruit or flavorless grain boiled into gruel— but there'd always been *something*. Selena's rationing kept their rations in check, and her bartering ensured they left every outpost or passing merchant with something to show for the encounter. She'd kept them going for months as the road grew worse and the outposts sparser. And here was Simon, alone barely a week and already stumbling onto famine's doorstep. Pathetic. His helplessness filled him with a corrosive blend of disgust and self-pity. Selena was better off without him.

Overcome with exhaustion, Simon slumped against a knuckle of basalt rising from the hardpan. He glanced back the way he'd come and noticed with a pang of despair that he'd lost the road. Not that it was much of a road to begin with, just a few ruts scored into the dirt by passing wagons. At some point, he must have veered to one side or another and carried on unknowingly. God only knew how far he'd strayed.

He cupped his face in his hands and sobbed.

When his eyes ran dry, and his chest ceased its hitching, he hoisted himself upright and perched atop the basalt outcrop to survey his surroundings. He didn't expect to see much. The wilds south of Fallowfield were as barren as the Middle Wastes, spared ransacking by the yellow locust only because there was nothing in the soil worth stealing. Hardpan spread out in every direction like a wrinkled bed sheet. Green-grey shrubs and anemic grasses clung tenuously to the soil, and curtains of emaciated dirt flapped up with every gust of wind. A clutch of old buildings jutted from the ground to the west, crumbling monoliths from the years before the Last War. Simon had ridden past a few of these on their journey south. Hopelessly poisoned places, all of them long since abandoned, their bones picked over by scavengers. Simon would almost certainly find nothing useful there, and could wind up befallen with bone sickness from the pre-War weapons leveled on insurgent towns. To venture all that way with diminished supplies was folly, an act of raw desperation.

And you're just desperate enough to try it, buddy. Sighing at this unfortunate truth, Simon stepped from the rock and began his long trek west.

His departure from the path grew increasingly evident. The southern road on which he'd traveled traced the remnants of an ancient riverbed, the memory of its dried-up waters lingering in the gentle downward slope of the land over which it passed. To the west, the earth had undergone no such leveling, and the crags and chasms grew denser and deeper and higher. Simon found himself clambering over sharp rises or skidding down steep bluffs, his shoes dislodging chunks of old stone and setting off tiny rockslides that heralded his arrival. The ground slept uneasily, and Simon feared his footfalls might cause some cataclysmic awakening—a canyon yawping open beneath his feet, or an avalanche of coarse rock grinding him to a gooey paste in its passing.

The gaps soon grew unbridgeable, the protrusions unclimbable, and Simon found himself taking long detours and struggling to reorient himself. Dust settled over every inch of him. An alkali stink filled his nostrils, which cracked and bled from the desiccating dust. He came upon footprints and followed them with a flicker of hope before realizing they were his own.

Despondent, Simon sat on the ground and found he lacked the energy to stand back up. A profound lethargy seeped into his muscles, dense as molten lead. Hunger squeezed his stomach into a wad of wet, pulpy misery. He clutched his belly and lay in the dust, moaning softly.

When the figure appeared, Simon assumed she was a hallucination. She was certainly strange enough: a girl his age or younger, black hair flowing to her waist in clumpy, matted ribbons. She wore a grey trench coat several sizes too big for her. Crude pockets motleyed its sides from lapel to waist, their bellies bulging with bits of scrap.

A leather satchel dangled from one shoulder. Her eyes hid behind tinted goggles. She studied him with her head cocked to one side, her intentions as opaque as the lenses shrouding her eyes.

"Hey, are you okay?" the apparition asked.

Simon groaned. Talking seemed much too painful, and he felt no real need to engage a product of his misfiring psyche in conversation. The figure approached, the scuff of her soles against the dirt audible in the near-stillness. She squatted next to him, unscrewed the lid from a metal canteen, and offered him a sip. He puckered his lips on reflex, expecting the figure to fade away.

Instead, the apparition pressed the canteen to his mouth—its rim warm and smooth and unquestionably tangible—and drizzled in a swallow of clean, fresh water. He nearly spat it onto the ground in shock. His lips sealed it in at the last second. He coughed into his arm. The girl slapped his back until the coughing subsided and held out the canteen again. Simon took it himself this time, sipping carefully.

"It's good," he rasped, shocked by the gravelly honk that was his voice. Who knew vocal cords could go out of tune so quickly? He cleared his throat, and his next words sounded a little more normal. "Thanks a lot."

He took another swig, longer this time. As his thirst abated, fresh discomforts shouldered in to take its place. He clutched his stomach as a cramp warbled through him and shivered. The girl touched his forehead and chewed the side of her lip.

"We'd better get you warmed up. Come on."

She bent forward and scooped him up in a single neat motion, interlocking her arm with his so they stood shoulder to shoulder. Simon stumbled along beside her, his feet tripping over every rock and crevice. The girl bore his weight easily. Simon marveled at her strength; in his diminished state, it seemed almost superhuman.

They rounded a cap of wind-smoothed stone and came to a rift in the desert's knobbly crust. No more than a fingers-width at its tapered end, it widened as it ran, spreading into a canyon thirty feet across. Simon peered over the edge. The crevice bottomed out after fifty or so feet into a bed of pebbly earth.

"Goin' gets a little tricky here," the girl said. "But we'll take it slow."

Chunks of ballast and granite formed a crude staircase into the rift. Simon would have found it perilous even in peak health, but the girl descended as if down a gentle slope, her stride almost casual. Simon matched her footing as best he could, leaning on her whenever his balance faltered. His stomach sloshed with every surmounted precipice, but they made it down without incident.

Compared to the stone and hardpan that scabbed the higher terrain, the earth at the base of the canyon was rich and spongy. Though a far cry from garden soil, it lacked the desiccated snakeskin texture of the surrounding landscape. This ground had known water and remembered it in its pebbly deposits and soft undulations of clay.

The girl led Simon around a few bulges of stone toward the corner where the two cliff faces intersected. Rocky overhangs blocked the sun and the lower walls tapered inward, leading to a cragged aperture. A gust of chilly air whistled through the gap. Simon eyed the cavern warily.

"Come on," the girl said and led him forward. Too tired to resist, Simon swallowed his unease and walked in step with her.

The tunnel bent this way and that, tracing an ancient subterranean stream. Fractured columns of light lanced through cracks in the ceiling. A dusty, metallic smell filled the air, threaded with acrid whiffs of old smoke. The smoky undertones grew more prominent as Simon, and the girl rounded a final bend and entered a high-ceilinged chamber. A dwindling cookfire burned in a ring of stones, unfurling ribbons of white smoke toward the long, jagged crack snaking across the ceiling. They seemed by the looks of it to be in an extension of the canyon, a narrow appendix where the two cliff tops briefly parted before resuming their intimate tectonic embrace.

An old man sat cross-legged before the fire, turning a spit over its smoldering coals. He turned his head to the girl, revealing a weathered face from which a long hook nose burst like an outcrop of stone. A swath of scar tissue mottled the right half of his face from cheek to chin.

"A visitor," the man said.

"I found him passed out in the flats," the girl explained. "He was heading for the city, near as I can tell."

His gaze floated toward Simon. "You ask him why?"

"Didn't seem right to question him. Best get him warmed up first. Here you go, pal."

She sat him before the fire opposite the old man, drew a sheet of dun cloth from a wicker basket, and draped it over Simon's shoulders. The material was fibrous and itchy, but he cuddled into it regardless, savoring the warmth it lay over his bones. He wrapped it tighter around himself as the girl crossed the cavern to a steel hand pump thrusting up from the pebbly soil. She worked the handle up and down. The fulcrum creaked in its socket with every downswing. After a few pumps, the spout sneezed a jet of water into a tin bucket. She gave a few more measured strokes and water began to pour out more steadily. Simon watched the process closely, partially out of his innate interest in the workings of anything mechanical and partly to avoid making eye contact with the old man, who watched him intently.

The girl returned with the bucket and set it near the cookfire. She dipped her canteen into the water and offered it around, first to Simon and then to the old man. Both drank: Simon eagerly, chugging nearly half the bottle; the old man gingerly, his face pinched and slightly pained. He wiped his mouth and handed the canteen back to the girl.

"Introductions'd be good now, don't you think?" he said. His eyebrows arched solemnly, though a small curl of his lips implied more teasing than admonition. The girl shrugged her bag from her shoulders and plopped on the ground next to him.

"Right, sorry. I'm Emily. This here's my dad, Otis."

The old man frowned. "You didn't even introduce yourself?"

"He was keeled over! What'm I supposed to do, check his brands?"

The old man scratched his scar. "I suppose…"

This exchange slipped by Simon largely unnoticed. His attention fixed on the old man. *That's her dad?* He looked old enough to be her grandfather. Fascination drew his eye, while his painter's instinct found several subtle signs to bolster the claim. He wasn't, on closer inspection, quite as old as he first appeared. His face, though lined with wrinkles, was firm, his skin unblemished with the discolorations of aging. He scratched his neck with his left hand, which lacked an index and middle finger above the first knuckle. The remaining fingers were thick and gnarled, prehensile tree roots.

Emily and Otis stared at Simon expectantly. He felt a moment's panic before realizing he still hadn't told them his name. "I'm Simon. Thanks for your help. I don't think I could've gone any farther on my own."

Otis warmed his hands—one crippled, one whole—over the coals. He wiggled his fingers and resumed turning the spit, tucking his mutilated left hand out of sight beneath the blanket. "If you don't mind me asking, where exactly was it you were goin'?"

Simon sucked his teeth. Life on the road had made him reluctant to hand over even the tiniest scrap of information about himself. But he needed all the help he could get, and while telling strangers where he'd come from could get him in trouble—recent history had taught him that particular lesson—he couldn't see what harm could come from saying where he was going.

"I don't know for sure," he said. "But my first guess is Juarez."

At this, father and daughter looked at one another. Information passed between them wordlessly, conveyed by the subtle semaphore of family. Otis cleared his throat.

"Don't mean no offense, but you ain't equipped to make it twenty wheels with what you got on you. And Juarez is closer to two hundred."

"I know," said Simon. He told them about the incident at the *pueblo*, how his sister and their guide had been taken and his inadvertent robbery. The girl chuckled at this before being silenced by a look from her father. Simon made no mention of where he'd come from nor where he was originally headed, and the pair didn't ask. He sensed curiosity in the girl, but she restrained herself—or else her father's presence did it for her. Since beginning his travels, Simon had grown aware of a de facto code of conduct among travelers that softened the abrasion of personalities constantly bouncing off one another. It was the same etiquette that kept him from asking about the old man's injury, or what the two of them were doing out here in the middle of the badlands.

When he finished his story, Otis clucked his tongue and tugged contemplatively at his septum with thumb and forefinger. "I'm right sorry to hear about your troubles. It's a hard thing, losing family."

"I haven't lost her yet," Simon said, his tone a bit sharper than intended. He studied his knees, spots of warmth blooming on his cheeks.

"Course not, course not. But you've a long way to go, and you ain't gonna get there with nothing but a few cups of water and the shoes on your feet. We'd best get you kitted out, point you in the right direction."

"You'd do that?"

"I don't want you on my conscience, boy. And sendin' you out onto the road without a sack full of provisions'd be good as thumpin' you dead." Otis leaned forward and sniffed the carcass on the spit. Evidently satisfied, he hoisted the shaft from its supporting posts and scraped it onto a tarnished brass pan with a hunting knife. He used his crippled hand for the operation. It handled the blade deftly despite its truncated digits, moving with the adaptive agility of the abnormals displayed in the curio caravans that crisscrossed New Canaan, their glassed-in enclosures stuffed full of armless boys and girls with fingers fused into lobster-like claws. Such unfortunates were common in the east—bred, his parents told him, from the bad air lingering from the Last War—but the government kept them largely out of sight, shunting them to rural workhouses or stowing them in basement hospices to live out their dwindling lives. Except Otis's deformity didn't look like a birth defect. His finger stumps were too abrupt, the borders of his mutilated cheek too well-defined. Simon tore his eyes away as Otis divvied up the meat into three portions, which he served on slates of smooth grey stone. He noticed with a pang that his meal was the biggest: Grace's was a bit smaller, Otis's mere scraps. He urged himself to refuse, to offer back most of the largess, but hunger slapped aside his pride. The first bite exploded with flavor. Simon scarfed it all, not wondering until he was finished what exactly he was eating.

"Thanks," Simon said, wiping his mouth. The words felt pathetically inadequate. "For everything. I really appreciate it."

"Don't mention it. You should probably rest up now. We'll get things sorted tomorrow."

Though bereft of rooms in the traditional sense, the cavern had been parceled into sections by the accumulation and positioning of furniture, most of which appeared to have been built from scavenge. Emily led Simon to an alcove deeper into the cave, where a strip of translucent polyurethane yellowed with age hung from the ceiling, offering a vestige of privacy. A loose assortment of fabrics collected in piles on the floor, resembling nests more than beds in their hodgepodge of textures. Emily took some blankets from one of the piles and laid them neatly on the ground one atop the other until they formed a makeshift mattress. Simon lay on it and squirmed himself into a comfortable position. Its limitations were evident—the layered fabric couldn't entirely mask the pits and nodes brambling the cave floor—but exhaustion plumped them into something resembling heaven. He folded the covers over himself and plunked into sleep like a stone tossed down a well.

Part II: Los Marcados

10: Insulted Flesh

Consciousness returned to Selena in fragments, discrete packets of time that stopped and started with the labored arrhythmia of a dying heart. Scenes played out before her in perfect fidelity, interspersed with fugues of immeasurable length.

She was outside, a dry wind scraping across her cheeks. The hooted exchange of a marketplace rattled the adobe walls of a cobbled courtyard. A crone with a triangle of flesh missing from one nostril poked a bony finger in her mouth and pried her teeth open. Rough fingers held her jaw in place to prevent her biting down. The crone shook her head at an attendant and hobbled off.

She was in a long corridor lit by torchlight, their orange flames spinning webs of light and shadow. Hands gripped her in a dozen places, handling her as one might a piece of furniture. She raised her left fist to strike her nearest porter but found it shackled.

She was on a gurney wheeling over rough stones. Iron rings

pegged her arms and legs down in half a dozen places. Someone threw a switch, and fluorescent light jabbed blindingly into her eyes. She squinted against it until a man's head eclipsed the bulb. A cotton mask obscured his face from the nose down. He held a strange device in one hand. It looked like some sort of weapon, perhaps a compact blowgun built to launch poison darts from a short distance. He fiddled with knobs and fastenings along its slender barrel.

The intermittent drip of her thoughts coalesced into a tiny stream, a rivulet of light and heat and pain trickling down the center of a vast black void. The stream widened into a river, washing away the darkness bit by bit until she emerged from its current, dripping but alive.

She was in a cell carved from naked earth, its rough-hewn walls powdered with dirt. A chain bound her left leg to a post driven deep into the floor. A patch of rug-burn misery sizzled across the left half of her face, stretching from her cheekbone to her eyebrow. Her mouth felt as if it had been scrubbed with steel wool. She coaxed some spit up her throat, sloshed it around her mouth, and spat. A wad of gooey redness splattered the floor.

A glance around her revealed four walls, an iron door, and little else, unless she counted the chain and her clothes. Light poured through two barred windows set high in the back wall. Folding the fingers of her right hand into a composite digit, she probed her body in a dozen places, checking for injuries to bones or deep tissue. She found nothing beyond the standard nicks and bruises—apart from the vast stinging welt on her left cheek, which she knew better than to mess with.

A hollow click sounded in the door's steel belly. It swung outward, admitting a tall, slender man dressed in a suit of thin cotton dyed a charcoal grey. A yellow cravat cinched his collar to his neck. He had the prim bearing of a banker or government envoy, though he moved through the cell with an easy confidence Selena wouldn't expect of a bureaucrat. Propping the door open with one foot, he grabbed a stool and set it down several feet in front of Selena. She eyed the man as he sat down, glanced at the chain around her ankle, and judged she could just about reach him if she sprung. She filed this information away for future reference and met the man's gaze blankly.

The man reached into a pocket and removed a glass vial. He flicked open the stopper and rattled two tiny white pills into his cupped palm. He held these out to Selena with one hand while the other refitted the cap, slipped the vial away, and withdrew a small flask from the breast of his jacket.

"These will help with any pain," he said, shaking his hand invitingly.

Selena's eyes flicked to the pills and back to the man's face. A fine growth of close-cropped hair darkened his jaw. He tossed the pills into his mouth, downed them with a swig from the flask, and wiped his lips on his sleeve. This demonstration complete, he offered Selena another two pills. She reacted just as she had the first time. The man shrugged.

"Suit yourself." He pocketed the pills. "So long as you don't get an infection. You don't get a say about *those* pills, I'm afraid. Not to worry there, though, Alphonso's quite good. I imagine everything's been cleaned." He leaned forward, hands pressed together in ersatz prayer, elbows propped on narrow thighs. "So. I'm told you put quite a hurting on Thorin's thugs. Took over six of them to subdue you. I don't usually make acquisitions on hearsay, but I've got eyes in his circle, and I trust what they see. You're a fighter?"

Selena said nothing. Her face might as well have been carved from the dirt wall behind her. The man's mouth lifted in the same tiny smile.

"You're a fighter alright. Everything's always gotta play hard. I dunno how you stand it. Me, I much prefer the go-along-to-get-along approach. Might be worth trying. Just a thought."

Her stone visage stared back, silent and unchanging.

The man gave a fatalistic shrug. He reached in another pocket and withdrew a drawstring pouch containing a crumbled mixture of tobacco. He sprinkled a few pinches into a curl of paper and worked it into a cigarette.

"You're new here, so let me give you a bit of a rundown. Name's Eric Todd. I'm from away as well. Came here from New Dixie. You know it? Dominion of West Georgia, far side of the Delta Sea."

He struck a match and touched the flame to the tip of his cigarette, which balanced on his lower lip. The flame wicked into the paper as he drew breath. He shook it out and tossed the spent matchstick onto the floor. Twin spirals of smoke curlicued from his nostrils.

"Guess not. Anyway, the New Confederacy don't cotton to slaves anymore—pretty funny, you know the history. But never mind.

Different story here. The *marcado* trade's big business and you've gone and gotten yourself caught up in it. Never mind the whys and wherefores. They don't make much difference, and you don't seem too keen to tell 'em anyhow. Point is, you're now property. Sorry to put it so bluntly, but it's a thought you best get used to, and for some folks it takes a while to sink in.

"Now obviously, this changes some things in your day-to-day, but don't go letting your imagination run away with you to any dark places. Some owners mistreat their property, but I'm not one of 'em. Never saw much point in it. Why collect fine china if you're just gonna smash it to bits? Same is true for people.

"You see, I'm not a pimp or a plantation man. Not at heart, at least. I'm a collector. I see things of a type, and I buy 'em. That's not such a bad attitude, as far as owners go. You probably don't feel that way right now, but give it time. You'll meet the other girls soon enough. They'll set you straight."

He placed his hands on his thighs and boosted himself upright, tugged a few wrinkles from his shirt cuffs, and flicked a mote of dust from his sleeve. He reached into yet another pocket and pulled out two objects, the first of which he tossed at Selena's feet. A single key clattered against its iron keyring.

"For the chain. The door'll be unlocked. Come out whenever you're ready. I expect you'll want to run, so I might as well tell you now that it won't work. You'll be picked up as soon as you reach the nearest town. My sigil's well known, you see."

He hefted the second object he'd taken from his pocket, a small disc of polished metal, and flicked it like a large coin. It landed in a puff of dust next to the keys. He tipped an imaginary hat and left, closing the door softly behind him.

Selena scooted forward, the links of her chain jangling, and grabbed the metal disc. It was surprisingly light, made not of steel but of some chintzy metal alloy too insubstantial to serve as a weapon. Its edges were rounded, negating any use as a cutting tool. She held the object to the light dribbling through the nearest window and caught sight of her reflection, which answered in a stroke two of her many questions:

What the man had meant by sigil, and why her face stung.

Bright blue slashes marked her cheek and forehead. She took them at first glance to be wounds succumbing to some unknown infection, but a closer look found the skin, though raw and slightly inflamed, was unbroken. They weren't wounds at all, but tattoos of two sleek blue arches tapered to points on both ends, curving downward in parallel on either side of her left eye—the upper arc above the eyebrow, the lower tracing the cheekbone. She ran her fingers along their paths and studied her hand, as if expecting the blue ink to have leeched into her fingertips. They brought back nothing, no blood, no blue dye.

She observed her face a while longer, absorbing the depth of the affront foisted upon her. It wasn't the marks themselves that bothered her. She had marks aplenty already, the knot of insulted flesh that was once her right ear not the least of them. But those were scars, and scars were earned. A tattoo was different. A tattoo was vandalism.

She hurled the circlet of reflective metal at the wall. The thin plink it made as it struck its target was deeply unsatisfying. She wanted to break something, but everything in the room seemed unbreakable by design. Even the stool, which Eric Todd had neglected to take with him, was of stout construction, a squatting thick-limbed thing carved from a single chunk of hardwood. She kicked it anyway, sending it skittering against the wall with a din more viscerally appealing than the metal disc, but just as fruitless.

Her rage momentarily blunted, she slipped the key into the chain around her ankle and was surprised when it turned easily. There seemed no further use to the key so she threw this too, though she could summon no real malice behind the gesture and the key clanked down before it reached the wall. Her aggression, unspent, soured into lethargy. She slouched from the room, hoping to find someone to hit.

An opportunity presented itself just outside the door, though Selena had no cause to pursue it. A young woman leaned against the wall opposite her chamber, thick arms crossed over a wide chest. She wore a leather jerkin and pants sewn from strips of weathered hide, both garments the washed-out brownish no-color of the cavernous hallway. A chain of baubles—tiny dolls knit from spun hair and bits of salvaged plastic—hung around her neck in a spasm of color, as if to make up from the plainness of her dress. Her hair had been knitted into sleek tubes threaded with bits of colorful string. The tendrils flowed toward a single nexus at the back of her head, where a strip of rawhide choked them into a common stream. Twin lines like blue claw marks marred her cheek and forehead. They were identical in shape to those on Selena's face but a lighter, greener shade of blue, perhaps to better contrast with her mahogany skin.

"So, you met Mr. Todd, huh?" she said, by way of introduction. "He's a bastard. But less of a bastard than all the others. My name's Mary Catherine. The girls call me Mary."

She extended her hand and Selena shook it. Her palm was dry and rough with calluses, her grip firm. They pumped hands up and down for a moment, an awkward pause stretching between them.

"You got a name?" Mary prompted. Selena felt a twinge of guilt at her impoliteness.

"Selena."

"Silent Selena, huh? Well, that's okay. They call me Mouthy Mary sometimes, so the contrast works nicely. Who picked you up? Harriers? You from one of the factions, or were you just on a trader's caravan with shit luck?"

"It's complicated."

"Well, it just got a whole lot simpler for you, so there's that. C'mon, let me show you around." Mary walked off, assuming Selena would follow. After a moment's hesitation, and for want of other options, she did.

Mary issued a steady stream of commentary as they walked, offering a desultory description of life in Juarez. "Todd's got two kinds of girls: bruisers and beauties. You're a bruiser if I ever saw one. No offense."

"I'd be more offended if you called me a beauty."

Mary laughed. "Fair enough. I'm a bruiser too, in case you couldn't guess. It's the better gig of the two, in my humble opinion—but I'm guessing the beauties feel the same about theirs, so it all works out in the end. You speak *Mejise*?"

"No."

Mary tisked through closed teeth. "Pity. But you'll get by. A few of the girls speak *Llanures* okay, and I can always translate for the others until you pick it up."

"*Llanures?*"

"You know, plains talk. What we're speaking now."

Selena pursed her lips. She'd never heard the term plains talk before, but when she moved to correct Mary, she realized that she had no satisfactory word for her own language. There'd been no need for one in New Canaan, where inflection varied between Salter and Seraphim, but the same tongue was shared by all. She felt at once repulsed by and drawn to this strange lacuna, poked it the way a tongue probes the gap left by a missing tooth.

They ascended a staircase and emerged into a small courtyard. A broken fountain with a dry, cracked basin leaned atop a stumpy pedestal. The fountain's original subject, a granite angel whose lips puckered to spout a playful jet of water, had been knocked down and cast aside. It lay in several fragments beneath the fountain's bulbous underside.

In the angel's place stood a robed figure cobbled together from bits of wood and ceramic, its head a grinning human skull. It clutched a scythe in one twine and wire hand, while the other held a dried gourd painted in blotches of brown and blue. A host of candles slouched half-melted at its feet, while offerings filled the basin below: coins, beads, baubles, flower heads pressed into delicate crowns, poppets made from twigs intricately wound together, bundles of dried herbs bound with string.

As Selena and Mary walked past, an old woman hobbled to the altar. She knelt and uttered a prayer, her eyes shut tight with devotion. A palsied hand drew a copper coin from a pouch and set it reverently atop the pile. The woman stood and wiped a tear from her wrinkle cheek before carrying on her way.

Mary led Selena through an onion-domed archway onto a cobbled thoroughfare. Wooden boardwalks lined it on both sides, their planks warbling beneath the steady footfalls of pedestrians. Relics of bone and metal hung over nearly every doorway, adding splashes of texture to the otherwise flat adobe. Men in ragged clothes stood before thin-legged tables, hawking skulls or bits of crude taxidermy. A dozen rattlesnakes fanned across one display like a selection of fine leather belts. The proprietor cast a showman's inviting hand over the wares and winked at Selena knowingly.

"This here's *Calle de Jefes,* the main drag. Most of what you're after you can get here. Go where you want on your free time, so long as you stay in town. Don't try a runner. Every peon in every town in a hundred wheels knows all the major marks, and none of them are stupid enough to harbor anyone who's got one." She tapped the tattoo on her face. "They'll spot this beauty right here and turn you in quick as anything. Harborers get hanged."

"You ever try it?"

Mary snorted. "Please. Runners are for captures. Girls born into it got more sense."

"You were born a slave?"

"It's *marcada*. Calling someone a slave around here is a good way to get punched."

"Sorry. You were born *marcada*, then? Your parents were the same?" Selena found this thought particularly horrific. Being taken prisoner as an adult was bad enough. What chance did a newborn have?

Mary seesawed her hand back and forth. "Not exactly. Me, I was a ward to a plantation family. The Montenegros." She spat the name as if it were something bitter she'd dislodged from between her teeth. "All the joy of bein' a *marcada*, but you get to call your keepers ma and pa. Fuckers treated me like dirt. Scrubbing floors, doing laundry, brushing the tangles out of their shitty kids' hair. Still, I was a citizen, which meant I was outta there at eighteen. Figured I could hack it 'til then, when I was still a kid. Then I grew tits, and Papa Montenegro started getting handsy."

Selena shuddered. "You fight him?"

"Nah. I poisoned him. Wife and kiddies too. Put arsenic in the sugar dish. Wards weren't allowed sugar, you see. Too expensive." She flashed a lupine smile. "Mr. Todd bought my way outta the gallows and gave me my stripes. There's another perk of bein' a plantation ward for you—no *marcado* or *marcada* who raised a hand to her master'd ever get out of it alive, I don't care *who* was payin' their way.

Still, could've been worse."

"Could've been better, too."

Mary shrugged. "Better's a mug's game. You'll drive yourself nuts with it. Time's better spent steerin' clear of worse."

Calle de Jefes widened into a diamond-shaped plaza. More vendors like the ones they'd passed dotted its fringes, the larger ones cloistered in booths or backed by makeshift trellises hung with garlands of skulls and pelts. At the center of the plaza was a raised platform on which half a dozen men stood naked, their sagging skin mapped with faded tattoos. A series of chains bound each man to his neighbor by the ankles. Their genitals drooped like lilacs in parched soil. They exhibited neither shame nor pride in their nudity, but rather a bovine indifference that Selena found more disturbing.

Apart from the naked men stood a man in black and yellow robes. He orated rapidly in the Juarezian tongue—*Mejise*, Mary had called it—while motioning to the captives on his right, his lower half obscured by a podium jutting from the stage floor. A crowd of onlookers pressed toward the platform on three sides. Occasionally one of them would bark something at the orator, who would point at the speaker and continue his flood of verbiage unabated. The process continued until the orator struck the podium with a gavel.

A plump man waddled onto the stage. A spiral of gold threaded the outer ridge of his ear from helix to earlobe, and diamond studs formed tiny horns atop each eyebrow. He pushed an index finger into one man's mouth, pulled down his lower jaw, and peered inside. Satisfied, he led the daisy chain to the back of the stage for further inspection while a fresh lot shuffled into place, this one an assortment of men and women. Selena looked away and was grateful when Mary led her down a side street, and the stage fell out of view.

They came to a long low building near the center of town. Its walls curved upward to a rounded roof, which couple with its rounded porthole windows gave it the appearance of a half-submerged submarine.

Inside, the building was spartanly furnished but lighter than Selena expected, its portholes admitting crisscrossed shafts of light. A single room made up most of the interior, though a door set in the far wall hinted at more private chambers. Beds lined either wall. Selena counted fourteen, all of uniform manufacture, slim iron frames ribbed with wooden slats beneath thin, lumpy mattresses. The standard issue extended no farther, and each station was ornamented with various personal effects. Crates and stacked lumber served as makeshift nightstands, and several beds sported quilts sewn from bits of stray fabric. The room was spare apart for these assembled possessions, with one notable exception: in the far corner, opposite the wash basin, stood an altar garlanded with coins and candles and wreaths of dried flowers, above these offers stood a skeletal figure much like the one Selena had seen in the courtyard earlier.

Two girls sat across from one another on the foot of their beds, leaning into a conspiracy of giggles. They were Mary's opposite in terms of build, with slight shoulders and round hips and long shapely legs. Todd's sigil bracketed their left eyes, though the arcs appeared smoother and lighter than Selena's. They shot Mary a brief glance of acknowledgment before continuing their conversation, then gazed with more interest when they noticed Selena standing beside her.

Mary spoke to the girls in *Mejise*—Selena recognized her name among the thicket of foreign syllables, so she assumed she was getting an introduction—before switching back to her native tongue.

"This is Eleanor and Theodora. Remember what I was telling you about beauties and bruisers? Well, my girls here are beauties in a nutshell."

The girls rolled their eyes but didn't protest Mary's statement. Not that there was much to protest; the girls were indeed beautiful, their fine bones and soft skin as out of place in this chapped and ugly city as orchids in an ash pit.

"Please to meet you," said Theodora, her voice smoky with sibilance. She was the darker of the two, her skin a faded umber, her long hair lightly kinked. Eleanor—fairer-skinned, her narrow arms folded with oscine delicacy—merely nodded.

"I'd expected more of a crowd," said Mary. "Where is everybody?"

"Mr. Todd having the party for planter families. He wanted his girls to serve the drinks."

"What, even the Princess?"

Theodora's smile suggested Princess was more insult than honorific. "You think Todd keep his prize pearl locked in some drawer?"

"I'm surprised she went, is all." Mary scratched the back of her head. "How'd you two get out of it, anyway?"

"We have a match," said Theodora.

71

Selena looked from one girl to the other. She couldn't imagine what sort of match these two could participate in. Surely, they weren't fighters—they had the bearing of porcelain figurines, bits of meticulous sculpture that would crumble under brusque handling. They looked a few years older than Selena, yet she thought of them as girls, not women, the latter term too load-bearing for such fragile materials. Selena didn't think often of her looks, but at that moment she felt acutely aware of her missing right ear, the grease-dulled yellow licks of her unshorn hair, the scuffed shell of grime that callused her arms from finger to elbow. Her self-consciousness prickled. She curled inside it like a hedgehog behind its quills.

"Good timing. We can show Selena here your work."

Theodora clucked her tongue. "She is more in your line, no?"

"She'll see me soon enough. Still important to get the whole picture."

"She will get it today," said a voice in the doorway. It spoke in soft tones but its timbre was abrasive. It sounded the way metal tasted, harsh and sour.

The speaker stepped into view. He was a small, trim man in a suit of impossible antiquity, its once black fibers faded to a thin incorporeal grey. His head was bald and smooth as a river stone, his jaw a slab of basalt fused to its bottom. He regarded Mary with his left eye only, as his right was little more than a sightless blotch of yellow-white fluid.

"Well hey there, Trejo," said Mary. "Boss didn't invite you to his party, I guess. Bit rude, wasn't it?"

"Perhaps if I were not needed as babysitter, I could attend such functions. Thea, Ellay, your show begins. You should be dressed by now. Cat, you will show the new girl to the bench and get on your own gear. You shall also fight today."

"Thanks for the notice," Mary grumbled.

"Speak to Mr. Todd. I can only tell you what I know when I know it. Thea and Ellay perform at third chime. Your match is at fourth. Do not be late." With this pronouncement he left, the clack of his hard-soled shoes receding. Mary spat on the place where he'd stood.

"Asshole," she muttered. She shrugged aside her annoyance, as if shifting a burden to a more comfortable position, and turned to Selena. "Well, we should get a move on. Second chime was a while back. Come on. It's time to show you the Iron Circle."

11: Fresher Parts

The room was full of cobwebs.

They covered everything, thick strands binding chair to desk and desk to wall, drooping from the weight of dirt and dead flies. Curtains of pale silk choked the wan light dribbling through the windows, wringing out every quanta of warmth and color until only a dirty grey residue remained.

Simon leaped from his chair with disgust, shuddering as the silken threads gave way with a wet tearing sound. He stumbled, braced himself on the desk. His fingers sank into half an inch of pale, stringy moss. He recoiled, arms held stiffly out to avoid accidentally brushing his tainted fingers against a yet unsullied bit of skin.

Where am I? But even as the question surfaced, he knew. This was The Mayor's office, far larger than he remembered it, distant walls vanishing into a fog of grey-white webbing. He strained his eyes against the mist, and it accommodatingly parted, revealing a shadow play embroidered with gashes of garish color—reds mostly, and the glitter of silver and gold. The door opened and Selena charged into the room. She wore the trim grey dress and leather shoes of the Seraphim, New Canaan's ruling caste. On her breast sat the empire's emblem, a white cross within a garland of green thorns. Simon opened his mouth to call her name, but all that escaped was a click.

A second figure formed behind Selena, oozing from the shadows and coalescing into a beastly shape with quicksilver eyes. It loomed over her with fingers outstretched. They were long and slender and cruel, and from their tips dripped death.

Simon yanked open a desk drawer, revealing a silver revolver atop a velvet pad. He grabbed the gun, raised it. It seemed to exist in a different atmosphere, one with the viscosity of rancid syrup. He steadied the gun with both hands and fired.

The expected roar of the shot never came. Instead, there was a shrill creak, the protest of rusty metal. He pulled the trigger a second time, a third, each time praying the cylinder would settle on a loaded chamber and each time sounding the squeal of dying hinges.

Simon awoke with a jolt. A glaze of sweat covered him from chest to ankle. He kicked off his blanket and fumbled for his glasses. His finger met glass, and he slipped them on. Vague blotches resolved to a crystalline image. He never felt wholly awake until he had his glasses on, as if the fault in his vision lay not in his cornea but his consciousness, the swimmy blurs he saw a residue of dreams.

He left the alcove and entered the main part of the cave. Emily stood at the hand pump, working the lever with broad, forceful strokes. Damp air gasped from the spigot, flecked with dewy bits of moisture scarcely large enough to survive the brief downward trip into the bucket without evaporating. Eventually, she gave up the effort and inspected the bucket's contents. It was less than half full. She noticed Simon and nodded a distracted greeting.

"Need any help?" he asked.

"Not much we can do. Pump's spent 'til the aquifer fills back up."

Simon chewed his upper lip. Her frustration, though not directed at him, made him uncomfortable. "Well, at least you got something to drink for now."

"It's not for me," she said and walked off. Simon wasn't sure if he was supposed to follow. After a moment's pause, he did.

They emerged from the cave into the murky grey-brown light of an overcast midmorning sky. The earth formed a path where frequent footsteps had trodden it flat, and they followed it to a gap in the canyon's right wall, where the caprices of a long-dead river had carved a basin in the alkaline earth. The slow accumulation of minerals had lent the basin's soil a loamy, porous quality absent in the rest of the arroyo. From this earth rose a collection of crops—mostly corn and beans and some sort of gourd, though there were other plants Simon couldn't identify.

Emily poured the bucket over the front-most row. Water trickled through a guard affixed to the lip of the bucket, which funneled the flow through a narrow spigot. She worked in increments, meting out hydration dribble by dribble. When the spigot ran dry, she upended the bucket over the unquenched soil, tapping its bottom to dislodge any stubborn droplets from its riveted seam. She swung the bucket idly by its handle and studied the ground. The dark patches of wet earth were already drying.

"How many trips have you made out here today?"

"This was my fourth."

Simon whistled. "How will you ever get enough out of one bucket to water all this?"

"I won't. Look." She walked Simon around the front row and into the field. The ground grew drier as it went, tufts of greyish loam crumbling to tan clumps of dust and clay. The stalks of corn rising from them looked wan and brittle, wilting leaves hiding vestigial ears of inedible grain. Bushes hung limply from defeated shoots, their leaves dust-dry and crumbling. The few bean pods that had managed to grow were black and withered. The desolation was nearly absolute. Of the crops Simon could see, all but ten percent or so were doomed if they didn't get a decent watering soon. Even those plants that had received their share bore the parched, concave-cheeked countenance of famine victims.

"I don't get it. How'd they grow in the first place?"

Emily motioned to a squat steel box at the far end of the field. One of its panels lay in the dirt nearby. A pair of legs jutted from the exposed chassis. Their knees bent, and Otis emerged from the box. Dirt and grease marked his upper body like hastily applied war paint. He wiped his forehead and tossed a wrench at the ground. The earth absorbed the blow with barely a sound.

"God damn this piece of shit," he growled. He noticed Simon and tamped down his frustration, his lips pursed with poorly concealed embarrassment. He picked up the wrench and wiped it off with a cloth.

"What is that?" Simon asked. He peered into the metal aperture, performed a quick survey of the parts it contained. The circuitry was fairly simple, a few strips of silicon capsuled in plastic casing. Wires linked the disparate components in a tangled loop around a column of copper eight inches in diameter. The central pipe rose from the earth directly, while the rest of the box sat on a foundation of gravel and chipped stone. "An irrigation pump?"

Otis arched an eyebrow. "Good guess. She gave out a few weeks ago. No way to get the crops enough water without her."

Simon hunkered down on the balls of his feet to afford a better view. "Did you build this?"

Otis gave a bitter laugh. "I can't even fix the damn thing."

Simon leaned into the chassis, hoping to spot an easy fix—a loose screw or torn wire. He traced the connections from the motor to the bank of photovoltaic cells on the pump's flat roof. The connections seemed solid. He ran his thumb along the solar panel's translucent membrane, checking for accumulated dust that might inhibit light absorption. His thumb came back clean.

Gripping the exposed chassis for leverage, he wriggled inside. It was tough to inspect the smaller components without an electric light. He slid the faceplate from the largest circuit board, wincing as the brittle plastic nearly snapped from the pressure. Age had ossified its once-supple molecular bonds, rendering them fragile as glass. He ran his finger along the circuit's copper tracings, expecting to peel back a curtain of dust. Instead, his fingers came back damp and tacky. A moist film collected under his fingernail. He held the substance under his nose. It smelled sour and metallic. A few more actions confirmed his suspicions.

He emerged from the pump. Emily and Otis stood over him, their faces pinched and grim. Simon ran his tongue along the front of his teeth and gave his diagnosis.

"The gasket at the top of the inflow pipe's got a leak in it. It was pretty small, but water got into the circuit board and corroded everything."

"So does that mean it's toast?" Emily said. She squeezed Otis' hand. He squeezed back silently.

"The circuit board is, yeah. Maybe not the rest of it." Simon rubbed his chin. "Can you tell me exactly how the pump worked? Not in a technical way or anything, but just how you turned it on, how long it ran for, that sort of stuff."

"I never had to do anything to it," said Otis. "It was runnin' when we moved in here. The folks farmed this valley before us musta done it. Woulda been during the Last War, is my guess. They were long gone when we showed up. The field was still here, though. Overgrown and full of yucca and creosote, but healthy as anything. We hoed out the weeds and sowed the good crops and tended it ever since."

"Did it run the same time every day?"

"No, it could come on any time. It seemed to know when the soil was getting dry."

Simon nodded. "That part could be tough to repair. But if the compressor works and the power works, then all you really need is some rewiring. It wouldn't be automatic anymore, but you could switch it on manually when the soil gets dry and switch it off once it's moist again."

"And you can do that?" Emily asked. She looked at him with something like awe. Simon chewed his lips and drew a few quick patterns in the dirt with the toe of one shoe.

"I think so. But the stuff in there's pretty rusted up. I'd need some fresher parts, and those can be hard to get."

Emily and Otis exchanged a glance. Almost imperceptibly, Otis nodded.

"I can get you what you need," Emily said.

12: Cheap and Strong

The bar was dim from the moment Marcus stepped through the door, and it only got dimmer the farther inside he went.

This suited him fine.

Shards of anemic, dust-flecked light jabbed through its front windows—empty frames lined with the jagged remnants of panes long since shattered. They faced the far wall of a narrow alley, and the light that passed through them had already been battered by bends and forks and mounds of trash that marked the alley's winding path, leaving little more than splinters of luminescence to pierce the bar's dank interior. Their penetration was scarcely subcutaneous, and as Marcus descended, his eyes switched gears to the wispy orange glow of tallow candles smoldering in hammocks of broken crockery. Cobwebs of smoke dangled from the ceiling, their stinging strands catching on Marcus's face and forcing his eyes into slits.

A dented piece of reflective metal hung behind the bar, collecting scraps of residual light and sprinkling them over the assembled bottles.

A woman in a leather jerkin stood behind the counter, exchanging chitchat with a trio of drunks whose positions on their stools were at various degrees of precariousness. The barkeep spoke with easy banter, though her hand was never more than a foot away from a short steel rod she kept half-hidden in a lip at the countertop's edge. It was nearly invisible in the bar's crepuscular glow, but Marcus's eyes were well-honed, and they spotted it effortlessly. He could scarcely fault her for her prudence, as the slab of meat she'd hired as a bouncer was slumped at the end of the counter, his wages pouring down his gullet as if out the bottom of a hole-ridden bucket.

He flagged down the barkeep and ordered a bottle.

"Of what?" the barkeep asked.

"Does it matter?"

The barkeep handed over a scratched-up glass vessel with a V-shaped chink in its lip. The bottle was unlabeled, its contents clear and anonymous. Marcus swigged it until it burned too much to continue—a state achieved with acceptable promptness. He pulled a handful of *pesos* from his serape and thrust them into her hand. She took the money and offered him an empty glass. He waved it away.

Marcus exchanged a few hollow pleasantries with revelers on his way to the backmost table. He was almost surprised to find himself addressed and responding in *Mejise*, a language he'd spoken most of his life but that felt more than ever like a foreign tongue.

Securely nestled between columns of wood and shadow, he began absolving the bottle of its sinful contents—a task he set about with diligence and determination. When it was done, he set the bottle aside and took stock of his drunkenness. It was, to his mind, inadequate. Likely the bottle had been watered down, its caustic effects drawn from cheaper, non-intoxicating additives that left him with a sour belly and an unfortunately robust sobriety. Without alcohol's beguiling aegis, he had no choice but to think of his predicament

Of the *Jefes* who ran Juarez, why was it Thorin who'd had to grab power? Why not Delgado, who wielded his authority with something like justice? Or Evangelista—a canny kleptocrat, perhaps, but one too set in his ways to unweave the status quo. Thorin's coup was the worst possible outcome—but also, Marcus saw in retrospect, the likeliest one, perhaps even the only one possible. Delgado and Evangelista had held the edge in strength and numbers, but it was always Thorin who'd been the most ruthless. Unencumbered by empathy, his mind could move with a viper's stealth and speed, slithering through cracks in the unspoken agreements the other *Jefes* considered impenetrable.

Ironically, it was these qualities that drew Marcus to Thorin in the first place, to seek his services as a lender where the other, more conservative *Jefes* would balk. It was a decision that, when recalled, still left him aghast at its reckless stupidity. He'd known Thorin's word was worth less than the rancid air in which it sounded, but he'd counted on the *Trinidad* to keep the man's venal caprices in check. In so doing, he'd sold his foolish self into slavery without even knowing it. Usury was one thing, but how could one free oneself from debt bondage when the man who held that debt wouldn't accept payment? So long as Thorin was in power, Marcus was as good as *marcado*. Unbranded, perhaps, but no less owned.

Marcus knew someone was coming several seconds before they arrived at his table. Inebriation could make him fumble-fingered, but it couldn't sheath the ever-drawn blade of his awareness—and he was far from inebriated anyhow. His left hand slipped silently beneath his serape while his right lay by the bottle in a loose C-shape, a casual posture that could morph it into a cudgel in a single neat swipe.

The figure scraped a chair over the floorboards, drawing four parallel lines in the straw strewn about as a prophylactic against spills and vomit and—on more colorful nights—blood. Strings of greasy black hair dangled over his forehead. Sunken, yellow cheeks revealed the contours of his skull, and sores studded the outline of his smiling lips. He wore a dustcoat several sizes too big for him, its hem filthy from dragging over miles of hardpan.

"Welcome home, *primo*," the man said. "If I can call you that. Two days, and I have to hear about it from some dickhead *pandilleros*."

"It's hardly been two days," Marcus retorted. "Besides, I've been busy." His eyes flicked to the bottle, back to the man's.

The two men laughed. There was genuine warmth in the sound, though it lay atop a much greater coldness, the embers of a campfire lit on the tundra. Marcus's smile soon wilted from the chill. "What's happened to you, Emilio? You look terrible."

"You should find yourself a mirror, *calaca*, before you tell me about looks." Emilio's smile invited Marcus to share the joke but received nothing in reply. He glanced to the floor, his tongue probing at the sores on his lips. "These are lean times. Especially for the trade."

Marcus nodded. Emilio's trade wasn't an easy one, and its

practitioners felt booms and busts as keenly as more orthodox tradesmen. Pickpockets may have little to fear from the constabulary—a neutered organization of overgrown watchmen even before Thorin's tenure—but their "clients" could be rough indeed.

"Leaner times I can't recall." Marcus batted the bottle back and forth. It glided on a cushion of spillage, leaving comet tails of moisture. "If it's money you're after, I don't—"

"Please." Emilio held up his hand. "I know what happened."

"How?"

Emilio shifted in his seat. "It doesn't matter. This isn't about money."

"How do you know what happened, Emilio?"

"Thorin's men are crowing about it, and he's done nothing to dissuade them. They say you're his dog, that you tried to buy your own freedom with a girl from the north."

Marcus's grip tightened around the bottle. He forced his fingers to loosen before they crushed the glass and cut themselves to ribbons. "My freedom was never sold. I was a debtor, not *marcado*."

"You think I don't know that?"

Marcus felt as if someone had used his guts as a tourniquet. There was no graver insult to a free fighter than to be called *marcado*, yet even this insult Marcus could bear. But to accuse him of offering Selena as barter, that was unforgivable. It was an abhorrent charge.

Is that why it chafes you so, whispered a voice. *Or is it simply a bit too close to the truth? It is because of you she is in the pits, is it not?*

The spindle in his belly gave another savage turn. Emilio laid his fingers on the back of Marcus's hand, beckoning him back from the darkest caverns of his memory.

"I'm not here seeking money. I didn't come to tell you about Thorin's nasty little rumors either—had hoped not to, in fact, though you'd've heard of them soon enough anyway. I'm here to ask you to come see your mother."

Marcus closed his eyes. "I'm not ready for that yet."

"If it's up to you, you're *never* going to be ready. And you may not have as much time as you think."

"Is she …"

Emilio's hand seesawed in the air. "Who can say?"

"Very well. Perhaps in a courtyard or café …"

"She can't leave her bed, Marco. She's much too weak. You'll have to go to her, not her to you."

Marcus raised his chin until the back of his head touched the seat behind him. He rubbed his face. The stubble he found there surprised him. How long had it been since he'd shaved? There'd been no opportunities for grooming on the back of Hector's wagon, and his mind had turned to other matters since.

"I'll go," he said, fixing his eyes squarely on Emilio's. He tossed the bottle to his cousin, who caught it easily, his quick hands moving on reflex. Marcus watched their deft tracings with a touch of pride. Emilio hadn't taken to knifework, but those clever hands were still crafted under Marcus's tutelage.

"What should I do with this?" Emilio asked.

Marcus flipped him a coin—his last. "Fill it with something cheap and strong. And bring back a second glass. I could use the company."

13: A Tough Old World

The Iron Circle was aptly named.

It sat in a sinkhole that, through judicious tunneling and the building of earthworks, had been converted into an amphitheater of impressive size. Rows of clay-rich earth sprouted upward in dozens of concentric arcs, their corners hewn into wood-lined benches and bulwarked with stone. The seats descended toward a stretch of hardpan demarcated into rough quadrants by faded lines of chalk. The shape of this inner plateau was formless; its boundaries jigged and contorted by architectural necessity. Offshoots jutted into the crowd where the edge of one bench had collapsed, while buttresses shoring another against a similar fate intruded inward.

Lending order to this chaos was a band of circular metal, two hundred feet in diameter. It formed a ring in the arena's rumpled heart, its steady curvature supported by steel posts every twenty feet. There was no door, no focal point, no break in its blue-black perfection. Combatants entered by clambering over or under it. Two did so now, pulling an appreciative roar from the crowd. Both bore marks of bondage on their faces: one a purple star with curved points as if bent from rapid spinning, the other three black bars stacked one atop another.

The star-faced man, the smaller and leaner of the two, held a strange weapon in one hand. Neither sword nor spear, it tapered steadily along its smooth metal length to a gradual point. Ten inches of tight-wrapped leather formed a crude handle at the butt end. Though three feet long, it seemed light, for the crouching man wielded it without difficulty.

The bigger man, his head shaved to pebble smoothness, bore a more conventional broadsword. Selena wondered where he might have found such a weapon. Clearly, it had been made in the days before the Last War—it was at once too well-forged and rust-eaten to be a modern facsimile.

The fighters circled one another. The smaller man moved in a frog-like crouch, his upper body nearly parallel to the ground, his knees bent at acute angles. The larger man matched him with a sidestepping march. He kept pace with the smaller man for a time and leaped without warning. His sword rose and fell with the swiftness of ricocheted lightning. The smaller man hopped to one side, his spear-sword jabbing out with equal speed. The larger man swiveled his hips with surprising grace, and the spear-point destined for his belly instead grazed the meaty flesh below his ribcage. The wound made a sucking sound as the steel tip pulled free, tearing the narrow bridge of flesh between its entrance and exit. It was an ugly gash, but shallow, and the big man seemed barely to notice it. He unearthed his blade and heaved a wide, open-handed strike. The smaller man dropped lower, and the sword whizzed over his shoulders. He stabbed out again, but this time the larger man was ready and sidestepped it all together. Their first clash concluded, the two fighters withdrew from range and studied each other, smiles of mutual admiration playing on their lips.

Selena leaned forward, engaged despite herself. She'd expected little more than brute force bludgeoning from the proceedings, but both men moved with the self-assured dexterity of real fighters. Their builds and styles put them at odds, an issue which usually makes some bouts ugly or lopsided, but both men had, piled atop their primary skill sets, the far rarer savvy to find sure footing on unfamiliar ground.

Their second clash proceeded like their first, a blitzkrieg tussle of grunts and feints and the whicker of steel narrowly evaded. The larger man scored a point this time, but not with his main weapon—a clean blow from the broadsword would have bisected the smaller man easily. He landed instead with a sharp kick to his opponent's abdomen, hurling him back and derailing a fierce jab of his needle, which had been on track for the hollow of the bigger man's ribcage. The smaller man landed with a wheeze three strides from the bigger man's feet. The larger man brought his broadsword down in a triumphant arc. The smaller man wriggled from its path with inches to spare, moving with a liquid scuttle that seemed almost to defy his anatomy. He hop-scotched to safety and whirled to his opponent, sword-spear brandished like the baton of a lunatic conductor.

The fight ended, as most did, with anticlimax: a misplaced swing, a seized opportunity, and the spear-sword skewered the larger man between the third and fourth rib. It traveled upward on a diagonal for a foot or two but stopped before coming out the other side. The smaller man made no effort to withdraw it, but sprung back empty-handed, allowing the larger man his final spasms of confused anger. He lurched like a stuck bull, swung his sword ineffectually at nothing, and collapsed. Only after a few feeble twitches did the smaller man inch forward and retrieve his weapon.

As the roar of the crowd reached its climax, Selena was surprised and faintly horrified to find her own voice among its chorus. She found fights to the death repulsive in both their morals and the waste they engendered, but the artistry she'd witnessed viscerally thrilled her. The arena was and always would be her home, and she would forever find some manner of solace there, whatever strange form it took.

A heavyset man beset with rings stormed into the ring. His every motion whispered with luxurious fabric. He stood over the dying man and kicked him several times, admonishing him in rapid *Mejise*. The large man did nothing to retaliate, but merely closed his eyes, ashamed.

His ire spent, the heavyset man made a twirling motion with one hand. Two men in vests of stiff leather shuffled onto the field, tectonic discs of muscle shifting beneath the skin of their legs. Both bore a tattoo of three black bars in the same position as the dying man.

Once the field was clear, two new fighters entered the ring. Selena recognized them instantly. There was no mistaking Eleanor and Theodora among the other competitors, whose shirtless figures presented various conglomerations of stooped and corded muscle. The girls, by contrast, wore flowing dresses woven from strips of sheer fabric—colors contrasted to distinguish participants at a distance. Theodora wore red, Eleanor blue. They bore no weapons, nor were their fists gauntleted or wrapped in stiff cotton to prevent splintered bones or dislocated knuckles—a practice so common in bare-knuckle fighters Selena would have thought it universal.

The crowd cheered them as loudly as they had the men, though their enthusiasm struck a different timbre. It was rounder and more jovial, pierced through with whistles. The girls acknowledged the attention with prim waves. They strutted toward one another, instants of bare leg flashing through gaps in their dresses' fabric. The crowd's jubilation reached a higher pitch.

Coins showered the ring, cast in a volume Selena would have thought impossible from such a grubby-looking group. The girls smiled and preened for the crowd, conjuring a fresh volley of coins, before strutting into fighting position.

What followed was not a fight, but its coquettish parody. A gaudy piece of burlesque theatre where feints and jabs never landed but instead snatched free ribbon after ribbon of clothing, revealing provocative bands of bare skin. Their faces pantomimed aggression, indignation, and triumph, taunting one another with handfuls of purloined fabric or crossing their arms over themselves with rosy-cheeked shame. It was acting of the broadest sort, but the audience lapped it up, eager to buy whatever nymphic myth the girls chose to sell them.

Selena became aware that she was a lone woman in a row of men, all of them frothing with glee at the spectacle before them. They laughed and cheered and stomped their feet, whispered innuendo to one another before dissolving into a susurrus of giggles, howled encouragement or advice in coarse *Mejise*. The salacious content of their requests oozed through the language barrier and into Selena's ears. She pressed her hands against her thighs to keep them from balling into fists.

The act reached its crescendo with both girls nude save for two parallel bands, the first hugging their breasts, the second shifting precariously over the curvature of their hips. They circled like wrestlers, arms raised, thigh muscles coiled and ready to spring. They leaped as one, clashed midair, and tussled to the ground.

Eleanor was quicker—either through honest athleticism or the scripting of the show. She pinned Theodora face-down, locked her arms behind her, and raised her to her knees in a posture of submission. The crowd foamed with anticipation. Sensing its mood, she cooed out a question in *Mejise* and cocked a hand to her ear, as if straining to make sense of the deafening cry that followed. The downcast eyes and clench-kneed shyness Selena had witnessed in the barracks was gone, replaced by a boisterous theatricality that drank in the crowd's gaze the way a plant drinks in sunlight.

A fusillade of coins pelted the hardpan at Eleanor's feet. She rolled her hand, inviting further offerings. When they'd arrived to her satisfaction, she reached down and with a flourish yanked the ribbon from Theodora's chest. Her pale, full breasts swung freely for an instant before she hid them behind crossed arms. Eleanor strutted before the crowd, holding up the top like the pelt of a rare and wily creature she'd felled. Feigning vengeance, Theodora crept up behind Eleanor and ripped her top off in kind. The two of them chased each other about the ring for a while before exiting to whistles and applause.

This time, Selena felt no urge to join in.

A group of skinny *marcados* bearing Todd's sigil swept through the ring scooping up coins, after which Mary took the stage. Her contrast to Eleanor and Theodora in bearing and dress was stark. She wore loose-fitting pants of thick worsted cotton and a leather vest bound shut with rawhide ties. She proffered no glimpses of flesh below her neckline save for her bare arms, which bulged with utilitarian muscle. A brass gauntlet clung to her right wrist, morphing her arm into a kind of battering ram. She performed a few quick curls with it to limber up as her opponent entered the ring.

Calling him an opponent was, Selena felt, putting it charitably. He staggered into place with support from two burly guards, each of whom had locked an elbow beneath his shoulder. The so-called fighter's feet wriggled in a crude approximation of locomotion, etching a meandering path of zigzags in the dirt. It was the sort of simulated walking one saw from marionettes in the hands of unskilled puppeteers. His right forearm ended in a wad of crudely-wrapped gauze, masking the stump where his hand had been recently severed. Purple veins bulged beneath raw, red skin. Sweat glazed his cheeks and forehead, and his dull green irises gazed out blearily from a thicket of bloodshot capillaries.

The guards let go of the man and gave him a quick shove in Mary's direction. He took three lurching steps and somehow managed to find his feet. The crowd showered him in ironic praise.

Mary moved in a competent boxer's stance, her right hand hanging slightly low from the gauntlet's weight. Her opponent embraced no such formality. He swung wildly with his remaining hand, delivering a swat-cum-karate chop that Mary deflected effortlessly. She faked with the gauntlet, and her opponent crossed his arms instinctively over his face, freeing her to hurl a few quick, brutal jabs to his undefended solar plexus. He bent forward, spewing a mist of sour, bloody air from his evacuated lungs. Mary threw a right cross. The gauntlet struck his face with a hollow crack. He staggered, arms flapping, and only just managed to retain his balance. Mary shuffled forward, her boxer's stance maintained despite its obvious lack of necessity.

Selena recalled Mary's phrasing from when they'd first met, the division of Todd's *marcado* into beauties and bruisers. She'd taken the categories as flippant or oversimplified, but they cut far closer to the truth's ugly core than she'd realized. Was this her future now? A choice between being a seminude drool-catcher or a carnivalesque implement of corporal punishment? Not that she was likely to get even that much choice, considering her missing ear and less-than-buxom frame. She touched the spot on her cheek where Todd's mark sank into her skin, an inky chain with endless slack that could be yoked tight in an instant.

Mary's fight ended when she broke the prisoner's jaw. She left amidst the applause, which seemed less for her than for the pain she'd inflicted on her opponent. The crowd jeered and hurled bits of garbage at his prostrate body as manacled servants dragged it from the ring. Two men entered, and the spectacle resumed its more traditional course. The fighters moved with the same savage grace as the men who'd preceded them, but Selena took no pleasure from the display. She shouldered her way along the row and clambered down to the underpass that allowed performers in and out of the arena floor. Mary and the girls spotted her just as they passed the archway where the tunnel met the stands. She waved.

"There you are. You catch the show?"

"Uh huh."

"How was it?"

"Not what I expected."

Mary shrugged. "There's worse out there, believe me." She motioned past the archway to the Iron Circle with a nod, where several men were erecting a wooden scaffold. A timber beam rose from the platform, supporting a braced L bend from which hung a pair of metal pulleys. A stout rope threaded the mechanism, ending at one end in a noose.

Two burly men stepped into the ring, lugging between them a thin and wretched *marcado*. Dark rings circled the prisoner's eyes.

Manacles bound his hands behind his back. His thin feet scraped reluctantly over the hardpan, half stepping and half dangling. The two guards carried him impassively along, indifferent to whether he walked or dragged. He gazed up at the crowd like a rabbit in an empty field, head snapping from side to side as he surveyed the convocation of eagles circling overhead. His skin blanched beneath the crosshatched yellow-black bars blotting his cheeks.

"You wanna know why *marcados* don't run away?" Mary asked. "Just watch this guy."

"He ran?"

"And killed one of the *cazadores* who tried to bring him in, to boot." Mary shook her head, lips pursed in sympathy. "Poor bastard."

An impresario in garish clothes addressed the crowd. Selena understood none of what he said, but it was clear from his gestures that he was detailing the *marcado's* various transgressions. As he spoke, the two guards lowered the noose and fixed it around the *marcado's* neck. The *marcado* struggled, but there seemed little fight left in him and a few smacks set him to whimpering acquiescence. The larger guard unhitched the rope from its metal cleat and pulled. The noose cinched tight, pulling the *marcado* to his tiptoes, where he struggled for balance. His pale face grew red and shiny with strain. He remained that way as the impresario finished his pronouncement, flourishing his hands like a stage magician. The second guard grabbed the rope, and the two of them hoisted the *marcado* aloft. His legs kicked wildly, probing in vain for purchase. His mouth flapped open and shut with the loose-lipped idiocy of a fish on dry land.

He remained like that, wheezing through a pinhole esophagus, while the impresario strolled to the Iron Circle's border and collected a peculiar weapon from a pair of waiting attendants. It resembled a scythe, but with a stouter and more rounded blade. A tight wrapping of leather thongs formed a handle near its bottom. The impresario hefted the weapon, spun it a few times in his nimble fingers, and approached the choking *marcado*. He bowed ceremoniously, raised the weapon and in a single smooth motion drew the blade downward, carving a gash from solar plexus to groin. He added a second perpendicular cut above the hips, forming an inverted T shape, and stepped back as the loosed offal spilled from the *marcado's* filleted belly.

The *marcado's* wheezing took on a raspy, retching quality. His legs kicked more fiercely at first, then hardly at all. A stink of blood and ichor wafted through the auditorium, dampening the applause and driving the nearest spectators from their seats. The rest stayed to watch his spams before gradually growing bored and filtering out into the surrounding streets. Selena turned from the spectacle. Mary caught her eye with a slight bob of her head.

"You're here for keeps, pal," she said. "Best get used to it."

Selena's gaze remained fixed on the stage. She heard rather than saw Mary removing her brass gauntlet, marking the snap of clasps unfastening, the rustle-flutter of its leather strap unbuckling, the near-silent whine of its hinges swinging open. She turned from the Iron Circle and watched as Mary unwound a strip of maroon cotton padding from around her forearm.

"Okay, so it wasn't that pretty. Neither is life. What'd you expect?"

"More or less what I saw, I guess," Selena admitted.

"Exactly. It's a tough old world out there. Faces are gonna get punched in no matter what you do about it. And personally, I'd rather be the one doing the punching than getting the pounding."

Mary finished unwrapping the padding. She held it to her face and sniffed, her nose wrinkling at the sour smell of it—an odor Selena's nose could catch from ten feet away. She threw it aside and began rubbing the feeling back into her forearm. Eleanor and Theodora appeared from a nearby alcove, their stage attire replaced with shapeless dresses that made them look almost childlike. They chatted with Mary in *Mejise* for a minute before remembering that Selena couldn't understand them.

"Sorry," Theodora said through an embarrassed smile. "I am at the *Llanures* not so good."

"It's okay," Selena said. "Go on." In truth, she didn't feel much like talking. She preferred to be alone with her thoughts, as unpleasant as they were. Now that she had a free moment to look beyond her immediate predicament, her mind turned once again to Simon. She feared for him far more than for herself, a position that was part selflessness and part arrogance. If it came down to it, she truly believed she'd trade her life for his, but she likewise believed that she handled hardship far better than he ever could, and so leaned into it with a bitter sort of pride. She preferred to ignore the latter fact, as it wasn't terribly flattering, but she couldn't erase it. It was an essential component of the equation that governed her actions.

A single sharp handclap brought her back from her thoughts and silenced the chatter between Mary and the other girls. Trejo stood in the doorway, his face exhibiting an impatience that Selena was beginning to think was simply his default expression.

"Enough nattering. Your work in the Circle is done for the day, and Mr. Todd is entertaining. He expects you to present yourself immediately. Wear your best things, and don't dawdle. Our coach leaves in thirty minutes." He repeated most of this in *Mejise*, as the first pass had clearly been for Selena's benefit.

"What's Selena supposed to wear?" Mary asked. "She ain't gonna fit into Theodora or Eleanor's stuff, and I've only got the one dress."

"Have no fear," Trejo said. "I have spoken with our tailor. He will take her measure in good time, but for now, he's sorted something that will work just fine." At this, he turned to Selena and smiled.

Somehow, good cheer made his ugly face even uglier.

14: A Touch of Intuition

The broth was well-seasoned and savory despite its leanness, but Simon couldn't enjoy it. Guilt soured every bite. Could he really eat these people's food while their crops failed and the desert closed around them? Without irrigation, not even the greenest of thumbs could coax crops from such blighted soil. They would need every scrap of pulse and grain to sustain them, and here was Simon, chipping away at those vital stores one spoonful at a time.

I'll make it up to them, he assured himself. *I'll fix their irrigator. Once that's running, they'll have all the food they can eat.*

Assuming he had correctly identified the problem.

Assuming Emily could find the parts he needed.

Assuming something else more irreparable hadn't gone wrong.

Assuming the water table hadn't receded beyond the machine's intake.

Assuming the crops weren't too desiccated to save.

Assuming the weather cooperated.

Around and around the thoughts swirled, a closed loop of anxiety feeding on itself, gathering speed. Simon shook his head briskly, knocking himself free of its tracks. He took a spoonful of soup from his bowl. His anguish must have shown on his face, for Otis smiled apologetically across the coals of the cooking fire.

"It ain't much, I know. But it'll keep you going."

"What? No! It's good." Simon shoveled in a mouthful, wincing as the hot broth burned his tongue. "I was just thinking of something else."

Otis nodded. "Wish I could say more to comfort you. Juarez is a hard place. Sounds like your sister's a survivor, though. Could be she'll make out alright." His eyes dropped to the embers as he spoke.

"If anyone can, she will," he agreed, expressing more confidence than he felt. He shifted his weight, and the data stick dug painfully into his thigh. The weight of his responsibility was an almost physical thing, a lead sinker chained to his innards. How could something of such incalculable importance be entrusted to him? Selena was its rightful bearer. Simon was an assistant at best; at worst, he was dead weight. He was utterly lost without her. He might as well toss the data stick in the nearest hole and be done with it. It's not as if he could ever make it to the Far Sea on his own.

Otis' eyes snapped to a fixed point on the horizon. His body stiffened. The bowl of his spoon hung inches from his lips. He set it back in the bowl uneaten and stood, skinny legs creaking on their hunger-stiff joints. Simon tried to follow his gaze but could see nothing for several seconds, until a tiny figure appeared over the lip of the canyon. How Otis had presaged her arrival, whether by subtle cues in the environment or the strange entanglement of father and child, Simon couldn't say.

She clambered down the canyon's steep cliff face, descending with light-footed hops despite the large sack she held over one shoulder. It gave a pendular lurch to either side with her every step. Watching her made Simon's stomach lunge in sympathy, but though the weight looked considerable, Emily didn't seem to notice it at all. She reached the canyon floor with a final jump and jogged over to Otis.

"I think I got everything," she said.

"Really?" Simon asked. His list had been expansive and padded with wishful thinking. He'd really only counted on the wire and a couple of simple components she could scavenge from broken pre-War electronics, items he'd highlighted as essential.

"I think so. I mean, I didn't know what the stuff was exactly, but your drawings helped a lot." She opened the bag and held it out for inspection.

Simon rifled through the sack's contents and gingerly removed a coil of copper wire. It was pristine, machine wrapped on its original spindle, its nonconductive jacket glossy and unbroken. Never before had he seen such fine material—even in New Canaan, where metallurgy had been rediscovered with modest competence, new wire was a rough and patchy product, its lengths warbling between gauges and looped around spindles by hand.

Emily studied Simon's expression. "Is it okay?"

"Who made this?" Simon asked. "Where did you get it?"

Emily looked to Otis, who paused a moment before asking his own question. "Do you think it'll do the job?"

"I'll have to see what all is in here," Simon said, taking the sack. "But it's a good sign."

He spread an old blanket out over the ground near the irrigator and set about itemizing the sack's contents. He removed each piece, studied it, and placed it in its proper place on the blanket. His sorting was idiosyncratic, adhering to no one attribute but rather following the intuitions of his own emerging design. With the exception of a few smashed chips Emily had grabbed as insurance, all the components were pristine and machine-built. The precision of their crafting made them unmistakably pre-War, yet they bore no hint of oxidation, nor the desiccation or fading or brittleness that marred every other bit of salvage Simon had seen. A clear, sweet-smelling oil coated most the metal, but the parts were otherwise perfect.

He roughed out a schematic in the dirt using a three-inch bolt as a stylus, pausing occasionally to confirm the details of a part or compare the design against the irrigator's components. Several times he had to change his approach to adapt to the existing structure, and a few of the more clandestine boards flummoxed him altogether. A manual would have made things far easier, but any such document had either been lost or rotted to dust long ago. He would have to make do with logic and intuition.

The lack of tools presented another challenge. He could neither weld nor solder anything in place, relying instead on bolts, twine, and the judicious wrapping of wire insulated from its neighbors by shims of wood or glass. He used a similarly jury-rigged system to measure potential difference and amperage—though "measure" was perhaps too lofty a term. Rather, he tested the presence of current in a circuit by shorting it with a bit of copper wire and waiting to see if the filament got hot. He dropped his makeshift voltmeter with a cry the first time its molten charge surged under its thin insulating coat, but afterward, the near-burn brought him some comfort, as it meant the panels were at least generating electricity. The question was whether or not he could harness it.

Finally, after several grimy, sweaty hours, he emerged from the chassis to find Emily and Otis standing over him. Anxiety played over their faces, jolts of it escaping with every nervous fidget of their fingers. Simon wished they would stop staring at him. The hope in their eyes was corrosive, eating away at the scaffolding of his confidence.

"Is it ready?" Otis asked.

"Well, I mean, I haven't tested it yet…" Simon pondered his schematic, tidied a few lines that had been smudged by the wind. "I was thinking of trying it now, though."

He inched toward the irrigator and knelt next to the access port where the exterior panel had been removed. The device had no manual power switch that he could see, designed as it was to run automatically, but Simon hadn't liked the notion of working on a device that could switch itself on or off at the whims of some internal program, and so had wired a simple breaker into the main power line.

He ran his thumb over the trigger that, if pressed, would complete the circuit.

"It might not work, though. I've never worked on this sort of motor before, and I couldn't say for sure whether—"

Otis put a hand on Simon's shoulder. It was a gentle gesture meant to soothe, but Simon could feel the strength slumbering in its work-thickened tendons. He swallowed audibly.

"Right. Here goes."

He flicked the power on. The three of them stood, drowning in the flood of silence that followed. Simon wiggled the connectors.

"It could be just a loose wire. You never kno—"

A low thrumming rose from the earth. The motor whirred, and the compressor rattled with an alarming chorus of pops and thuds before settling into a steady chugging rhythm. Endless seconds passed as humid air pissed out the irrigator's half-mile of perforated plastic hose. Simon chewed his lip. A gurgle sounded in its subterranean plumbing, and staccato jets of foam-flecked water hissed through the holes. The pressure abated, and the jets settled into a near-silent trickle. Simon stooped over a nearby stretch of hose, pressed his thumb over one of the tiny apertures.

"I was hoping for better flow," he said. "I might be able to fix it by upping the voltage."

"I think it's fine, Simon," said Emily. She held her father's hand, looked up into his weathered face with an expression of merged concern and wonder.

Otis was weeping.

15: Private Demons

Selena looked at the dress as if presented with photographs of a ghastly murder. Trejo extended the garment toward her, his smile widening at her reaction. He gave the dress an enticing wiggle.

"I hope it is to your liking," Trejo cooed.

"You can dangle that thing in front of me all day, there's no way I'm wearing it."

The other girls made a loose semicircle around Selena and Trejo, bearing witness to the confrontation with varying degrees of reluctance. Theodora shifted from foot to foot, forearms crossed over her belly and clutching opposite elbows. Eleanor chewed her lip, struggling to follow their exchange in *Llanures*. Mary appeared the calmest of the three, though tension revealed itself in the reflexive curling and uncurling of her fingers. The three of them had already donned their party attire, providing concrete examples of Selena's own reluctance. Satiny crescents scooped Eleanor's breasts into tight orbs, their naked tops quivering with her slightest movement. A slit appeared at her breastbone and widened until it reached her navel, forming a teardrop of bare midriff. Theodora's neckline plunged to the top of her abdomen, offering a wedge of cleavage to anyone in eyeshot, while strips of sheer fabric offered hypothetical cover for her hips, through which the contours of her underwear could be clearly seen. Mary's outfit was less revealing, though the term was of course relative—much of her was still on prominent display. Selena looked from them to the red and gold monstrosity Trejo dangled before her. Behind it, Trejo's smile sank into a bitter, flat line at Selena's ongoing obstinacy.

"No more delays. We must depart."

Selena sized up Trejo. A compact man, but hardly weak. Some men adopted stiffness as a false form of strength, as if bearing and posture, if constantly upheld, could lend a future blow greater power. Selena didn't count Trejo as this type. His was a frame rigid with potential energy, a bowstring pulled taut and ready, at the slightest twitch, to fire. Selena still thought she could beat him, but there would doubtless be consequences for her impertinence.

With a snort of disgust, she snatched the dress from its hanger and marched to the far end of the room, where pelts strung between wooden struts formed a crude changing screen. Beside her hung a sheet of polished metal that served as a mirror for the girls of the barracks. Selena made a point not to look; even through its scratched and hazy lens, a glimpse of herself in that outfit would've been unbearable.

She emerged a few minutes later with as little fanfare as she could muster, hoping the other girls—and above all Trejo—couldn't sense the depth of her discomfort. Trejo looked her up and down with a gaze devoid of the slightest lust, as if assessing a bit of second-rate livestock he'd gussied up and hoped to pawn off onto some unwitting buyer. He shook his head, pulled a tuft of yellow cotton from his bag, and affixed it to the side of her head with a hairpin. After a bit of mussing, the folds of cotton bloomed into a shape roughly resembling a flower, the petals of which obscured her mangled ear. Stepping back to inspect his work, he spat through his teeth, mumbled something in *Mejise*, and shrugged in a manner suggesting he'd done all he could. Selena absorbed this treatment silently, anger shifting behind her face like magma beneath cool crust.

Trejo ferried the girls into a covered wagon drawn by a pair of stout grey mules. He hopped onto the wagon's perch and spurred the mules into action. Sunlight dribbled through the canvas roof, suffusing the material with a yellowish glow and filling the cabin with shadowy half-light. Selena tugged the hem of her skirt as low as possible, hoping to cover another inch or two of leg. She leaned across the aisle to Mary.

"I thought you said we were bruisers," she hissed through clenched teeth.

Mary shrugged. "Bruiser or beauty, every girl's gotta play hostess sooner or later. Trust me, it's not so bad. You serve drinks, you have a chat—and given you don't speak *Mejise,* you won't even have to do much of that."

"I doubt it ends there," Selena said darkly.

Mary shrugged. "Not always, no. *Pesos* can change hands. But it's not mandatory. In fact, Mr. Todd kind of frowns on it. He'll look the other way if a fellow *casero* gets a bit handsy, but he doesn't let things get too far. It's one of his quirks. His best one, I'd say."

Selena didn't reply. She wasn't sure how "handsy" a guest she could tolerate, but the reassurance that Todd wasn't running his own private bordello was some small comfort, at least. Mary, perhaps sensing Selena's discomfort, settled into uncharacteristic silence. The wagon rocked on its wooden frame, its steady undulations amplified with staccato jostles whenever the wheels hit a rut or bump.

The *haciendas* perched on the high ground at the southern end of *Nuevo Juarez* proper, their stately verandas facing the town below as if surveying it with a proprietary air. Selena watched them roll past through portholes in the canvas until the mules turned up a curving path and toward Mr. Todd's. It wasn't the biggest, but it was more elegant than most, its lawn artfully sculpted with creosote and cacti, a desert analog to the sultry rooftop gardens of New Canaan's Seraphim. Marble columns—clearly pre-War, given their size and symmetry—held its terracotta awning aloft, their piebald lengths polished to shine, and statues of winged creatures from forgotten myths stalked its perimeter in frozen silence.

The wagon juddered to a halt, and the girls descended, maneuvering their dresses with a skill that denoted frequent practice. Selena struggled with hers, catching the hem on an exposed nail and pulling a loose thread from the seam. She yanked it free, winced at the sound of ripping fabric, and followed the others onto the verandah. A pair of burly *marcados* stood to either side of the door, filling a role that fell somewhere between valet and guard. The taller of the two nodded to Trejo, opened the door, and ushered them inside in a single smooth motion.

As she entered the *hacienda,* Selena felt a momentary chill pass through her. It took her a moment to discern its cause: the place reminded her of the Mayor's manor. It bore the same trappings of antiquity, with wainscoted walls and filigreed molding and paintings hung in ornate frames. But though the content was the same, Selena spotted differences in execution. Mr. Todd's rooms were tidier and more sparsely furnished, its collections and furnishings curated rather than stored. There was a care to their selection that felt paradoxically effortless, as if the choices had been made reflexively by some automatic impulse. Selena was familiar with the rigid boundaries of class imparted by New Canaan, the unbridgeable gap between Salter and Seraphim, and Mr. Todd's effortless décor could serve as one of a dozen silent badges denoting his membership to the uppermost stratum of the society in which he dwelled.

Mingled conversations drifted in from some distant corner of the manor. The other girls knew their way, and Selena followed them, gritting her teeth as the noise grew louder. Her hands kept curling into fists, and she had to force them time and again to loosen. She smoothed her dress against her thighs and tugged at the material to keep it from clinging.

They crossed an archway and entered a ballroom with a vaulted ceiling. Chandeliers hung overhead with an air of otherworldly weightlessness, celestial jellyfish imported from some far-flung alien ocean. Beneath them drifted shoals of partygoers, their wrists and fingers clinking with loops of precious metal, their well-fed frames shawled in brightly-colored fabrics. They reclined on antique furniture or clustered around hip-high tables, trading banter and plucking *hors d'oeuvres* from trays. Selena spotted a few women, most of them in puffy gowns and clinging closely to their husbands, but the guests were predominantly male.

Gender was more evenly split among the *marcado*, its delineation obvious at a glance. The men wore matching charcoal suits and cravats the color of rust. Their tattoos were tiny and discreet, positioned below the ear or peeking out the cuffs of their shirtsleeves. They scuttled from group to group, silently proffering canapes from silver platters balanced on the tips of their splayed fingers, ignored and interchangeable.

The women, by contrast, preened, bare flesh framed by slim cuts of multicolored fabric. There were at least a dozen of them, their cheeks branded with Todd's blue lines, their young bodies sheathed in wrappings of fine silken cloth. They shared few characteristics apart from their youth, bearing round hips and sleek legs and skin shaded from mahogany to freckled alabaster. Hair flowed down backs or piled in arabesques of startling complexity. Jewels glittered in navels. They seemed never to stand or sit but to pose, their bodies moving with a control that Selena would've found impressive if it weren't so disgusting.

A heavyset man in a beige jacket caught a girl by the arm and swept her into his lap, his conversation with the man next to him continuing unabated. He placed a meaty hand casually, almost absently, on the girl's breast. The girl wriggled up closer to him, her lips composed in an artful smile. A revolted shiver traced up Selena's back.

"Move, girl," Trejo growled, prodding her with a bony finger. His words skimmed over her cheek in a gust of sour air. "Make like the others. I don't expect miracles, but fake it as best you can. And play nice. Girls who bite get bitten back twice as hard."

With these words of motivation, he gave her a brisk shove toward an assembly of guests.

Selena stumbled a bit before catching herself, her fighter's equilibrium offset by the chorus of fabrics sounding around her waist. She tugged the hem of her skirt and waded into the murk of their conversation, her teeth bared in something that she hoped resembled a smile. The man who was speaking—younger than the rest, his angular face rounded by a neatly sculpted beard—gave her a brief glance. A man to her left ran his hand over the curve of her hip but otherwise ignored her. She clenched her fists. Bright flecks of pain flashed along her palm where her nails dug into the skin. His fingers continued their exploration, tracing the ridge of muscle along her abdomen, venturing downward to pinch a bit of thigh. Selena's fists strained like wolves at weak and fraying leashes.

Mary shouldered into the narrowing gap between Selena and her accoster, her voice bright and jangling. She exchanged a few easy words with the guests, nudged one in the ribs, and led Selena from the fray. Her hand slid down her wrist and gently but insistently pried her fingers free of the hard knot of knuckles and rage into which they'd tangled themselves.

"You've got to relax. You stand there looking sour like that, it just encourages 'em. You can get away with a lot if you just act coy about it. Insult 'em, rebuff 'em, slap their faces. They think it's a game."

Selena shifted in her dress, tugging here and there at stray bits of fabric. "Easy for you to say. I don't even speak *Mejise*."

"Yeah, and they don't speak *Llanures*. Call 'em a bunch of dough-faced pigfuckers. Tell 'em their dicks are so tiny they couldn't satisfy a flea. They won't know the difference. Just *smile* when you do it."

"I *am* smiling."

Mary gave her a sympathetic shake of the head. She placed her fingers on Selena's cheeks and kneaded them into shape, pausing on occasion to study her work. After a few minutes, she dropped her hands.

"We'll get there."

She shepherded Selena through the party, snatching cheese and fruit and fluted glasses of brandy from trays, exchanging flirtatious barbs, and waving at attendees without stopping in any one place long enough for wandering hands to settle on her. Occasionally she'd flag down one of the other girls and exchange a few bits of information—which of the guests had had too much to drink, which had been calmed by a decorous member of their party or stirred into greater lasciviousness by youthful male boasting, who was doling out *pesos* to girls with a bit of cleavage to show, and who bore around his eyes the signs of a hunger that could be easily and inadvertently nudged into violence. She and the others traded these notes in economical bursts, pausing only a few seconds to keep Trejo from chewing them out for lollygagging when they should be chatting up the guests. It was a complex and sophisticated maneuver, and Selena recognized in it the feints and topographic considerations of a good fighter's footwork. Strange how she could be so graceful in one arena and so clumsy in another.

As they drifted about the room, Selena noticed one woman who was never privy to the grapevine of nods and motions and sisterly snickers. She stood aloof near a marble-clad pillar, the fingers of one hand resting against the side of her slender neck. The others kept apart from her, repelled by some unacknowledged but fundamental force. Her black hair clung to the back of her head and a tightly-coiled bun. Most of the girls would have been called pretty—Selena was the outlier in this respect—but hers was a stiffer, more regal beauty. She looked to Selena like a tribal deity, her likeness carved by worshippers from the heartwood of some nameless jungle tree.

Selena found her attention drawn to the woman and would glance her way whenever they passed nearby. Eventually the woman, perhaps sensing a sudden and sustained interest in her person, raised her head and locked eyes with Selena, who winced away as if caught peeking through a stranger's curtains at night. Mary, noticing this exchange, gave a sardonic smile.

"The princess shootin' you daggers?" she asked.

"No, nothing like that," said Selena. She felt a slight affront at the tone of the question, as if the tall girl needed defending. "Who is she?"

"Same as you and me," Mary drawled. She grabbed a pair of drinks from a nearby server, handed one to Selena and sipped at the other. "Nowadays, at least. Grace Delgado. She was sister of one of the three *Senadores,* heads of the city's ruling families, back when there were three. Thorin was set to toss her to the brothels after he took power, but Todd put his bid in and got her instead. About the luckiest break you could imagine from where she stood, but you'd think she was sulfur mining come day and takin' johns three holes at once come night by the way she pouts. A hard knock mingling with us poor *marcadas,* I guess."

Her description finished, Mary dismissed the tall girl with a sniff. Selena's own gaze lingered. She set her eyes on a spot to the girl's left and observed her in the periphery. The former *Senador's* sister shifted from heel to heel, arms crossed over her belly, hands clutching opposite elbows. Her movements were furtive and incomplete, gestures half-made and rescinded, as if she'd been placed in a new body and still working out the controls.

A man in a red jacket swaggered over to Grace. Spirals of gold filament threaded the rim of his left ear, and a diamond stud sat atop his right nostril like a glistening pimple. He moved with the bandy-legged strut of a man who's far drunker than he realizes. His thick lips parted to reveal a set of large yellow-white teeth accompanied by a single golden incisor.

He said something to Grace and wiped a hair from her forehead. Having completed this task, his fingers continued their southward journey, descending along her jaw and leaping from neck to breastbone, where they adopted a slower, more luxuriant pace. They veered east, snuck beneath her dress strap, and pulled it from her shoulder, revealing a wedge of creamy skin.

Grace absorbed this treatment with none of the dry ripostes or giggling good-humor of the other girls, who'd honed their particular defenses over years of such onslaughts. She looked appalled, her disgust masked by only the thinnest veneer of frozen civility. Selena noted her stiff arms, her clenched jaw, the balling of her fingers into futile fists. Her nerves sung in tandem.

Selena approached the two of them. The man remained focused on his task, his fingers creeping past the strap to rummage deeper inside the dress. Grace snapped her eyes from the man to Selena and back but remained otherwise motionless. Selena watched for a moment longer, raised her glass, and calmly upended its contents over the man's head.

The glass was small, containing only enough liquid to wet his hair, but the effect of her action was outsized. He staggered back as if she'd clocked him, eyes blinking through a daze. Selena made no effort to slip away, but merely stood, her empty glass dangly by its stem from between two fingers.

Mary rushed over, draped an arm around the man, and led him away from the scene. Her free hand gesticulated madly, painting elaborate scenes in the air. She led him to Theodora, who leaped nimbly into the role of fretting conciliator, mopping the liquor from his hair and cooing over the state of his jacket in a manner he seemed to find quite satisfactory. The few guests who'd noticed the exchange watched with amusement. Mary returned a few minutes later.

"Okay, I think I smoothed that over, though I owe Theodora a big favor now. What the hell was that about?"

Selena shook her head. She couldn't say exactly why she'd done it. Certainly, the drunk's behavior wasn't the worst she'd witnessed at the party so far. Nor could she say the other girls were less in need of intervention on their behalf—they hid their discomfort better, but most were enjoying the party no more than she was. There'd simply been something in Grace's manner that cried out for a response— and something in Selena's that cried out to give it. The two cries had met, anonymous yet oddly unified, the sympathetic howls of dogs in the night.

Mary cupped Selena's shoulders. "You've gotta quit acting like you're at the bottom and things can't get worse for you. Trust me, they can." Her eyes flicked over Selena's shoulder. "Case in point."

A hand closed around Selena's wrist and yanked. Trejo snarled, his humorless face puckering with rage.

"With me, girl," he hissed.

Mary caught Selena's eye and mouth a single word: "Easy." Selena bit her cheek and nodded.

Trejo dragged Selena from the manor and out into the street. Selena expected to be tossed to the curb, but they reached the road, and Trejo kept going, eyes deadlocked on some unknown target in front of him, limbs rigid as iron. She trotted to keep up, hating the subordinate feeling of being escorted like a misbehaving child, but not quite daring to break his grip. Pouring the drink on the guy had been an overstep. She didn't regret it, but she didn't care to compound the insult either.

They came to a stable near the edge of the manor's property. Trejo banged on the door and shouted something in *Mejise*. The hostlers scuttled like beetles beneath an overturned rock, grabbing saddle gear and leading palfreys and hitching up a covered wagon. They worked fast, and after only a few minutes of Trejo's glowering a harried coachman, his hair disheveled into spikes like a rooster's comb, leaped onto the perch and readied the horses to ride.

Trejo opened the coach door and shoved Selena inside. He climbed in after her, slammed the door, and barked a couple of syllables at the coachman. Selena didn't catch them, but the coachman obviously did, for he snapped the reins and the horses trotted off.

They rode in silence. Trejo folded his arms across his chest and pouted, as if the outing were Selena's idea and he was a little brother dragged along for the ride. Just looking at him lit a flame beneath the kettle of Selena's rage, which threatened to boil over. She leaned against the coach wall and looked out the window instead.

The coach rolled away from the *haciendas* and into the heart of Juarez. It followed *Calle de Jefes* past the plazas and the amphitheater and continued until the peasant hovels on the town's northern fringe came into view. It turned down a narrow road and wound through courtyards and alleys, spilling onto a narrow strip with cobbles crumbling to gravel and boardwalks warped and rotting. Adobe buildings pressed close on either side, blocking out the afternoon light. Lanterns burned on iron posts, bathing the street in oily light.

Trejo climbed out of the coach and Selena followed. He led her down the boardwalk and through a pair of swinging doors.

The shadows from the street thickened into gloom. It rolled like mist through the long low-ceilinged room. Corn oil lamps glowed on tabletops, their feeble light flickering like distant stars. Men sat around the tables, playing cards and downing drinks. Bars of this sort were usually raucous places, the walls echoing with guitars and fiddles and off-key singing, patrons leaning over steins and shouting to be heard. Yet the atmosphere in this bar was almost funereal— not sad, exactly, but muted. Occasionally a table would break out in a collective chuckle at some comment, but overall the noise was minimal.

Past the tables, a green curtain divided the room into two. Trejo brushed past it into the rear of the building. Here the light was better, corn oil lamps replaced by lanterns of brighter-burning rendered fuel, but the effect made the room seem even dingier somehow, granting greater depth to the shadows and spotlighting the rumpled floorboards and discolored patches of grime.

The room flared out to either side like the top of a capital T. A bank of doors ran along the far wall, each five or so feet from the next. Some were closed, but most stood open, revealing tiny chambers containing a steel-frame cot with filthy linen, a wooden side table, and a woman chained to the bed by her ankle.

Selena watched as a middle-aged man with a wide-brimmed hat worn low over his eyes approached one of the doors. A woman accompanied him, her gray hair drawn back in a severe bun, her figure sculpted by a corset and buried in ten pounds of lace and satin. She motioned to a slim, brown-haired girl in one of the rooms and said something to the man. He responded with a question, which the proprietor seemed to answer to his satisfaction, for he handed the woman a stack of *pesos* and entered the chamber, unfastening the buttons of his shirt as he went. Selena saw the girl's face in the instant before the man closed the door. A look of bored resignation lidded her eyes, though beneath it, Selena sensed a flash of something darker, a feeling the girl probably had to smother on a regular basis.

Trejo walked Selena down the length of the hall, his slow strides ensuring she had ample time to soak in all the details. The girls varied in color and size. Most were young—some much younger than Selena; she spotted one with straw hair and gimlet eyes who could have been no older than ten—but a few were middle-aged, their stretch marks and wrinkles buried under drifts of masking powder. Two were visibly pregnant, their swollen bellies hiking up the hems of their skimpy shirts. What united them was neither age nor physique, but instead a rough cast of their faces and a hollowness behind their eyes, as if they were not flesh but living mannequins. None smiled. The coy, satiny ambiance of Mr. Todd's party was nowhere in evidence. Todd's barracks felt a little like a harem, even if the central male never partook. This place felt like a prison.

"These women are all *marcada*," Trejo explained. "Men with the brand have many roles. Women, not so much. Their keepers rent a chamber for a small fee. Men come and pay the house, and the house pays the keeper. It is very profitable. This house is well known, but it is far from the biggest. And there are more every week."

They left the way they'd come. Selena exhaled, glad to be gone from that horrible place, but Trejo's determined stride suggested he wasn't done with her yet. Sure enough, they passed the coach and made their way down a narrow passage between two buildings. Too tight to be properly called an alley, it was more of an architectural abscess, a hollowing in the adobe begun by age and widened by vandals seeking passage through the building to whatever lay beyond. An earthy, spoiled smell wafted through the gap, reminding Selena of a root cellar with poor drainage.

They emerged in a courtyard of sorts. Sheets of moth-eaten canvas hung from poles hammered into the adobe, forming a crude awning. Planks of punky wood balanced between cinder blocks served as benches, on which sat a dozen haggard women clothed in rags. They turned their faces up to Trejo and Selena for a moment before returning to their private endeavors: mumbling to themselves or scratching figures in the dirt or simply moaning out notes in a constant and ever-modulating chorus of misery. A woman in a grey robe tended to their sores, daubing them with a rag soaked in acrid-smelling liquid.

Many of the women were disfigured in some way, scarred by violence or disease or a mixture of the two. She saw women without fingers, women missing eyes, women with gashes from cheek to chin. Women whose teeth had crumbled into brownish rubble, whose bodies bulged with tumors, whose noses had rotted off their faces, leaving a messy black hole like a cruel and sightless third eye.

"Welcome to the retirement home. Pretty, isn't it? Clients are sometimes screened, but signs are missed, and most girls catch something sooner or later. And of course, you can't screen out the men who want simply to cut a woman, to hurt them in some way to pay for private demons they can't explain."

Trejo held his arms out expansively. "All this may have been yours, girl. It may be still. It is by the grace of one man that you aren't in one of those chambers, chained by the ankle, and you spurn him with your childish behavior. Such gratitude."

"A slave is a slave."

"You think Mr. Todd is your enslaver? Fool! Mr. Todd is your *savior*. You'd do well to remember that next time you are asked to perform and think it better to pull some petty stunt. There are always more chains waiting for those who don't listen."

With that, Trejo led Selena from the alley and back to the coach.

The ride back to the barracks was as silent and unpleasant as the ride out had been. Trejo resumed his sulky posture, arms crossed, lips pursed. Selena had expected a smug smile to break through in the wake of his scolding, but he seemed if anything even gloomier than before. Nor were Selena's spirits all that high. Part of her knew Trejo's little demonstration had been bluster—if Todd wanted her gone, he'd have simply tossed her out, not made a big show of it—but she wasn't foolish enough to see the threat as entirely idle. Life under Mr. Todd was unacceptable, and she would need to escape eventually. But it was one thing to plot your climb when you were already at the bottom. Her trip to the brothel had opened a crack in the floor, giving proof to the knowledge that as deep as the chasm currently seemed, there was still a lot farther to fall.

16: A Grim Patchwork

Barring all other information, you could always tell where you were in Juarez by the quality of the roads.

The city's provisional government, all but neutered in its other areas of influence, maintained a flawlessly cobbled thoroughfare through the city's center. The route thrived at the behest of the city's merchants, who insisted on good roads to facilitate trade. The *pandilleros*, who skimmed protection money from the merchants freely, were likewise supportive, as well-dug channels allowed the river of commerce to flow unmolested. Its north and south streams formed an estuary at the city's main plaza, its pristine surface spilling along nearby streets in a tangle of sandstone tributaries.

Beyond these areas the cobbles grew cracked and uneven, their seams buckling from the slow undulations of the earth, individual stones pummeled into powdery shards or pried up and taken for some unknown purpose. Past the untended cobbles the roads turned to gravel, beyond the gravel hardpan, and at the hardpan's fringes a slough of dirt that morphed into mud with every rainfall, churned by passing carts and hooves and feet before drying into a wasteland of hillocks and furrows and axel-snapping crevices.

The hospice sat at a bend in what could have perhaps once, with a degree of charity, been called a road. Scraggles of tarwort broke through the crusted earth like the hands of dead men prematurely buried. Their gnarled fingers tugged at Marcus's serape as he stepped over them. He paused at the threshold, wincing inwardly at every sign of the building's dereliction. Cracks twined up adobe walls, gaping wide enough in places to admit a probing finger. Broken windowpanes cowered behind plywood eyepatches or else stared, lensless and blind, at the road. The door, chewed by rot into an amorphous, splintery shape, hung tenuously from rusted hinges. Marcus raised his hand and knocked lightly on the punky wood. He knew to enter without knocking and expected no reply, but savored the additional moment outside that the motion afforded him. He waited a few pointless seconds, drew a breath, and entered.

Inside the building was one large room. Nooks and alcoves offered some semblance of demarcation, but most of its floor space consisted of a single L-shaped sweep of dull tile. A sooty dimness coated everything. The Grey Sisters had done what they could to combat it, whitewashing the plaster walls and polishing the metal fixtures to a lusterless shine, but they were too few and too overworked to make any real difference, and the room itself seemed to conspire against them, its sharp corners swallowing light. Agave blooms died slow, pointless deaths in chipped vases. A dry, sour odor clung to the under-circulated air.

Marcus made his way down the corridor. Their footsteps echoed off the tile floor, adding a backbeat to the chorus of moans and coughs and laryngitic wheezes rising from the cots. Small, weathered-looking women in grey smocks paced the floor with brisk efficiency. These were the Grey Sisters, a religious order of women in spartan attire who gave solace and care to the city's most vulnerable residents. Though funded only sporadically by alms and all but destitute, they were competent clinicians and tireless in their efforts. They greeted him with a few whispered words or warm but frugal nods. Marcus walked with his head down, avoiding their gaze.

Despite the absence of rooms, the Grey Sisters had made some effort to give each patient their own space. Curtains or plywood dividers offered patchwork privacy, and each bed was oriented independent of the others, eschewing the typical dormitory style in favor of something a bit cozier. Marcus couldn't fault the Grey Sisters for their efforts, for they toiled with unyielding if stoic compassion, their services rarely respected and never fully repaid. He'd never heard of one mistreating her wards or shirking her duties, never known a soul, no matter how bereaved, to speak an ill word against them. But they repulsed him all the same in their open-armed embrace of mortality, which he found slightly grotesque, almost profane. Death—natural death, that is, outside of the fighter's circle—should be a quick and private affair. What sort of person willingly walked among its gardens every day, tending the bitter seeds time or circumstance had sown until they reached their macabre bloom?

Still, he'd brought his mother here, hadn't he? That must tell you something about the Grey Sisters. *Or about you,* muttered a voice in his head.

Her bed stood near the far end of the corridor, its left edge pressed tight against the wall. Grubby curtains hung from the ceiling, in one instance bisecting a window to partition its light between her and her neighbor. Apart from the bed, her only furniture was an upended bucket serving as a nightstand and a small Lucite table bearing a statue surrounded by candles. The statue depicted a woman with a skeleton's face, her empty eye sockets enigmatic, her teeth clenched in the mirthless grin common to skulls. Garlands woven from reeds and twigs hung about her neck, their dry twists festooned with bones and baubles and dead snakes dried into strips of leather.

"What is that doing in here?" Marcus asked, his voice low and sibilant.

"The Sisters brought her."

"They had no right to do so. This is a hospice, not one of their shrines."

"Your mother asked for her, Marc. She gives her peace."

Marcus pursed his lips. He'd never adhered to the worship of *Santa Muerte,* though she was revered often among those in his profession. Personally, he found the beatification of death unseemly and naïve. Death had been his business for many years; he could tell you there was nothing holy about it. A man was so much wet slop in a rubbery sac. Poke a hole in the sac, and a bit of the man leaked out. Make enough holes, and he drained away to nothing. It was a biological function, no more transcendent than screwing or shitting. He had seen many deaths up close—slow deaths and fast deaths, deaths by blade and bullet and fire, clean deaths by garrote and messy deaths by fist or boot or bludgeon, stupid deaths from carelessness or ill luck and tragic deaths by disease, just about every sort of death you could imagine—and not once had he ever found beauty in any of them. Honor, perhaps, but never beauty.

"Marcito?" croaked a voice. A head swiveled on its lumpy pillow. Marcus studied its face with sadness and a resigned lack of surprise at its disrepair. He approached it as one might a childhood home long abandoned, its paint peeling, its fixtures cracked and faded, the slow shift of its foundation bending once firm angles into warped and droopy joints. The bedrock of fat and muscle had eroded further since his last visit—months ago, or could it have been years? Surely not—and the skin above it hung loose. Eyes looked up at him through a grey-white film.

"Marcito."

His mother smiled. Her teeth startled him with their healthy whiteness. He took her hand in his. Bones and ligaments rustled beneath the skin like a bundle of twigs loosely bound. A sharp squeeze could snap the lot of them.

"Hello, *Madre*," he said. The *Mejise* came effortlessly now. She spooled it out of him, a bedridden Clotho spinning him backward into her distaff. "How are you feeling?"

"Oh, you know. It changes day to day. There is pain, sometimes, but the Sisters are kind." The words were spoken lightly, as if over a tea of wild herbs in their cottage on the *hacienda*, the pot burbling contentedly over the hearth fire. The cottage that had been hers, once, the meager and well-earned spoils availed to dutiful peasantry after a lifetime's service. The cottage that should be hers still, with its blinds lowered against her fading health, its linens washed and pillows plumped by the younger homesteaders who paid homage to their elders, as she had once done to hers. The cottage that had been snatched away as collateral against a foolish son's debt—the wicked spawn of his arrogance and an ill-fated, catastrophic wager—leaving her prey to the austere mercies of the Grey Sisters.

"That's good, mother," he said.

I was supposed to free her from this. The prodigal son, returning in triumph to amend for past sins. Some triumph. Some amending. What a joke. He squeezed her hand gently and winced at the flash of ill-concealed pain on her face. To think her so frail. He'd barely tightened his grip at all. *Such a strong boy you are,* chided a voice. *To make a sick old woman cringe at the faintest touch.* He could do no good here. He wished he'd never come. His touch gave pain over comfort, his presence brought only bad memories. He was a Midas of misery, a killer so saturated with death that its bitter fluid leeched out of him wherever he went, staining all he touched.

"It's good you are home. I fear for you so when you travel. It's a dangerous world."

"That's so."

She looked as if she had more to say. Her lips pressed together, their corners turned downward. Marcus leaned forward to better catch her words, but for whatever reason, she left them unspoken. Perhaps she'd never intended to speak them in the first place. She closed her eyes and settled deeper into the creases in her thin mattress. Her breath escaped with a rumbling *harrumph*, a sound of sudden yet anticlimactic collapse. Marcus wondered if she'd gone to sleep, and if so whether he wanted to wake her. There seemed so much to say, but when he primed his lips to say it, he found the words absent. Years of unvoiced thoughts congealed into a mushy grey pile in his head, their meaning dissolved into incomprehensibility. Only their mass remained: enormous, suffocating, immovable.

He stood for a moment over her bed, watching the steady rise and fall of her chest beneath the blanket—a grim patchwork of threadbare cloth, but clean and neatly pressed; the Sisters did what they could. Her hand still gripped his lightly. He set it on her lap and began to withdraw his fingers when her grip tightened for an instant.

"Light a candle for me, Marcito," she said, her voice little more than a whisper.

Marcus glanced over to the statue of *Santa Meurte*. She grinned back at him, eyeless yet anything but blind.

"Of course, mother."

He drew a matchstick from a tin bowl at the corner of the table and studied the array of candles, his thumbnail scratching absently at the match's sulfur head. They came in many colors, some whose purpose he knew, others not: gold for money, red for love, purple for healing, brown for wisdom (*a good candle for your sake, fool*), green for justice. He found a purple candle burnt lower than the others, lit the match, and touched its flame to the blackened wick. It caught easily. He paused, the matchstick burning down toward his thumb and forefinger, and lit the green candle as well. Healing first, but let there be justice.

The match's flame crept toward his fingers. He shook it out and tossed the spent stick into another bowl kept for that purpose. Strangely, he felt a little better for having completed this bit of silent liturgy, though the green candle was a poor substitute for his true desires. As this was a place of healing, the table held no black candles, but it was a black candle that Marcus wanted most of all. Leave justice to the barristers and night watchmen.

Black was for vengeance.

17: Magpie Theology

Selena lay on the cot—her cot, she supposed, though she felt no more at home here than at the grubbiest traveler's inn—and studied the atlas of cracks and stains charted along the barracks' stucco ceiling. Her dress, hastily torn from her body at the earliest opportunity, lay in a rumpled pile on the floor. Around her the other girls undressed more carefully, picking spots of dried food from lapels and smoothing out creases with saliva-dampened thumbs.

"Moping's not gonna do you any good you know," Mary said. There was reproach in her voice, but she softened it with genuine sympathy. "You'll only make yourself more miserable."

"I doubt that's possible."

Mary sniffed a small laugh. "Look, the parties don't come around all that often. And besides, you get used to them."

Selena grunted a noncommittal reply. In truth, Mr. Todd's parties were not chief among her concerns at the moment. Her worry went far deeper, past her own predicament and to the data stick that was now—thanks either to her keen foresight or profound ignorance, she wasn't sure which—in Simon's possession. She prayed he would continue on to the coast without her and not just hole up in the *pueblo* to await her return—or worse, stage some hopeless attempt at rescue. Their job was to reach California before New Canaan did; nothing else mattered, not even their own lives. She'd tried to make this clear to Simon, but she could never be sure how much he was listening. It was up to him now. The thought filled her with dread for his safety and envy at his importance.

With the data stick out of her hands, her mind turned to the more immediate concern of her escape. The most obvious play was simply to flee—to pull a runner, as Mary had put it. She wore no chains and slept in an unlocked room, and Juarez had no walls or gates or checkpoints. But skipping town was only the first step, and her next moves were trickier: she'd need supplies enough to survive days or weeks in the wilds, currency to buy more when she reencountered civilization—assuming she eventually would—and, perhaps the greatest challenge of all, directions. She knew which way was west, but "west" was a big and brutal country that would abide no missteps. What's more, the very reason for her journey was no longer in her possession. She could reach the coast and have nothing to show for it if she didn't find Simon first, and there was no telling where he might be.

Perhaps she could reach him somehow, leverage Juarez's regional network to her own advantage. Mr. Todd seemed like an influential man. Maybe she could hold him hostage, use him to get a message out to Simon. But even if he somehow managed to find Simon, what would prevent him from using her brother against her? Moreover, how would she manage to hold Todd in the first place? This wasn't her city—she had no contacts, no power, didn't even speak the language.

That left one more choice: waiting. The more she learned about Juarez and the indentured caste system that had swallowed her, the better equipped she would be to plot her escape. But waiting was agony, each inert second a hot ember in her belly, searing her guts and weighing her down until she buckled beneath its molten payload.

Indecision swirled endlessly in Selena's mind. She yanked the plug and let it drain into its subconscious cistern, where it would sit in silence for a while before burbling up again. Her attention turned to the women with whom she shared the barracks, the twitter of a dozen conversations in *Mejise*. The atmosphere was surprisingly convivial, less a harem of slaves than an all-girls boarding school after final bell. They'd let her be after she returned, perhaps sensing her turmoil, but once she sat up, a few girls came over to chat, their words pecked out in pidgin *Llanures* or smoothed into coherent sentences by Mary's translation, while others acknowledged her with a flick of the wrist or nod.

The hum of conversations cut off as Grace stalked into the room, her dress billowing about her hips. None of the girls looked her way or acknowledged her overtly at all, though the intent of their silence couldn't have been more apparent if they'd scrawled it on a piece of paper and nailed it to her forehead. Grace ignored them all in turn, undressing as if alone. She put on a plain cotton dress to replace her ornate party attire and removed the pins holding her hair in its elaborate twinings.

Brushing a lock of hair from her forehead, she crossed the room to the statue of the skeleton woman perched in the corner. She knelt before the altar, lit a match, and touched the flame to the wicks of several candles gathered about the strange deathgod's feet. Thin bands of colored smoke rose in wavy paths to the ceiling. A strand of mumbled prayer unspooled from her lips, a faint drone that jumped on occasion with flourishes of melody.

The other girls noticed, their conversations falling quiet one by one, until the room turned silent apart from Grace's prayer. Muttered whispers followed, syllables rasping like whetstones on knives.

Two of the girls rose to the nods of their confederates and marched over to the statue where Grace knelt. They grabbed her under the armpits and hurled her toward the center of the room. She landed with a thud on her tailbone. The two girls loomed over her. One of them brandished an index finger in her face and shouted in machine gun *Mejise*. The former *Senador's* sister absorbed the fusillade silently.

Eventually, the girls stopped berating her and returned to the flock, impish smiles breaking through their scowls. Conversation resumed. Selena nudged Mary and leaned forward, strangely afraid of being overheard.

"What was that about?"

"The girls don't like princess types praying to *La Santa*."

"You mean that statue?"

Mary narrowed her eyes. She seemed genuinely offended for a moment, though she masked it with an ironic eye roll. "*Dios mio,* northy, you really aren't from around here, huh? That 'statue' is a shrine to *Santa Muerte,* patron saint of serfs and *marcados.* A *Senador's* sister's got no right to light a candle to her, not even a deposed one. *La Santa* is ours."

Selena nodded as if she understood. She'd spent her childhood choking down the magpie theology of New Canaan's *Final Testament,* and so knew better than to question the finer points of religious conviction. Her eyes drifted past Mary to Grace Delgado, who made no second attempt to approach the shrine—though she did look its way as she leaned against the wall, her lips twitching with the contours of an unspoken prayer.

Part III: The Vault

18: A New Hole to Work With

Selena walked up the cobbled path to the *hacienda*, her shoulders pulled back in a deliberate gesture of confidence. It was a posture she'd learned to wear unconsciously since she first began frequenting the street fighting rings in the slums of Jericho, a subtle reclamation of the space to which few men felt she was entitled. Through the years it had taken on the worked-in comfort of a ratty but well-loved sweater, but as she donned it today, something seemed off with its cut. The hem pinched where it should softly hug, the sleeves hung past her fingers with spaghetti limpness. She'd been branded only a week, yet already the ink on her skin had eaten its way inward, staining her mind with its indelible accusation of caste.

The door was solid oak and hard enough to sting Selena's knuckles as she knocked. The creak of aged floorboards signaled movement inside. The door opened a few seconds later. Trejo regarded her with his one working eye, its broken, pupil-less twin squinting blindly into the middle distance. Though he and Selena were of a height, he had a way of appearing as if he towered over her, his basalt jaw a pitiless and unscalable cliff-face.

"Mr. Todd didn't mention you'd been summoned," he said.

"I wasn't. I came to talk to him about something."

Somehow Trejo's smile made his face even less friendly. "That's how you think this works, hmm?"

"Why wouldn't it? I've got something to tell him and I wanted to do it to his face."

"A *marcada* don't tell, girl. A *marcada* don't even ask. Sometimes, maybe, she pleads. Mostly she just shuts up and does as she's told. You've a cot and a kitchen, which is more than most in your position get. Or have you forgotten our little excursion already? I suggest you go back to it and thank whatever death-god you worship for Mr. Todd's kindness."

Selena opened her mouth to respond, but a voice behind the door beat her to it.

"Trejo? Who's that at the door?"

"No one, sir," Trejo replied. He spoke with his teeth clamped together.

Mr. Todd peered over Trejo's head at Selena. His smile was warm enough, though tinged with a patronizing gleam Selena didn't like.

"Why, if it ain't our newest little foundling. Let the poor girl in, Trejo. No need to stand on ceremony."

Trejo's face suggested standing on ceremony was very much in order, but he acquiesced with a stiff bow.

"Right this way," he mumbled and slid back to permit her entrance.

Mr. Todd led her into a cozy annex off the main hall. The room hadn't been used during the party and so was new to her. It retained the grandeur of the entertainment areas, but on a cozier scale more suited to private chats than grand soirees. A stone hearth dominated one wall, a pair of antique swords hanging crisscross over the mantle. Armchairs formed a lazy half-circle around the fireplace.

Selena took the seat nearest the wall. Beside her, a mahogany bookshelf bore a series of matching leather-bound tomes with pristine spines. She glanced at the titles, noted a common author between them.

"Who's Charles Dickens?"

Mr. Todd laughed at the question. It was a teasing laugh, but one without real malice, the sort of indulgent chuckle one gave to the unwittingly funny comments of a young child. Selena didn't care for it. Personally, she would've preferred a genuine insult.

"Greatest writer there ever was," he replied. "Or so I'm told. Reading makes me dizzy. The words all jump around on me. You know how to read?"

"Yeah."

Mr. Todd smiled. "Then perhaps one day you'll read 'em to me. We can both get ourselves a little education."

Selena gave no response to this.

"So what've you come to see me about?"

"It's about the Iron Circle. I'm guessing it's only a matter of time before I get my own turn in the ring."

"That's right. Give Trejo a few days, and he'll have something sorted for you."

"I've seen the sort of fights he arranges. I'm not interested in doing a striptease or doling out punishment to petty criminals."

Mr. Todd studied her, his head tilted slightly. His index finger curled along the sloping flesh beneath his lower lip. "Well ain't that something. My girl's got standards. What are you interested in, if not performing for your audience?"

"The Iron Circle's a fighting ring, isn't it? I want a fight. The sort the guys put on to open the show."

"I'm afraid my girls don't really do those sorts of fights."

"Then put me up against someone who does. Man, woman, I don't care. As long as it's an actual opponent."

Mr. Todd touched his fingertips together, making his two hands into a kind of gridiron. "I must say, that isn't the sort of request I'd expected. I've had girls who caught a touch of stage fright, girls who wanted to show a little less skin. But girls asking to brawl with the Brothers of the Iron Circle? That's a mighty queer request."

"Look, I'm not asking to shirk or anything here. I'm a prisoner or whatever, I get it. But that … performance business isn't me. If it's recognition you're after, I can get it. But I can only do it my way."

"What makes you think I'm after recognition?"

"Fine, money then."

Mr. Todd motioned around him. "Does it look to you like I'm hurtin' for money? The plantation pulls in plenty."

Selena blinked. Curiosity threw her momentarily off point. "Then why?"

"I've got my reasons." His fingers bent and straightened, drawing his palms in and out. "You have any idea what happens to girls who got tossed in the pits with all that scum? Sleeping in piles on the dirt with the biggest, baddest, nastiest fighters you could name? It doesn't happen much because they don't last long. I recall one hacked off her own nose with a bit of broken glass. Wanted to make herself less appealing, you see. All she did was give the boys a new hole to work with."

"I'm not asking to move in with them. I just want a proper match."

Mr. Todd clucked his tongue.

"No, I'm sorry, I can't have it. I've made an investment in you, and I don't intend to squander it by having some knucklehead pound your pretty face to a pulp."

"Someone already beat them to it," Selena said, pointing to her ruined ear.

"An ear's not a face. And while you may not be a siren like Theodora or Eleanor, you're still not a pain to look at, you don't mind me saying. Best we keep it that way." Todd slapped his hands on his thighs and stood. The sound was apparently a signal, for Trejo scurried in an instant later. "Let the monsters have their scraps, girl. You're under my wing. Enjoy it."

Selena made her way out before Trejo could set his eager hands on her. She sensed no lust in his reaching fingers, but a keen disdain that was, somehow, even more unpleasant.

"Oh, and one last thing," Mr. Todd said. "I'm happy you came to see me today. It gave us a chance to clear a few things up, get to know each other. In the future, if you ever have anything else you'd like to ask me, best to go through Trejo. He'll treat you right."

He winked at her and turned to face the unlit hearth. His eyes remained fixed at the empty fireplace as she left the room.

19: Tendrils of Hope

The gorge grew shallower as it squiggled west, rising with the land until they reached a common height and the fissure tapered shut like a wound poorly healed. A steady wind chased phantoms of dust along the plains, harrying them from their cracked sandstone tombs. The land here was even more lifeless than the *pueblos* he'd fled, a feat Simon would scarcely have thought possible. The tufts of creosote and tarwort had vanished, replaced by anonymous spiny weeds that put Simon in mind of yellow locust.

Crows cawed sardonically from the branches of a dead tree. Simon picked up a stone and threw it at them. It fell several feet short of the mark. He tried again and scored a blow against the tree's knotted trunk. The birds flew off with an indignant ruffle of their wings, screeching their hoarse, inscrutable expletives.

Simon was beginning to feel he'd made a mistake. The impetus for his journey had been vague in the first place, driven more by curiosity than any concrete plan. He'd simply wanted to know where Emily could have gotten such pristine parts. And Emily agreed to show him. What he might do with those parts or where he might take them he had no idea, but at hearing the offer some long-stalled gear in his brain had started turning, setting the two of them in motion.

They'd left the next morning, supply bags loaded with boiled cornmeal, twists of sun-cured crow meat, and bottles of water made of a thin, brittle plastic that, once transparent, had clouded into a piebald translucence the color of sour milk.

A cuesta banded the earth to their right, and they scrambled up its crumbling face. Atop the ridge lay the ruins of a pre-War highway, its paved face weathered into chunks of tar-clotted gravel. The road led them through the rising foothills to a cleft in the rocky outcrops, where the remains of a pre-War town went about their long slow slide into rubble. Town was perhaps too grandiose a term: the buildings—what was left of them—formed a parallel procession along the crumbled fossil of the highway, a dozen or so limpets clinging to a behemoth's dead belly. Shards of brick and rotting lumber collected in the narrow thoroughfare, a steady accretion of refuse that would one day choke the pass entirely. Simon doubted such a tiny place would boast any former industry, let alone one with stores that could be plundered after so many years had passed.

Emily stepped nimbly over the slough of rubble and hopped through the sagging archway of what had once been a building. Its façade had long since fallen down, revealing concrete bones turned osteoporotic as time dissolved their rebar marrow into rust and oblivion. The result had an ugly, anatomical cast, a fractured skull with the face peeled away. The remains of the ceiling littered the floor, while the walls bowed inward as if in grief at their passing. Dust, stirred by the constant eddies of the wind between the chasm walls, barbed the air with its creosotic tang.

Simon sneezed into the crux of his elbow and wiped the reddening skin beneath his eyes. His eyelids felt like tissue paper, as if the slightest pressure could tear them in two. It seemed a cruel irony that his allergies would flare up even here, in this awful dead place.

They entered through the building's gawping mouth. The remnants of its inner walls stood only ankle high in places, but Emily treated them as solid boundaries, tracing the halls as if the house were unbroken. Simon wanted to ask Emily what they were doing here, but he restrained himself despite the urge. He'd agreed to follow her and would have to trust her methods, however strange they might seem.

His patience was soon rewarded. Crouching in the far corner of what was probably once a kitchen—the shards of ceramic tile mixed in with the other detritus was a clue—Emily thrust her hands into the debris and grabbed hold of a plastic tarp. She tugged on it a few times and swept it to one side, revealing the top of a cement staircase.

Surprised, Simon stomped twice on the ground. The floor felt solid beneath his feet. There was no telltale thump to suggest a lower level. How could a suspended floor remain unbroken after so many decades of neglect? Puzzled, he chewed the corner of his mouth and followed Emily into the darkness.

The descent took longer than expected, sinking through a dozen feet of earth and concrete before entering a stark subterranean chamber hewn from bare earth. Stone columns ribbed the walls, steel struts binding one to the next. Simon glanced up uneasily through the gloom at the untold tons of dirt and stone hanging above him. *That explains why the first floor's so solid.* He just hoped it stayed that way while he was down there.

Emily removed a small device from her pocket. She clicked a button, and a cone of white light shone from the glass bulb at its tip.

"Where'd you get that?" asked Simon. Flashlights weren't exactly foreign technology to him, but he hadn't expected to see one so far from Jericho.

"You want one? Wait a sec, you can have as many as you want."

She led him to the room's dim recesses, where the beam of her flashlight honed upon an enormous steel door. It stood eight feet high, hogging every inch of vertical space between floor and ceiling, its bulk wedged into a metal frame eight inches thick. Its face was without feature save a single wheel—a device that looked more to Simon like the master control valve for some vast urban reservoir than the latch for a door—set in its precise center. Judging by its size, Simon guessed it would require at least two grown men to move it, but Emily seemed undaunted. She stood on tiptoe to grasp the wheel and turned it clockwise. It spun silently on well-oiled bearings.

She gave the door a push and it swung inward. Intrigued, Simon studied the door as he passed. His engineer's eye noted the sturdy hinges as thick as his wrist, the brushed copper contacts between door and frame that suggested an electromagnetic seal, the interior deadbolts for manual reinforcement once inside. Clearly whoever built this place wanted it to be well-defended, but didn't want an unexpected power failure to make it their tomb. He nodded in silent admiration to his anonymous predecessor.

Bare earth gave way to concrete and metal, all of it curiously preserved. Simon ran his finger along the wall. He expected porous stone but felt instead a smooth lacquer. A steel grate held him half a foot above the tunnel floor. Rust nibbled at its myriad weld pools and speckled brownish patterns along its length, but here too the material held up better than expected. Emily's footsteps rang along the grating, a sound Simon only noticed when it stopped. The beam of her flashlight fixed him in its gaze.

"You coming?"

"Right. Sorry."

Simon scurried behind her to a bend in the tunnel, where the corridor opened onto a chasm of yawning black space. Emily felt along the wall for a switch and threw it. Banks of sterile white light ignited overhead. Many of the bulbs had burnt out, but enough remained to reveal a subterranean chamber twenty feet high. Simon wondered what power source they might be drawing on. Solar panels on the cliffs overhead? Geothermal energy? Deep-cycle batteries charged a century before, their long-dormant electric payloads unthawed through some long-forgotten process?

The steel grating became a catwalk that circled the chamber's perimeter, feeding staircases that zigzagged down to the floor below. Sturdy plastic crates filled one corner of the room. A few of them lay scattered about the floor, their lids pried off and contents removed, but most remained sealed and stacked in tidy columns eight feet high. Emily clattered down a nearby staircase and slipped past them to a bank of a dozen-plus doors set in recessed frames. She motioned to the lot of them like a merchant displaying her wares. Simon chose a door at random and went inside.

The room was no wider than the doorframe, a pantry with shallow ledges running elbow high along both walls. Above the ledges hung dozens of high-powered rifles, their sleek barrels bloated with scopes and shrouds and extended magazines.

"There's no bullets, before you get too excited," said Emily. "Whoever was here last took 'em all before they sealed the place up. Dad thinks it was one of the militias, during the Last War. Guess they had more guns than members by the end."

"What happened to them?"

Emily shrugged. "Who knows? Whatever got 'em didn't get 'em here, though they left in a pretty big hurry. Took the food and the ammo but left the rest. They sealed it up tight, so they probably figured they'd be back. Didn't work out that way, though."

The other rooms were similar to the first, their contents less outwardly arresting than the rifles but ultimately—to Simon, at least—more exciting: banks of small plastic drawers heaped with bolts, nuts, screws, and nails; coils of copper wire spun tight around cork cylinders; anonymous white jugs heavy with oils and solvents; resistors, capacitors, and diodes of every sort; an armory of hand tools, from pliers with wire-stripping notches to screwdrivers with exotic triangular tips. His exploration brought him around the room to its far end, where a concrete archway fed into a second chamber even larger than the first. He had only just passed its threshold when the chamber's contents stopped him mid-step.

Transit in New Canaan was basic and communal—the upper-class Seraphim took the mag-train while the plebian Salters and their middle-class minders the Shepherds walked—and the scarcity of fuel and paved roads made personal vehicles a rarity, but Simon had grown up among the elite and recognized an automobile when he saw one.

But these were not the sleek wriggles of quicksilver chrome that well-heeled Bishops used to putter about the Outer Baronies, affectations of the eccentric rich. These vehicles had purpose. Iron grills snarled across hoods of olive-green metal, steel plates bobbing on outsized chassis. Cabs sank into armored frames, limiting the driver's view to a foot-high band of reinforced glass. They showed their age more than the tools, their tires sagging and their undercarriages flecked with rust, but they retained a look of ferocity subdued but unbroken—circus lions eyeing their trainers with quiet, patient hatred. Simon half expected them to roar to life as he approached, imprinting their decades of captivity on his pulverized bones.

"Do they work?" Simon asked.

"No. I've tried 'em all. Not so much as a flicker from any of 'em."

"Do they need fuel? Is it an electrical problem? Or do you think it's more structural?"

"How should I know? I flicked all the switches and nothing happened. Beyond that, I've got no clue."

"Can I take a look?"

Emily presented her hand, palm up, in a "be my guest" motion. Simon licked his lips. In the back of his mind a plan was already growing. He pruned back his expectations as best he could, told himself that there was no point in planning before he'd even checked the engine blocks—the things could be totally gutted for all he knew, nothing but the hollowed carapaces of long-dead machines—but the tendrils of hope sprouted quicker than he could trim them.

"How long can we stay here?" Simon asked.

"Well, we've got enough food and water to last us a few days at least."

"And that's for two of us, right?"

"Yeah. Why?"

"Listen, I know you've already helped me a ton, but would you be able to get more supplies? You can go about your business otherwise, I'd just need them before I run out."

"Of course. You're the reason our crops aren't toast already. But what are you going to do here for a whole week?"

"I don't know yet, exactly," Simon said, though this wasn't strictly true. He knew what he wanted to do, all right.

He just didn't know if it would work.

20: A Tide of Blood and Bone

The ring felt bigger once you stepped inside it.

As a spectator in the upper rows, it seemed big enough, a circular arena more suited to team sport than a one-on-one brawl. In the tunnels below the stands, it grew bigger still, the narrow confines and the susurrus of a dozen fighters preparing their bodies for their personal wars stretching its iron contours into a parched and hostile wasteland. But once Selena stepped into the ring itself, and the weight of a thousand pairs of eyes pored over her, the unbroken ramparts of crowd-roiled adobe swelled to the size of a country. And she knew in the deepest chambers of her heart that none may pass beyond its unbroken, noose-tight border unless their toll had been paid, and that the only currency the Circle recognized was blood.

Selena stood just outside the ring's geographic center. There was a grandeur to this place she'd never encountered in any fighting venue before, a weight that was awful and terrible in the oldest and truest sense of these terms, and as the guards dragged into the ring the human scab they called her opponent, she felt an anger rise in her, not just at the things they'd done to her and were making her do—though these factors were present, too—but at the way they'd cheapened this place, wrung the honor from its proceedings and contorted them into something petty and perverse.

She looked to the other fighters waiting in the tunnels surrounding the circle. Her eyes moved past the *gladiadores* with their motley array of rust-flecked death weapons and the *blanco* bruisers seeking a frisson of infamy and settled on the elite clutch of talent and muscle congregating in the northern alcove. Mary had told her about these men. They were *Los Hermanos del Círculo de Hierro, marcado* warriors of renown who, over years of unparalleled spectacle and flirtation with death, had shed their marks of bondage and become slaves to the Circle alone. Such stories had naturally inflamed Selena's imagination, though freedom took years to earn.

One *Hermano*, his hair lathered with oil and bound in a tight braid down his back, noticed her staring and responded by raising his hand to his lips and waggling his tongue between his second and third finger. A tattoo danced on his right cheek. Once a greyish shape of some sort, it had been blotted out by a red X set in a like-colored circle, beneath which writhed a small, elaborate squiggle. He dropped his hand and winked at her.

Shaking her head, she returned her attention to the man she was supposed to fight. He could barely stand unaided. Some dreadful disease had eaten away his nose and most of one cheek, leaving in their place a yawning red cavity rimmed with a greenish-brown crust. The guards—or perhaps attendants was a better term—unlooped his thin arms from their shoulders and shoved him forward. He collapsed to his knees and coughed, spewing a mist of bloody phlegm. One of the guards gave him a prodding kick to the tailbone to get him moving.

He staggered to his feet and gazed about, seemingly unsure where he was and why so many people were staring at him. A fringe of matted hair hung down over one eye, while the other floated in a film of yellowish ichor. After a few seconds of reflection, he raised his hapless fists, thumbs tucked into the hollow formed by his curled fingers. Selena shook her head in disgust. A punch from those hands would land like jelly and snap his thumb at the first knuckle.

Selena approached the man without caution. She didn't deign to raise her arms in a fighter's stance, nor move on the balls of her feet as she would against a real opponent. Her every motion lacked the spectacle of combat, in which the tension of the fighters' muscles coils the audience tighter in sympathy. She stood a few paces from the man, arms at her sides. The man cringed behind his raised fists.

As seconds passed and nothing further occurred, the roar of the crowd settled into a murmur. Selena's opponent peeked out from between his fists. A few spectators shouted taunts, their general meaning obvious despite the words being in *Mejise*. Selena yawned and scratched her chin. This brought several more jeers, which encouraged several more, and soon the individual insults coalesced into a single amorphous growl of displeasure. Selena's opponent glanced back and forth between sections of the crowd, his eyes swollen with fear.

Selena grabbed her opponent's left wrist. His skin was hot and clammy, its greasy expanse flecked with patches of flaky, dry crust. Suppressing her revulsion, Selena brought the man's arm up behind his back and, with modest but steady pressure, eased him to his knees. The man obeyed without struggling. Whatever spirit his disease hadn't eaten away had been beaten out of him by Thorin's strongmen. He was defeated before he'd even entered the Iron Circle. The least Selena could do was signal this defeat gently.

She laid him on the ground and pressed his shoulders into the dirt. He seemed to get the message, for when she released him, he stood slowly, nodded at her in uncomprehending thanks, and scuttled out of the circle. She imagined he wouldn't get far and would likely face his punishment in some other form. There was nothing she could do about that, but at least she wouldn't be the one providing it. In recognition of this resolve, she stepped back and raised her arms to the crowd, beckoning their ire.

The crowd obliged, hurling incomprehensible epithets and pounding their fists on the railings. Selena ignored them, summoning her inborne Seraphim's hauteur. She set her eyes instead on the clutch of fighters awaiting their own bouts, scanning for an ideal target. There was no shortage of options, but Selena was choosey. It would have to be someone who appeared unbeatable, and he would have to be among *Los Hermanos*.

One presented itself almost immediately. The *Hermano* who'd gestured obscenely at her before the fight was now tapping his friend on the chest with the back of his hand, signaling his derision at the spectacle before him. She scoped the topography of his muscles, sized up his potential speed and power, noted points of weakness: long hair and beard for easy grabbing, an offset knuckle that would weaken his left jab, a peculiar slope to his jaw hinting at an old break. He commanded respect from his peers, which meant he was good—but also meant he was cocky. Selena was good, too, and no one here had seen her fight.

She approached him with casual strides, thumbs tucked into the waistband of her pants. He smirked as she loped over the iron circle and cleared the remaining distance between them. She stood uncomfortably close, her eyes level with his chin, gazing up with a defiance that denied the slightest difference in their sizes. He cocked his head to one side and spoke a query in *Mejise*. She knew it for a question for its rising cadence and guessed its derogatory nature by the simian guffawing of his compatriots. In response, she smiled, took his vest in her hands, and noisily blew her nose into it.

The man's smirk flattened into an ugly line. Its ends peeled upward a moment later, purporting a levity that didn't match his eyes. He wiped his vest clean with one hand and flicked the snot from his fingers. Selena walked back into the ring, turned, and beckoned him forward.

For a moment he seemed uncertain. He whispered among his fellow fighters, likely asking what this crazy woman was up to and if he would face any consequences if he taught her a lesson. Ultimately, he seemed to decide it was worth the risk, for he jogged forward and vaulted gracefully over the Iron Circle. Selena studied the ease with which he'd heaved himself aloft, one-armed, and wondered if she'd made a serious miscalculation. The thought remained with her only a moment before the red wave of impending combat crashed over her, a tide of blood and bone that drowned lesser emotions in its merciless fathoms.

Unsanctioned, the fight had no formal beginning. It simply *was*, a fluid conflict that burbled to the surface with her gauntlet-throwing sneeze and gushed into full-on combat.

He tested her with a few open-handed blows, not quite ready to dignify her with a fist. She swatted them aside like so many bothersome mosquitos.

He marched forward, shoulders squared, in hopes of muscling her about the ring. She threw a high jab to his face, pulled the punch, and delivered a punishing shovel hook to his solar plexus.

He woofed out an incredulous breath and stared, gobsmacked, as her second jab connected with his lips. She didn't pull this one, and the blow rattled his teeth in their sockets. He closed his hands around his head and shuffled away from the flurry that followed.

A lupine voice in Selena's head howled for her to press her advantage. She ignored it. His power was still untested, and her ruined ear remained a weak spot. A hook from a lead-armed fighter could flatten her. Better to take things slow and steady.

Scenting blood, the crowd leaned into the fight, a thousand chants and cheers and admonitions pouring from its myriad mouths. Her opponent glanced at a few spots in the stands, testing the timbre of their response. He rolled his shoulders, raised his fists, and came at her fast.

No kittenish slaps this time. His fists were tight, and they landed hard. Selena felt their impact rattle through her arms. She hurled back a few jabs and a cross, landed half, but took a slashing blow to the cheek that split her skin and left that hemisphere of her skull ringing. They collided in a formless scuffle, a snarl of grapples that wouldn't take, until Selena shoved the man away and took the free instant that followed to settler her stance.

Her opponent surged forward immediately, raised his left arm for a haymaker, and threw a right kick instead. It was a swinging blow, not chambered but whip-fast and delivered with power. Selena cocked her hip at the last second to divert the blow away from her liver to the hefty sheath of muscle below it. It connected with a savage thwack that sent her sprawling. She scrabbled for her footing, lost it and turned the fall into a roll, hurling herself upright before he had a chance to press his advantage.

He tried to take her off guard, but she'd been knocked down many times before and had studied the awkward grey art of regaining your equilibrium before your opponent got his foot on your throat. She met his charge with a palm strike that threaded neatly through his dukes and slammed the bridge of his nose. Cartilage crunched. He gritted through the blow and kept charging, his hooked arms scooping her up and hurling her to the ground. She landed on one knee, sprung forward, and hammered his abdomen. He rained closed fists onto her back, strikes whose crudity belied their savage power. She slid back, hoping to put herself in range to throw a solid cross, but he pinned her arms to her sides and squeezed. Several inches taller, he managed to contort the bulk of his weight onto her back, pressing down on her spine with agonizing force.

The pressure grew. Selena fought to free her arms, but his grip was tight, and the few punches it allowed were powerless. Black spots bubbled along the fringes of her vision. A few more seconds and they would narrow to pinpricks. Her ears rang with a high and howling wind. With a desperate lurch, she worked her forearms up and clawed at his face. Her opponent laughed, kissing at her scrabbling fingers. He said something taunting in *Mejise*. Finally, she seized his beard. A firm tug assessed her grip and found it sufficient. He snarled at the discomfort but continued his squeezing assault.

With a final tweak to her grip, Selena hurled her face forward. Her forehead struck his nose. A brittle snap filled the Iron Circle. She smashed her forehead into him again and again. Blood and mucus flecked her face, running along the rivulets of sweat that lined her cheeks, fluids mingling in the horrible intimacy of fighting at its most vicious.

She delivered a final slam and released him. His knees buckled like hinges with the pins pulled free, spilling him onto the dusty ground. He lay there for a moment, blood dribbling from the shard of red meat his nose had become and congealing into mucusy curds about his beard.

Selena hedged back, fists raised. This wasn't an official fight, which meant there was no way to say exactly when it ended. She watched the man arch his back, his eyes narrow to slits, and his mouth part to emit a huge and bellowing laugh. He kicked his heels and pounded the dirt with his fists, cackling hysterics into the open air. A confused murmur drifted through the crowd.

The man raised himself to his feet and tottered over to Selena, his gait still a bit unsteady—or so it appeared. Selena had used the same type of feint on many occasions and did not drop her guard. He held his palms out in a supplicating gesture. Selena studied him wearily.

They remained that way for a moment, neither moving, until the man's hand snapped out and grabbed Selena by the wrist. She yanked her arm back but was unable to break his grip. In a single fluid motion, he held her arm aloft and pivoted to stand beside her, the two of them facing the crowd. He shook her fist as if waving a trophy and motioned to her with his free hand, imploring the crowd to acknowledge her.

Cheers buried the Iron Circle in a rockslide of sound. Selena glanced warily at her opponent, who met her gaze with a flash of his large and red-flecked teeth. His nose had swollen into a hideous tuber bulging from the scraggly thicket of his beard. She half expected him to try and sweep her arm back in some petulant, elbow-shattering bit of revenge, but he simply let her hand drop and disappeared back the way he'd come. Selena soaked up her applause for another moment and, afraid to overstay her welcome, slipped out of the ring and into the underpass where some of Mr. Todd's other girls had watched the proceedings.

None of them spoke. They stared at Selena, their faces windswept and alien. Selena turned to Mary Katherine. "That went pretty well, I guess."

"Pretty well? That was Paulo Aguilar! He's a Brother of the fucking Iron Circle!" Mary's excitement abated. She chewed the corner of her mouth. "Uh, did Mr. Todd tell you to call him out like that?"

"No. Why?"

Mary said nothing. She looked away, fingers smoothing out stray strands of hair. The other girls did likewise. Only one continued meeting her eyes: Grace Delgado, her head tilted slightly on her long regal neck. Selena stared back, projecting neither hostility nor friendliness. After a few seconds' pause, Grace gave a small nod and walked away down the corridor.

A familiar hand closed around her bicep. Trejo's breath hissed hot and sour in her ear.

"With me."

"You could just ask, you know," Selena said. Trejo didn't' listen. He was off, dragging her behind him like a disobedient child. The last time he did this it had infuriated her, but for some reason. his silent fury struck a comic note in her this time, and she had to bite her lip to restrain a peal of giggles. *What the hell is wrong with me? There's nothing funny here.* And yet the laughter built in her belly. She felt overcome by the giddy fatalism of an explorer who, having cast ashore on an uncharted beach, set her ships alight behind her, resolved to live or die in the new world.

After a short jaunt in a carriage chilly with Trejo's bitter silence, Selena found herself marched up the stairs of Todd's *hacienda* and set down in a chair opposite him. The glib, slightly patronizing bonhomie of her first visit was nowhere in evidence. Trejo bowed stiffly and left. Todd ignored him, his glare locked squarely on Selena.

"I've just had a most interesting conversation with my messengers regarding your little performance this afternoon. The last time we spoke, I'd had it in my mind that you and I'd reached an understanding. It seems I was wrong."

"Looks like it," agreed Selena, picking at a loose thread in the arm of her chair.

Todd pinched the bridge of his nose. "Then let's be clearer, shall we? I told you I didn't want you to fight in the Iron Circle. And the first time you get in the Circle, what did you do?"

"Why was I there, if not to fight?"

"The same reason many of my girls step into that ring. To put on a show. Which you did in the most half-assed way possible. Then, for an encore no one asked for, you went and challenged a Brother of the Iron Circle to a fistfight."

"Challenged and won," Selena clarified.

Todd chuckled. "You're amused. I'm glad. We'll see how funny you think it is when one of the pit boys gets you pinned. And it'll happen. I don't care how fast you were in that Circle. No one's fast forever."

Selena cocked an eyebrow. "You're saying I can fight again?"

"Can? Try *will*. You're an upstart young girl who, unprompted, bested one of the greatest fighters in the most elite segment of the entire Iron Circle. The crowd won't accept anything less, and I can't find it in myself to care about your well-being any longer. I've rescinded my protection. You're still my *marcada*, but the beasts of the Circle can do what they want with you. It's all one to me."

They sat in silence for a moment, Selena unsure what to say next and Todd clearly uninterested in saying anything at all. He sipped morosely at clear liquid in a fluted glass and stared into the unlit hearth.

"I guess I should say thanks."

Todd laughed, a single ashen cough of humorless noise. "I'd tell you to hold your thanks for a couple of weeks if I even wanted them in the first place. Which I don't. We'll see how happy you find this new arrangement once word gets out. You think there's chivalry among the *Hermanos*? If so, you're in for a very rude awakening."

"Okay."

Todd shook his head. He seemed disgusted at his own amusement. "Get the hell out of my house, already. In every sense but your branded fealty, we're done."

Selena blinked into the sunlight. An otherworldly haze hung about her head, the fogginess one gets in dreams when the where and the why of things grows soft and tenuous, its edges smudging the more you touch them. She'd answered Todd's summons with an air of resigned fatalism, unsure what awaited her once she left his manor the second time—prison? An auction block? The gallows? Instead, he'd given her the one thing she'd asked for and been denied, the very object she stole from under his nose and was supposed to be punished for. She didn't even need to vacate her bunk! He said he'd rescinded his protection, but when in her life had she ever had any protection before? The events spun in her mind like a wheel on a broken axle, all jolts and wobbles and doubling back, drilling through her with its pervasive dizziness.

"Well, what the hell do I do now?" she asked aloud. The opportunity to even ask the question had been so unexpected, that the answer took a full second to arrive, as obvious as it was.

She would fight, of course.

21: Fools and Kings

Marcus was running out of places to drink.

It wasn't for a lack of money, though he had none: his reputation was known and respected through most of Juarez's assorted watering holes, and he could always eke out credit when needed. Nor had he been officially kicked out of anywhere—as if any right-thinking barkeep would dare. Rather, he abandoned them, drifting to the next friendly stool once the discomfort his presence caused his current bar's owners grew too obvious to ignore.

This discomfort was never consciously addressed, but Marcus lived and died by his ability to winkle out the innermost thoughts and intentions of those around him, and it never took long for him to pick up on them. Bartenders nodded too eagerly, their faces rigid with pasteboard smiles, and scrubbed compulsively at glasses that were clean five minutes ago. Patrons barked overfriendly greetings before disappearing to the far corners of the room. Tension buzzed in the background of every moment, a subconscious chord endlessly swelling in volume.

Marcus never had to ask if someone knew his current situation: it was clear everybody already did. Whether leaked from an observer or spread by Thorin himself, all of Juarez knew that Marcus was due to fight for the *Jefe* in the Iron Circle and that he'd thus far refused to do so.

His refusal was unspoken but potent. Each morning, when Thorin's porter called on him to attend his fight, he brushed past him and went somewhere to drink instead. It was the same story every day, without the slightest variation in the porter's tone of voice, or the benign expectation of Marcus's acquiescence. The porter—thin, young, his bronze-hued face shaved bald and emblazoned with green stars at either temple—displayed no anger or surprise at being so consistently ignored.

As a strategy, this was unsustainable. Any amusement Thorin found in Marcus's gall would sour into anger soon enough, and blood would follow—at least some of it Marcus's. Yet Marcus couldn't quite bring himself to care. Everything he'd felt since returning to Juarez— the anguish at Thorin's ascent to de facto emperor, the rage at his own impotence in the face of such a regime, the guilt at how the stains of his past had tainted those around him—lay buried beneath a rockslide of apathy. Let them come for him. Let them kill him, for that matter. He just planned to get his money's worth out of his liver before they did. This remained his sole objective: the overtaxing of an internal organ. As a *raison d'être*, it wasn't much, but you played the hand life dealt you. Only fools and kings believed they could slip in a phony card and not get caught out over it.

So, the porter kept coming, and Marcus kept ignoring him. The pattern of visits changed only once, when Manuel arrived in the porter's stead.

Marcus had made no effort to ingratiate himself directly with any of the *Senadors*. Tensions between the three had always been high, long before Thorin had planted the first seeds of his eventual coup, and forming alliances with one inevitably meant making adversaries of the other two—a losing proposition, overall. But while sycophancy wasn't his style, he did make a point to stay friendly with key figures in their *pandillas*. Sometimes these relationships were tedious affairs, the men in question arrogant bores turgid with self-importance, viewing anyone not of their rank and affiliation with varying levels of suspicion and disdain.

Manuel was a different case. A *teniente* in the *pandilla* controlled by *Senador* Delgado—himself the most pleasant of the city's three rulers—Manuel never lost the easy bearing of an unranked *blanco*. He'd respected Marcus without fearing him, which made their interactions loose and unrestrained in a way they seldom were for a man of Marcus's reputation. If Thorin had tried, he could scarcely have chosen an advocate more likely to persuade Marcus without rankling his pride—a fact that made Marcus suspect Manuel had come of his own volition, or perhaps even against Thorin's wishes.

"You need to stop this foolishness, *ese*," Manuel said. His smile, once as constant a staple of his face as the mole on his chin, was nowhere to be seen.

"There was a time when your idea of foolishness would be to greet Thorin with anything but a mouthful of spit. What happened, Manny?"

"Thorin's coup happened. You weren't here to see it. He's a coward in some ways, but crafty and willing to gamble. Delgado and Evangelista had forgotten this. They saw him as the blowhard, the jester, the bent prong of their trident, while he mustered just enough force to depose them. They were atop the gallows with their hands bound before they'd even fully realized he'd struck. There was resistance, but he tamped it down. Those who fought back died awful deaths. I saw a man live for two days without a strip of skin on his body, warmed by flames to keep hypothermia from ending his misery. I saw eyes gouged out, limbs severed and sutured back where they didn't belong. We saw it all—were made to see it all, so when Thorin called to us, the *torturadores* to his left and the *tatuadores* to his right, we all knew which one to choose."

"A sad story, Manuel. I'm sorry for what's happened to you. But never have I bowed to a *tirano*. I refused when there were three of them, and I refuse now there is only one."

Manuel grabbed Marcus by the shoulders and shook him. Few men outside his family would dare perform such a gesture. "You're still acting like *la paz inquieta* is there to protect you. But it's gone. The old rules have been erased, Marcito. Thorin rewrote them. And that means he wins every time. You're right that he wants you to fight under his banner—your name carries far in these parts, and it would be an honor for him. But you're not indispensable, and there are no other *Senadores* left to give you quarter."

"I ask for no quarter. If Thorin wants me so badly, let him come to me himself. I tried to pay my debt through envoys, and he denied me. Now he sends envoys on his behalf, and I give him the same treatment."

Manuel shook his head. "I pray for you, *ese*."

"My hand has never needed prayers to give it speed, Manuel, but thank you."

"I'm not praying for your victory in combat, Marcus. That would be a waste of time. I'm praying for you to see reason."

That had been yesterday. This morning the porter had been back, once more subject to Marcus's rebuff. With the return to routine, Marcus could almost convince himself that things wouldn't escalate. Thorin would continue to send the porter on his quixotic quest—perhaps as an inventive sort of punishment for a past slight—and Marcus would whittle away his days in penury.

But Manuel's plea continued to echo in the backmost chambers of his mind, and it was thus no real surprise when two men with pistols on their hips strode into the room and loomed over Marcus's table, their faces so composed and stoic they seemed scarcely human, pareidolic illusions glimpsed in chunks of stone.

The surprise came from the man who stepped in after them.

Thorin moved with a kingly swagger cribbed from some second-rate pantomime, shoulders swiveling with each outsized step. He took his position between his guards.

Only two, Marcus mused. *There was a time he wouldn't have come for me with less than a dozen men at his side. Has my shadow truly grown so small?*

Thorin rapped his knuckles on the table in front of Marcus. His rings struck the wood with a bracing clack, catching the attention of the few remaining patrons too inebriated to notice his presence beforehand. Those with less sodden faculties had already skirted to the nearest exit, or else tucked themselves into their drinks in an effort to be overlooked.

"You've been ignoring my summons, Marcus," Thorin said. "This is not appreciated."

Marcus shrugged. "I've been busy."

"I can see that."

He took the bottle from Marcus's table and held its neck between two fingers. It swung back and forth, the dregs of cloudy amber liquid swirling in its belly. He took a sniff of it and recoiled.

"Peh! What is this horse urine?"

He turned toward the bar and hollered at the bartender, whose bald head shrank into his hunched shoulders.

"You call this mescal? I've pissed finer drinks than this!"

The bartender nodded with a small tittering laugh and continued polishing the countertop with a rag.

Thorin took a swing and grimaced. "You debase yourself with this swill, Marcus. Why not allow yourself something finer?"

"Fine things are not without cost, *Jefe.*"

"There is no need for this self-inflicted poverty. You are the

168

best fighter the Iron Circle ever saw. We do not let our warriors go unrewarded."

Thorin put a hand on Marcus's shoulder and squeezed. Marcus suppressed a shudder of revulsion. He longed to brush the odious hand away, but restrained himself. It was a fine line he was walking—and given how little mescal remained in the bottle Thorin held, Marcus doubted his capacity to walk anywhere. He chose his words delicately.

"It seems to me, I can expect no reward no matter what path I may choose. I attempted to pay my debts to you in good faith, but this attempt was rejected. I am yours forever perhaps, but that doesn't mean you'll find me worth having."

"That is most unfair, Marcus. I have never been known to leave my debtors without their spending money. As *Jefe*, I take care of all my citizens. Does your mother not enjoy the charity of the Grey Sisters? These women practice their art at my pleasure. They could easily be stopped."

Marcus chose not to respond to this threat. He studied the table before him, losing himself in the whorls and eddies of its grain.

Thorin was a man who'd grown used to having his questions answered. He frowned. "I will ask one more time. There is a match awaiting you in the Iron Circle. Will you attend it?"

Marcus felt his inebriation leak away. It was a chilly, unpleasant sensation, as if he'd been enjoying a warm bath and someone had pulled a stopper from the drain, leaving him to shiver in naked sobriety. His fingers continued to tremble, but this was no more than playacting. Playing drunk was a great way to make opponents underestimate you—especially if you really *had* been drunk a few moments before. His switchblade gained sudden heft beneath his serape, its textured handle nuzzling against his ribs. He worked his fingers subtly open and shut, limbering muscles stiffened by drink. *So, the time has come,* he reflected. *I hope you chose your men wisely, Jefe. I shall put them to the test.*

Thorin heaved a heavy sigh and whistled.

A clutch of guards marched into the bar. In their center wriggled a lean man with a purple bruise blossoming on one cheek. Thorin stepped aside, and the guards hurled the man into Marcus's table.

Emilio's brown eyes gazed up at him, frightened and uncomprehending.

"Marcus?" he asked. "What's happening?"

Marcus's resolve collapsed. His fingers dropped clear of their quick-draw position. Had he forgotten how vulnerable he was? How much Thorin loved killing a man by cutting him in a place deeper than mere flesh, to winch guilt around his soul and torque it agonizingly tight? He stood, hands raised, palms out in a conciliatory gesture.

"Okay, *Jefe.* You win. I'll fight."

"You made your choice, Marcus. You must learn to live with the consequences."

"I'm sorry. I've changed my mind. I'll fight for you night and day. Pick the time and the man. Or men. I'll take on every fighter in the pits. I'll do it now." He came forward. Three of the guards drew their pistols and trained the barrels on Marcus's chest, forcing him several steps back. The remaining guards seized Emilio and positioned him face-down across the table. They pinned his left arm behind his back while stretching his right arm out straight. A burly man with braided hair and a notch missing from his left nostril grabbed the arm at either side of the elbow and pressed it firmly into the wood. Emilio grunted.

Moving with slow, measured strides, Thorin rounded the table until he stood next to Emilio's prostrate arm. He drew a large knife with a stout silver blade and contemplated his reflection. It was a hefty thing, more cleaver than dagger, its dull back edge weighted to lend extra force to the swing.

"Running a city is not such an easy thing, you know. Every peasant fancies that he would be a kind and just ruler, a man for whom statues are built and children are named. But it's not so simple as that, Marcus. It's not the day-to-day matters that pose a challenge. The paving of roads and passing of laws. One can hire good men for this and not trouble himself. No, the true challenge comes from this incessant need for *kindness*. Kind and just, they say. Kind and just. But kindness is a soft and dribbly thing, and justice is heavy and hard. One cannot build a just world on kindness, just as one cannot build a stone temple on a swamp. *Bedrock* is what's needed, Marcus. Cold and ugly and rough. But strong."

Thorin brought the blade down. It bit through sinew and bone and came to rest in the table's warped grain. Emilio's severed hand twitched a few times and lay still. The man himself was less docile.

He bucked in the guards' grasp, his shriek sharper than the blade that had maimed him. The guards gathered him up and hurled him to the floor, where he lay, weeping and cradling his ruined wrist. Thorin regarded him the way a child might watch a fly, after having pulled off one of its wings. He grabbed the severed hand from the table and held it to a nearby lamp to study it.

"Patch him up," he said, and turned to Marcus. "A porter will attend you at first chime. You will follow him where he leads and perform the task I've set out for you. You did not wish to fight in the Iron Circle? Then you shall not. There are other uses for your talents, and you may soon learn the value of your previous role. And if the chime sounds and you hear the bottle calling you instead …"

He tossed the hand to Marcus. It landed on the table with a wet thump.

"Just remember that, at the moment, this boy still has one hand left to him."

22: Otro

Selena's first sanctioned fight in the Iron Circle was almost her last. Her opponent was a hunched, wiry man an inch shorter than her, his thin arms knotted with ugly, utilitarian muscle. A tattoo blotted his forehead. Like Paulo's it had been crossed out with a thick red X, marking him as a Brother of the Iron Circle. He winked at someone in the stands and flipped him a two-fingered salute, an in-joke that set the larger man guffawing. Selena sized him up and thought him a weak second act after facing Paulo.

A paunchy man with a gold ring through his septum took the role of emcee, bringing the fighters to their positions and roiling the crowd with a frantic upward motion of his arms. He bellowed his patter in a polished jet of *Mejise* and bowed his way out of the circle, which Selena gathered was the signal to begin. Her opponent, more familiar with the proceedings, caught this a moment sooner than she did, and he pressed the gap to full advantage with a flying kick to her sternum.

It was an audacious move, insanely risky, and it paid out for him the instant his foot connected with her belly. Selena had never encountered such a blatantly gymnastic technique, and the sheer speed of it caught her totally off-guard. She grabbed his leg with both hands, but without a proper stance she could do little but guide the man's foot into her stomach.

The force of the blow rippled clean through her, rattling her spine and rocketing her to the ground. She landed badly. Her head struck the earth hard enough to dent the soil. A dark cloud settled over her vision, its fumes clearing slowly as she struggled to roll free. For a few seconds, she was all but blind. Ballpeen fists hammered her arms and shoulders, driving her back into the dirt. She lashed out with a heel and—by luck more than skill—connected with something hard. Whatever it was it knocked the man back long enough for Selena to regain her feet.

Blood trickled from a cut on her forehead and into the corner of her eye. She rubbed the rivulet with her thumb and blinked the stinging sensation away. The last thing she needed now was another distraction. Her opponent bounced on the balls of his feet, fists raised, and cackled to himself.

This was shaping up to be an inauspicious debut. It wasn't the risk of losing alone that bothered her—she'd lost many times before, and badly—but losing early and to such an improbable-looking opponent. In a public fight, optics meant more than most people gave it credit for. The crowd became an extension of you and your opponent, a twin-tubed umbilicus that could feed you energy as quickly as it could slurp it away. Selena had seen fights tip from one would-be victor to his opponent purely through the caprices of the crowd. If she went down here, all the ground she'd gained by beating Paulo would evaporate. Her victory would be seen as a fluke—or worse, a fix. Some pity play concocted by Paulo for his amusement, or to sucker people into loser bets.

Selena closed the gap between her and her opponent, she feinted low, lulled him into an easy jab at her jaw. He took the bait, cocky with recent triumph. She swatted his arm aside and drove a cross into his nose. Cartilage cracked. A trail of blood and mucus soaked her from wrist to elbow.

Her opponent staggered backward. His eyes warbled in their sockets, struggling to focus. Selena didn't give them the chance. She pulled her arm back, paused half a moment until his shuffling feet struck their most off-balance pose, and swung a haymaker into his right temple.

He hit the ground like a toppled statue. The crowd cheered. Selena dropped her stance. The tide of adrenaline went out, and a hundred aches bobbed to the surface. A fresh dribble of blood stung the corner of her eye. She raised her arms to the crowd. Her ribs screeched like rusty gates swinging in the wind. A black fog settled over her senses. It was fainter than the one that had come in the wake of the wiry man's kick, but visible all the same. When the emcee took her arm and moved to guide her gently from the ring, she felt an urge to go along. Instead, she pulled her arm free and shook her head.

"I want another one," she said. The hunger in her voice surprised her.

The emcee looked at her, perplexed. He continued to usher her off.

She reached deep into her brain and fumbled for the dozen or so phrases she'd learned from Mary, mental fingers closing on what she hoped was the right one. *"Otro, otro."*

The emcee shook his head. It was a gesture driven more by fright than conviction. *"No, no puedes, por favor.* Is too much."

"Too much? I've seen people die in this ring. You're telling me I'm disqualified because of a few bruises?"

"Si, but their keepers, they choose this. They are just *vacas,* yes? Meat for slaughter. You are Mister Todd's, and for him, this is not so. He does not like the violence for his girls."

"He made an exception. Why do you think I'm here?"

By then the spectators nearest her had turned her protest into a chant, banging their fists on the railing in time. *"¡Otro! ¡Otro!"* It spread through the crowd, seat by seat and row by row until the entire arena shook with its trochaic incantation.

"¡Otro! ¡Otro!"

The emcee tottered in a slow circle, mouth agape. He tugged at the corners of his mustache. His tongue poked out from between his lips and disappeared several times.

"Bien vale," he sighed. *"Otro."*

The crowd roared its approval. The emcee shuffled off, defeated, and fetched a fresh opponent. He was larger than the first, with a barrel-chested, simian build she'd faced many times before. A red X voided a wolf's head tattoo on his shoulder. Selena nodded. The emcee repeated his patter, though his delivery lacked its original enthusiasm.

Chastened by her wiry opponent, Selena approached her next

fight with more caution and won it easily. She knew all the notes, and she played them deftly, jabbing pressure points with hypodermic precision and contorting his punches into throws and eye-bulging holds. She won by tap out, not knock out, the big man's face pressed in the dirt as she twined his index and middle fingers into unendurable shapes, but the crowd loved it anyway.

The emcee emerged with two burly guards to escort the loser from the ring—vengeance from beaten parties was common in the wake of contested matches—and held Selena's arm aloft. She bathed in the accolades for a moment, turned, and spoke a single word loud enough for the crowd to here:

"*Otro.*"

The emcee looked like Selena had stuck a dagger in his side. He shook his head, mouthing protests he lacked the strength to voice. Already the crowd had seized Selena's conspiracy and taken up its two-note chant. He pinched the bridge of his nose and sighed.

"*Uno mas.* Uno. *Eso es todo.*"

The emcee slumped off and returned with a third appointment: tall, dark-skinned, and lithely muscular. He split her lip and chipped one of her teeth, but Selena bested him with a heel smash to the liver and an uppercut that sent him flat. By then she was bleeding from her injured ear and bruised in a dozen places. Her body felt like an engine running at 100 rpms past its limit, all rattling pistons and fraying belts and gears grinding at the edge of their endurance. The emcee raised her arm to signal victory and she had to bite back a scream.

"*No más,*" he whispered to her. "*Estas sangrando. Vuelve mañana.*

Tomorrow, please." Without giving her time to object, he pitched his voice to the crowd and hollered his pronouncement. "¡Más mañana! Ella debe descansar."

The crowd shrieked at the emcee as he made the announcement, hurling bottles and rocks into the field. For an instant Selena shared their wrath. She wanted to tear the throat out of this pathetic little man who dared to try and close his piddling floodgates on her. Her fists tightened, sending jolts of agony through her pummeled arms. The sensation calmed her—as unpleasant as it was, it settled like a friendly hand on her shoulder, a subtle warning to take things easy before she did something she'd regret. The truth was she'd pushed things far enough. Best to leave them wanting more.

Selena raised a conciliatory hand to the crowd, bowed to the emcee—her battered solar plexus whining—and walked out of the circle. The crowd continued to jeer the emcee, but the cries lost their hostile edge and became more sardonic. Spectators threw no more missiles, contenting themselves with catcalls bellowed through cupped hands. As Selena hoisted herself over the Iron Circle, the cacophony coalesced into a single repetitive cheer.

She made it to the underpass with a confident stride that dissolved the instant she was out of view. Her dragging feet snagged on a slight rise in the cobbles. She stumbled, caught herself with one arm, and slumped against the wall. The cool adobe felt wonderful against her skin.

"My god, girl. You really don't play, do you?" said Mary. She'd watched the whole thing from her spot in the alcove. Without asking to or being asked, she'd adopted a shifting role as Selena's coach, promoter, and ringside medic. She dipped a rag in a bottle of vinegar and dabbed the solution on Selena's lip. Selena hissed at its touch but didn't draw back. She tugged down the shoulder of her shirt to reveal a fresh cut for Mary to work on. Through the arch leading to the Iron Circle, Selena could hear the crowd repeating its short but passionate litany.

"What are they chanting?" she asked.

Mary raised an eyebrow. "Excuse me?"

"That chant. It's *Mejise,* right? What does it mean?"

"That's not *Mejise*. They're saying your name."

Selena turned back to the crowd in wonder. She'd grown so used to being hollered at in *Mejise* it hadn't occurred to her that she might understand. She thought back on all the fights she'd ever had and the wave of crowd noise that had washed over her. She'd been cheered and booed, clapped for and hissed at, mocked and lauded, but it had always felt somehow impersonal. She knew that it wasn't *her* the crowd was reacting to, but the event itself. They wanted blood and mayhem, and she was simply a well-stocked vendor of those particular goods. This was different. They weren't cheering in reaction to the spectacle they'd witnessed. They were cheering *for her.*

Somewhere in the deepest fathoms of her mind, an idea took shape. It wasn't a plan, but a possibility. Growing up as the daughter of two double agents in a country where a single misspoken phrase could lead to a brutal, protracted death at the hands of Templar inquisitors, Selena had become preternaturally attuned to the unspoken undercurrents that churned beneath the surface of even the calmest cities. And Juarez was anything but calm.

Her decision to compete in the Iron Circle, driven at first by a mixture of her never-truly-contained desire to fight and her petulant need to strain against any yoke placed on her shoulders, had taken on a more practical aspect. There was something here, something she could use.

She just needed to find out what it was.

23: Entropy's Clutches

A cold wind descended from the mountains. Acrid dust filled Simon's lungs, bringing every breath to the cusp of a cough without quite nudging it over. He itched his eyes and straddled the peculiar device they'd taken from the canyon vault. Mechanically, he understood it well enough—he'd gotten it running, after all— but when it came to actually using it, the thing might as well have plummeted to earth from a distant galaxy. Why had its designer given it only two wheels? It was sleek enough but lacked any inherent stability. He hauled it upright until the seat pressed snug against his thighs, his tiptoes barely scraping the ground.

"Okay," said Emily. "Now lift up your feet and turn the handle a bit."

"If I lift up my feet, I'll fall."

"You won't once the engine kicks in. It's only hard to balance when you're not moving."

With a final sigh, Simon lifted his feet and hit the throttle. The machine listed right and chewed up the gravel with a scream of its tires. Simon felt his equilibrium topple and hurled himself free, hitting the ground with a jolt and skittering across the hardpan for several feet. A splash of heat rent his elbow. Hissing, he cradled his arm to his chest and observed the injury. A patch of skin over the joint hung raw and tattered, studded with stony grit.

"This thing's impossible!" he cried.

"Here. Let me give it another try."

Simon relinquished the machine. Emily righted it and mounted the seat with a graceful swing of her leg. She stood astride it effortlessly, a feat Simon couldn't manage despite being two inches taller than her. She pushed off with her foot and gunned the throttle. The engine whirred, and she took off, legs tucked nimbly against the footholds near the rear wheel. She glided over the hardpan, a wheeled chimera, and described a quick loop of the saltpan they'd chosen as their testing ground. Her hair whipped behind her in a hundred black streamers.

She came to a stop next to Simon and dismounted. Her smile receded as she noticed Simon's dejection. She tugged a wrinkle from her jeans. "It's not so tough when you get used to it. You just need a bit more practice."

"I don't think there's enough time left in the world for me to get all the practice I need on that thing." He kicked a pebble across the hardpan, hands stuffed in his pockets. How on earth was he going to manage to ride that thing all the way to Juarez? He couldn't make it ten feet without falling over.

The plan had seemed so simple: jaunt down to Juarez, find Selena, and scoot away before anyone could stop them. The machine gave them a tremendous advantage in terms of speed—that is, if the driver didn't fall on his ass every thirty seconds. He could try using one of the bigger vehicles instead, but they'd take weeks to fix yet. And how was he supposed to hide it once he got within city limits?

He grabbed his hair with both hands and tugged until the pain brought tears to his eyes. Why was he so bad at everything? Selena wouldn't have struggled to ride the machine. She would've figured it out even quicker than Emily had. How many times had she rescued him from one mess or another, often of his own making? Now it was his turn, and he was failing miserably.

A gentle hand settled on his shoulder. Simon turned to see Emily beside him.

"There's another way to go about it, you know."

Simon sniffed. "How?"

"Let me go down there instead."

"You mean to Juarez?"

Emily nodded. "I've got the hang of this thing pretty well. I bet I could do it."

"But you've never even met Selena. How could you recognize her?"

"She's your sister. Plus, she's missing an ear. I doubt she'll be that hard to find."

Simon scratched his head. A shameful part of him felt relief at Emily's suggestion. He did his best to push it aside.

"I dunno. Isn't Juarez supposed to be a big city? You might have a hard time finding her."

"The same goes for you. At least I speak some *Mejise*. I can scope out the situation, get a message to her, maybe coordinate something for the two of you."

Simon shook his head. "I can't ask you to do that, Emily. It's too dangerous. This is my problem. I need to solve it."

"Yeah, and fixing the irrigator was my problem. And my dad's. We did a good job solving *that* ourselves, didn't we?" Her eyes settled on the ground at her feet, which she scuffed with the heel of her shoe. "If you hadn't gotten the pump working again, we'd've been sunk. Our stores could never last the winter. The beans are already bouncing back, and we'll pull in twice as much corn as we would've otherwise. You saved us, Simon. Let me try to pay back the favor."

Simon scratched the back of his head. Emily's offer was tempting. Accepting it felt a little like cowardice, but it was true that she was far more likely to make the journey unscathed than he was. And not just from her facility with the machine: she knew the region, had sojourned long distances across it before, and could speak the local language. As a traveler, she'd blend in with the crowd far better than Simon could ever hope to. And she'd volunteered to do it, hadn't she? Simon wasn't forcing her. He hadn't even suggested it.

"What will your dad think about this?"

"He doesn't need to know."

"Won't he notice you're gone?"

Emily shrugged. "I've been away from home before. He doesn't like it, but he knows it's necessary."

"How far away is Juarez?"

"I dunno exactly. A few days at least on foot. On this thing?" Emily gave the handle an affectionate tweak. "I guess it depends how far it can go without charging."

Simon ran the toe of his shoe through the dirt, drawing desultory patterns. "Each battery gets about four hours, I'd say. They take maybe six hours each to charge in full sunlight, but you can do 'em at the same time." *Assuming they don't crap out altogether.*

The batteries were truly impressive bits of technology, capable of retaining significant charges despite being drained for years. But nothing built could escape entropy's clutches forever, and any guesses he made toward the substances inside the batteries' casing—and how that substance might hold up to hard use—were just that: guesses.

"How many batteries can I take with me?"

Simon recalled the struggle he'd had lifting one of them. "I'd say the one running the motor plus one alternate. You'll need to save some space for food and water."

Emily nodded.

They hashed out the details as they made their way back to the camp. Emily walked the machine alongside her, its wheels spinning easily in neutral, and stashed it in a culvert once they neared the cave entrance. She worked a cupful of water from the pump and drank, nodded a brief hello to Otis, and filled a second cup for Simon.

"Hey, Dad."

"Hey there, sunshine. How's the work going over there?"

"There's some stuff he might be able to use, right Simon?"

Simon jumped at the sound of his name. "Uh, yeah. Yeah, I think so."

"It'll still take some fixing up, though," added Emily. "There's a lot of work for us to do."

"The boy's welcome long as he likes. Those crops are as much yours as ours, far as I'm concerned." The lines on his face deepened as he smiled. Simon made himself smile back. His face felt like it was made of clay, its every motion stiff and sticky.

Emily set her cup down near the pump. "We're going to stay at the vault for a while. It's too far to come back and forth all the time."

Otis squeezed her hand. "Take plenty of supplies. If anything gets dodgy, light the smokiest fire you can. I'll come runnin'."

"I know," she said and kissed him on the head. Simon saw the look that passed between them, the depth of their familial bond, and felt a nauseous squirt of guilt and jealousy. The latter feeling dissolved into the former, enriching it with its own fresh flavors of misery. *How many things can one kid feel guilty about,* Simon wondered. There had to be a cap somewhere.

Sure, sneered that familiar voice. *It's called suicide.*

Simon raised the cup to his lips. He wasn't thirsty, but the rim masked the quiver of anguish that passed over his lips.

Everything'll be fine, he told the voice. *Emily knows what she's doing.*

The trouble was, did he?

186

24: Sand in the Tank

Selena plunged her hands into the wooden bowl and sighed. The water in the basin was lukewarm and cloudy, but it soothed her knuckles all the same. She moaned with pleasure. Mary shook her head.

"I dunno why you do this to yourself. You ask me, you were better off actin' out Todd's little pantomime with the rest of us. At least I don't finish the day lookin' like I fell down a flight of stairs."

"It's complicated," Selena said, unsure whether this was true. Was it complicated? It was hard to describe, but ineffability wasn't the same as complexity. Her need to fight was simply there; trying to explain it to someone who didn't see it was like trying to describe color to a blind man. Analogy could only get you so far.

She'd finished two fights already today and was considering a third, though her hands all but pleaded for a respite until tomorrow at least. It was a punishing schedule, and she knew she couldn't maintain it forever, but it was paying dividends in the Circle. Crowds cheered her whenever she appeared, chanting her name had become a tradition, and she often found her hand shook and her back slapped whenever she went out on a busy street. Selena appreciated the crowd's affection, but she didn't really understand it. Her rise in a few shorts weeks was as precipitous as it was puzzling. Surely, she couldn't have been the only successful woman fighter in the Iron Circle's history—and even if she was, why did so many people care?

Once the stinging in her knuckles abated, she emptied the bowl and returned it to the vendor who'd lent it to her. The vendor, a middle-aged woman in a woolen serape, took it with a few words of thanks in *Mejise*. Mary translated Selena's polite reply.

"C'mon," Mary said as they left the vendor. "Let's go grab a drink."

The streets slumbered in their mid-afternoon lull, empty save a few *pensionados* and women in kerchiefs going about their shopping. The vendors had walked their carts to the fields and factories where the men worked, hoping to skim a few pesos from the *blancos* before they spent them on various vices in town. Lame and scrawny *marcados* skittered about on errands, their age or infirmary barring them from more fulsome work.

A man with no hands clutched a sack of barley to his chest, his spindly arms struggling to grip the package with their truncated appendages. A green star, its points loose and saggy with age, splashed across the left half of his face. He shot a haughty sniff at the beggars slouched across the boardwalks near the mouth of the plaza, who rattled rusty cans dug from pre-War ruins and showcased the sores on their chests and faces. A few picked at their scabs to start them weeping, the better to spur donations from any *blancos* inclined to charity. The hollow ting of lone *pesos* in their cups suggested a poor yield.

Selena fished a coin from her pocket and pinged it in the cup of a man with sunken cheeks and missing fingers. He glanced up vaguely in her direction, his eyes frosted with a milky film through which his pupils were barely visible. His mouth flapped open in a loose smile, revealing the brown and scattered relics of a once full set of teeth.

"*Gracias,*" he wheezed.

"*De nada,*" Selena replied, leveraging one of the rare fragments of *Mejise* Mary had taught her. As she walked away, she noticed some passers-by watching her with peculiar smiles on their faces. Had she misstepped by giving money to the beggar? Was he a con artist, his illness merely a bit of stagecraft and makeup? She scanned the faces of her onlookers for sniggers of derision or sneers of disapproval and found none. There seemed nothing but genuine warmth on their faces. Unnerved, she gave them a tiny wave and departed.

Despite the nearly empty streets, a crowd was forming in a nearby plaza. Thorin's burly *esbirros* had gathered around a public shrine to *La Santa Meurte* and were busily dissembling it. Around them, dozens of Juarezians watched the display with mounting anger. There were folks of every sort, old and young, men and women, *blanco* and *marcado*—only their disdain united them, evident in every muttered word. Selena didn't bother asking Mary to translate; their opinions were as clear as if they'd spoken in her tongue.

The *esbirros* paid no attention to the crowd. A stocky man swept his thick arms along the base, scattering offerings across the cobbles. Votive candles sputtered and died as they struck the ground, their glass holders shattering. A second *esbirro* worked the skeletal figure from her base with a crowbar. He struggled for a moment before the bolts gave way and the beleaguered saint rocketed into the crowd. An old woman with a pronounced hump dove to rescue the icon, but the *esbirros* batted her back and dragged it toward the offerings, which had been swept into a pile near the base of the deposed shrine. A thin man with iron studs through his nose and earlobes upended a bottle of translucent oil over the statue, struck a match, and tossed it onto the pile.

Flames wriggled through the statue, rending cracks through its skeletal face and turning its flowing garments to cinders. The crowd's outraged mutterings swelled a few decibels, but the *esbirros* stared them down, and they dared not advance. A curtain of smoke swept over the onlookers, drawn by the wind. The smell of scorched hair and burning marrow filled the plaza. The arsonist glared at the crowd over the burnt icon and bellowed in a deep voice:

"*Si quieres adorar algo, adora a tu Jefe.*"

"What's he saying?" Selena asked.

Mary, glowering, spat the translation on the cobbles. "If you want to worship something, worship your *Jefe.*"

A young *marcado* took off his shirt and used it to drag the statue from the pyre and snuff out the flames. A *pensionada* cradled the smoldering statue to her chest, murmuring something in a *Mejise* gone sloppy with tears. The *esbirros* reached down and tried to wrestle the statue from her grip, but the old woman held fast. They kicked her, spat on her, hurled insults and threats, but still the woman hung on. Shaking his head, one of the *esbirros* slathered a wooden truncheon with oil and touched it to the smoldering remains of the burnt offerings. Fire danced around its tip. He upended the bottle of oil over the woman and lowered the flame to her soaked back.

The torch flew from his grip. Before she'd even realized what she was doing, Selena had leaped over the woman and kicked the weapon form the *esbirro's* hand. It twirled end over end and disappeared into the crowd.

"Why don't you goons leave her the fuck alone?"

The *esbirros* regrouped and glared at Selena through narrowed eyes. She doubted they'd understood a word she said, but it was pretty obvious she wasn't complimenting them on their tactics. The middle *esbirro* took a step forward, studied the timbre of the crowd, and stepped back. He barked something unflattering at Selena in *Mejise* and withdrew. The crowd parted begrudgingly for him and his cronies. Apart from a few jeers and a bit of half-hearted shoving, they escaped unscathed.

Selena knelt down and helped the old woman to her feet.

"Are you okay, ma'am?"

The woman grinned, revealing a partial set of thin yellow teeth. She touched Selena's cheek and cooed.

"Uh, thanks."

The crowd erupted in cheers. Men fell to their knees and wrung their hands at her. Women wept. Selena stood awkwardly and absorbed it all, astounded and uncomfortable at the scope of their praise.

A lot seemed to happen all at once, but in the chaos, the crowd seemed to reach some sort of consensus and sent forth an old woman in a gingham dress as their representative. She held a votive candle fished from the wreckage, its left half-melted into a permanent slouch. A tiny flame danced atop its blackened wick. She presented the candle to Selena with a small bow.

"*Gracias,*" Selena mumbled, unsure what else to say. The woman spoke to her in impassioned *Mejise* and concluded by pressing a coin into her free palm. Selena tried to give it back, but the woman cupped her hand around Selena's and curled her fingers shut around the offering. She patted Selena's closed fist twice. The crowd cheered once more and began to drift away. Selena watched them go, the candle flickering in her hand. When their presence had dwindled, she turned to Mary.

"What was all that about?"

Mary rolled her eyes. "They're grateful, Selena. Can't you see that?"

"Yeah, but all I did was tell those thugs to knock it off. It was them as much as me who stopped it."

"It's not just because you stepped in, though. It's what you've been doing this whole time. It's who you *are.* Folks are saying *La Santa* sent you. That you're her envoy."

Selena blinked. "Sent me? Why?"

"She's patron saint of fighters and *marcados.* You're a fighter and a *marcada*. Her envoys are always said to be women. You're a woman." She made a rolling gesture with one hand. "It doesn't take much to start rumors in this town. Everyone's desperate to believe in something."

Mary toyed with her bracelets, tweaking the baubles and straitening the loops of twine that bound them. "I'm gonna head back to the barracks. I don't feel much like being out here anymore. You coming?"

Selena thought of her cot. It was tempting, but her blood was still up from the afternoon's fight, and it itched for movement. She shook her head. "No thanks. I'm gonna stay out for a while."

"Okay, I'll see you."

Mary headed off toward the barracks, leaving Selena alone with her thoughts. "The Envoy of *La Santa*," Mary had said. That was quite a gig. It explained some of the reactions she'd been getting around town. Combatants got a fair bit of respect in Juarez, particularly the Brothers of the Iron Circle, who'd worked their way out of servitude through the sheer force of their popularity in the ring, but the awe she'd encountered from townsfolk was of a different sort altogether. Then again, Selena supposed that if she met someone who she thought represented the incarnation of death on Earth, she'd hand her a little respect, too. She pictured the icon brooding in the corner of the women's barracks, her grin unknowable beneath the midnight sinkholes of her eyes. What did it say about her, to be considered the emissary for such a deity?

Someone tapped her on the arm. Selena half expected another candle, but the girl standing before her bore no gift she could see.

She was a short, scrappy thing, her narrow shoulders hidden beneath a pea green jacket several sizes too large. A pair of aviation goggles sat just above her eyebrows. Selena's twin reflections stared back at her from their scratched and brownish lenses.

"You're Selena, right?" the girl asked.

"Who's asking?"

"My name's Emily. Your brother sent me. Can we talk?"

The years Selena spent in the fighting pits of Jericho had taught Selena to never telegraph her reactions. As such, she stared dispassionately down at this strange elfin messenger, even as the words she'd spoken pinged madly through her head, each ricochet knocking free a new question. *Simon sent her? Is he okay? Is she lying? How would she know I have a brother if Simon hadn't told her? Could he have done it under duress?* She scratched a nonexistent itch on her thigh and shifted her weight.

"Talk about what?"

The girl shot her a look that Selena recognized well. It was a glare practiced exclusively by precocious children dealing with elders who said something irredeemably stupid. Selena had used it many times in the past and would use it many more in the future—even if a new generation of practitioners was already coming up behind her.

"About him rescuing you."

More ricochets, more questions. Selena gathered them up in silence. "We'd better find a place inside. Come on."

She led the girl under an awning and into a dim tavern. Vats of oil hissed behind the counter, unfurling the savory smell of frying *masa*.

She laid a few coins on the table and flashed two fingers. The server scooped up the coins and stashed them in a box behind the counter.

Selena jingled the remaining money in her pocket, which comprised the remnants of the weekly stipend Trejo supplied to Mr. Todd's *marcados*. She wondered if more would be forthcoming, or if the scant *pesos* to her name were the last she'd receive in light of her rebellion. Perhaps Mary was right about Todd, in a way—she doubted most masters gave their *marcados* spending money. *At least being La Santa's emissary pays a little,* she mused, tilting her candle to one side. The pool of wax around its wick crested its lip, sending trickles of liquid down its length, where they cooled into narrow ridges.

The server fished the pads of *masa* from the oil and flopped them onto molds of corrugated metal, where they hardened into U shapes. She grabbed two that had already cooled and spooned in a hash of *carnitas* cooked with various spices. Her hands worked effortlessly, balancing the *tortillas* with the grace of long practice. She handed the pair to Selena, who nodded her thanks.

They found a seat near the front of the tavern, far from its few patrons who preferred the dank coolness of its backmost corners. Afternoon sunlight slanted through its windows, years of which had bleached the wooden tables a ghostly, ashen white. Selena slid into a chair and set the candle down on its base. It wobbled a little but kept its feet. She handed the girl one *tortilla* and kept the other. The *tortilla* cracked on her first bite, spilling juice down her chin.

"So, you know where my brother is," said Selena, wiping her face with the back of her hand. "Why should I believe you?"

Emily shrugged. "Why would I lie?"

"That's the problem. I have no idea. Just like I have no idea why you'd be helping him contact me in the first place."

"Your brother helped my dad and I when we were in big trouble. I'm just returning the favor."

"Helped how?"

Selena listened to Emily's story. It matched what she knew about Simon's situation—his heading south alone, his lack of supplies—and his disposition. She wouldn't put it past him to fix a centuries-old irrigator he'd never seen before. The boy had his gifts, just as she had hers. The story could be true, or it could be a tangle of lies trussed to a few supporting facts.

"Okay. So Simon's alright. I'm glad to hear it. But what is it you want from me, exactly?"

The girl blinked, confused. "I don't want anything. I'm just here to deliver a message. Hang tight. Your brother's coming to rescue you."

Selena nearly spit out a mouthful of *carnitas*. Rescue? Emily had said it before, she recalled, but it had been so absurd she'd ignored it. Simon, rescue *her?* He had enough trouble rescuing himself.

He did okay when the Mayor had a gun to your head, scolded a voice. Her smile withered at the sound of it.

"You brought a message to me today. Are you able to bring one back?"

'Sure."

"Tell him to forget about me. The two of us have a very important

196

job to do, and now it's up to him to do it. He's got the ... he has everything he needs. I'll figure all this out on my own and meet up with him where we're going."

Emily didn't ask what the very important job might be, whether out of respect for their privacy or because Simon had told her already, Selena couldn't say. "I can deliver the message, but I'll tell you right now he's not gonna listen to it. He's got a plan to get you, and he's going through with it."

"Then you'll have to convince him not to."

"How am I supposed to do that? And even more, why would I want to? That's his decision to make, not mine. Not yours."

"You don't understand. The two of us have something very important to do, and we need to do it soon. I'm caught, so the task has fallen to him. I get that he wants to help me, I do. But he needs to think of the bigger picture."

Emily's nose wrinkled. "The bigger picture? You're his sister. If you guys were swapped around, would you really leave him to rot as a *marcado?*"

"I'm hardly rotting," Selena spat. She tinted the words with an anger she didn't feel, hoping to throw Emily on the defensive. It didn't work; the girl didn't budge.

"That doesn't answer my question."

Selena drummed her fingers on the table. *This kid's good.* She thought back to that moment in the tall grass, her eyes stinging with rage, the wound on her head still fresh-voiced and screaming. To Bernard's cackling threats against her brother, caught in the Mayor's web. To the data stick's terrible weight on her leg, the competing forces pulling west and south until she thought they might tear her in two.

"If it was absolutely necessary, then yes. I would."

Liar.

Emily seemed to hear Selena's internal reply, for she didn't bother refuting it. Selena rubbed her face.

"Okay, new plan. You're gonna have to tell him you couldn't find me. Or better yet, tell him I'm dead."

Emily recoiled at the suggestion. "I'm not doing that."

"Look, you think I *like* suggesting this stuff? You think I want my brother to think I'm dead? That I'd get a kick out of the pain it'd cause him? I hate it. But there's no other way."

"Sure there is. Let him rescue you."

A sound escaped Selena's lips, a bedraggled chimera somewhere between a laugh and a sob. "It's not that easy. This place isn't some prison. I could run off today if I wanted to. But I'm branded, and that means I'd be hunted everywhere I turned. *We'd* be hunted. If I fled with him, I'd be as good as tattooing this mark on his face too. I love my brother, but you don't know him—"

"I'm starting to think *you're* the one who doesn't know him," said Emily.

Selena swallowed. Something hard and bitter dropped into her belly.

Emily lowered her gaze to the table. "Look, lady, I don't know how well you know your brother. And I haven't known him that long, that's true. But I can tell you one thing for sure: he's coming to get you. Whether you cooperate or not, he'll be here. And if you hide from him or try to stop him, he'll come anyway, and he'll die. But if you work with him, who knows? Maybe you'll both make it."

Selena found herself giggling. A sense of detached amusement came over her, snipping her tethers and leaving her mind to float about the room. *Sure,* she thought. *Let Simon come. Let him bring a whole damn army. We'll burn this shithole to the ground and trample every* cazadore *foolish enough to stand in our way!*

The feeling receded, and she floated gently back to her seat. As she did, she thought of the crowds cheering her in the Iron Circle, of the townsfolk's reaction when she stood up to the *esbirros* trashing the statue of *La Santa,* of the look on the old woman's face when she presented her with the candle. The idea, first planted in the alcove of the coliseum, began to sprout.

Simon didn't have an army, of course. Neither did she, and she sure as hell wasn't about to raise one—it's hard to fire up the troops when you don't even speak the same language. As long as Thorin held firm to power, escape would be all but impossible. The engine of Juarez's vast slave market ran too smoothly, and the response to a runaway would be quick and coordinated. But throw a little sand in the tank, and the engine might backfire. Maybe not enough to break it all together, but she didn't need it broken. Just a little hiccup would do.

"Okay," Selena said, leaning forward. "I'll wait for my hero. But if he's coming, there's a few things I need him to know."

"I'm listening," said Emily.

25: The Sludge of Simple Murder

Marcus slid the epee home. It dimpled the flesh of the man's breast for the briefest moment before piercing skin and sinew, gliding neatly between the third and fourth rib, and taking momentary residence in the left ventricle of the man's heart. The conquered organ shuddered, a desperate pounding that resonated up the blade and into Marcus's knuckles, while the man he'd stabbed fixed him with a look of uncomprehending hurt. Behind the well-trained muscles of his face, Marcus recoiled at the man's silent plea. *Do you think I chose this? Do you really think I wish you dead? You're nothing to me.*

None of these thoughts showed on his face. Even his eyes were impassive, flakes of obsidian laid atop a corpse's eyelids. His wrist performed the slightest lateral twitch to quicken bleed-out and he withdrew the blade. The prisoner collapsed. Marcus could tell by the way his body hit the ground that he was already dead.

He wiped the flat of the epee along a rag cupped in his upturned palm, first one side then the other, moving in slow, deliberate strokes. He folded the cloth to mask the blood and used an unstained corner to buff away a bit of dirt near the hilt. The sword was not his, but he felt for it the kinship he held with all blades and did not want to see it mistreated. He bent it along a beam of sunlight, studying the path of the gleam as it crept up the blade. It glided true, finding no nicks to divert it or tarnish to diffuse it.

A pair of burly *marcados* dragged the body from the stone grate, where the last of its fluids dribbled into a reservoir. Water trickled through a channel beneath the grate, washing the ichor from the abattoir. It made a burbling sound that filled Marcus's ears in the silence between executions.

Thorin rose from his throne, hands spread exultantly. "Expertly done, Marcus. If execution is an art, then surely you are its greatest practitioner."

"Thank you, *Jefe*," Marcus muttered.

"No, I mean this truly." Thorin wandered as he spoke, his hands grasping in front of him as if in search of some nascent thought. "Any dog can butcher a man. Indeed, I have many such animals at my disposal. They serve their purpose. But it takes an artist to kill with grace, with elegance, to hone the line between life and death to a razor's breadth and puncture it neatly. Such work is necessary for a city-state to function. Such elegance must be seen."

Then why are we in your abbatoir, Jefe? Where only you, the dead, and a few marcados *can bear witness to my craft?* Marcus nodded noncommittally.

Finished with his wanderings, Thorin came to rest atop the stone grate where ten lives had ended since the sun rose that morning. Every one of them died by Marcus's hand, pierced by the silver-pommeled epee he still held in one hand.

It was obvious to everyone present that Marcus's new assignment was his punishment for refusing to fight in Thorin's name. Not just to stand in the Iron Circle against his will, but to serve as private executioner. Thorin sought to pervert his gift, to dip his talented hands in the sludge of simple murder, to make him beg for a place as Thorin's fighter. He had succeeded in items one and two, Marcus had to admit—but he would never succeed in the third.

On instinct, Marcus's eyes swept the room and marked the men in it, who they were and where they stood. The *marcados* stood at attention next to the throne. The nearest was over twenty feet away. Marcus could kill a dozen men before the swiftest guard would be upon him. His fingers tightened around the hilt, squeezing furrows into its leather grip. Thorin stood his ground, arms outstretched.

"This position doesn't demean you, does it, Marcus? It is not intended to do so. It is just that I need your services. And since you chose not to fight… well, you can still kill, can you not? That is still within your power?"

Blood pounded a galloping beat in Marcus's ears, driven by the audacity of Thorin's phony concern. His tongue circled the inside of his lips—an invisible gesture, as decades of practice kept his mouth a tight line and his tell hidden from view. He saw his arm raise the blade parallel to the floor, felt his toes curl *en pointe*, heard the whicker of air as he snapped forward, viper quick, his single fang screeching for Thorin's heart.

But atop this image, he saw the aftermath. Subdued by a thousand *marcados*. His fingers promptly severed, the better to avoid any tricky escapes or suicides. The mutilation, the gelding. The procession of everyone he'd ever known and loved into the Iron Circle. The cackling innovation of tortures old and new. Death drawn out beyond any hope of endurance.

"Yes, *Jefe*," Marcus mumbled. "My hand is yours to command." His voice, though far from jubilant, bore none of the interior strain that had nearly ripped his heart in two. Yet somehow Marcus guessed Thorin had seen it all the same. It showed in his smile, the grin of a boy who'd torn the tail from a scorpion and watched, amused, as it struggled hopelessly to sting him.

A pair of *esbirros* dragged a woman into the chamber. She wore a black robe that hung down to her ankles. Its shirt cuffs clattered with bones and teeth sewn into the fabric with silvery thread. A dozen skulls hung around her neck, strung through their eye sockets on a rawhide braid. Blood dribbled from her nose, and a bruise darkened the baggy flesh around her right eye, but she seemed unafraid. She locked eyes with Thorin as the *esbirros* denounced her.

"We've got one for you, Jefe. A *sacerdotisa*. She was preaching before an altar. In public."

Thorin shook his head. "Foolish woman. Must you sully my courtyards with your squawking? I allow you your little shrines in your homes, and make no quarrel with those who practice in private."

"Your time is coming, Thorin False-King. *La Santa* knows the blasphemy in your heart, and she is angry. Her signs are waxing."

Thorin pursed his lips. "You do yourself no favors, hag. But I admire your conviction, stupid as it may be. I sentence you to death. Marcus, you may carry out your duty."

The old woman shook free of her captors. They braced, ready for her to try and run, but instead, she stepped onto the stone dais, clasped her hands behind her back, and stuck out her chest. She eyed Marcus without pleading or anger or fright.

"Do your work, child. *La Santa* bears you no ill will, for you give me her ultimate blessing. It's his hands that shall taste my blood, even though you swing the blade."

Marcus did as instructed. It was a clean strike, and the woman didn't even shudder. She simply closed her eyes and fell limp as the blade split her heart. Thorin glowered at her corpse as if she were a stain on an otherwise pristine piece of furniture.

"They're growing bolder. My men work overtime clearing their filthy shrines from the plaza, and now we have a *sacerdotisa* preaching her nonsense in public. In *public*. Are they such fools, these death cultists? Are they really so keen to be martyrs for their little ash bin goddess?"

"It's that *luchadora, Jefe,*" explained one of the *esbirros*. "The rabble say she is an envoy."

Marcus's ear perked up. *The luchadora? Selena?* He fiddled with the sword's pommel, hiding his interest behind gestures of boredom.

"Those imbeciles really will believe anything," Thorin scoffed.

His voice sounded disinterested, even amused, but his face betrayed a deeper concern. He dismissed Marcus with a wave of his hand.

"You've done all I need of you for today. Enjoy your afternoon."

"Thank you, *Jefe*." Marcus turned to the door. He took a few steps before Thorin's voice snared his ear.

"Oh, Marcus," he said, pointing. "The sword."

"Right. Apologies, *Jefe*." Marcus swung the epee, his finger a fulcrum against the flat of its blade, and presented it hilt-first to Thorin, who brandished it with a few clumsy flourishes and slid it back into its scabbard. Marcus suppressed a smile at the man's incompetence. *You may own Juarez,* Jefe, *but I've met children who could best you with a blade.*

The sun slashed him with its frigid brightness, stinging his eyes while laying no warmth on his face. He shrugged his serape higher up his shoulders and walked into a dusty wind. The air tasted dry and sour, laced with alkali scratched from the salt pans to the city's north.

Marcus thought about the *esbirro's* words, his reference to a *luchadora*. Was Selena fighting in the Iron Circle? Last he'd heard Todd had snapped her up in an auction, made her part of his little sexless harem. There were worse places to wind up in this town, god knows, though that did little to assuage the guilt he felt whenever his thoughts turned to her. And what was all that about her being an envoy? Selena never struck him as a *santanista*. The good lady was all but unknown north of *Mejica*. If she'd converted, she'd certainly made a quick job of it…

A half-dozen *marcados,* all of them stripped to the waist despite the chill, hauled a wagon along the road. A *blanco* laborer traded coins with a vendor on the boardwalk, who scooped a *pupusa* from a sizzling iron pan, wrapped it in corn husks, and handed it to his customer. The *blanco* walked briskly across the road, nibbling at the *pupusa* as he went. Marcus caught his eye by chance as he passed and nodded minutely, the closed eyes and slight bowing of the head that was basic courtesy among *blancos* in Juarez. The laborer made a snorting sound and mumbled something. Marcus caught only one word, but it was barbed: *perro*.

Moving with unconscious speed, he matched pace with the man and grabbed him by the bicep. His grip stopped short of being painful, but it leveraged the steel cables that long training had wound into his fingers and the laborer couldn't break it without a serious struggle.

"Did you call me a dog?" Marcus asked.

The laborer swallowed. It seemed to take some effort. "No."

"You didn't call me Thorin's dog?"

The laborer shook his head.

"So, you're saying there is something wrong with my ears. Because you spoke clearly, even with a gob full of *pupusa*."

The laborer shifted his feet. His free hand held the *pupusa* at chest height. He seemed to decide denial was getting him nowhere, for he changed tactics. "Forgive me, Marcus. I misspoke."

"So you know who I am?" Marcus let go of the man's arm.

The laborer smiled. He rubbed his bicep with the pinky of his opposite hand, his remaining fingers clutching awkwardly at the *pupusa*. "Of course I do. I saw you in the Iron Circle many times. There is no one better with a blade in Juarez, I've often told folks that myself."

"So you know I'm no dog."

"Yes, yes, of course not."

"Good, that's good." Marcus's hand knew its business. At no point did the growing crowd notice it vanish beneath his serape. One instant it was empty, the next his switchblade flashed against his palm. He thumbed the trigger, freeing the blade with its sibilant *schwick!*

"Perhaps we should make it clear to these good people as well, hmm?"

Though the blade kissed only air as it left its hilt, it may as well have nicked a major artery, for the laborer's blood fled his face in an instant. He stepped back, his one hand still pointlessly holding the *pupusa.*

"No, Marcus, please ..."

"A good start," cooed Marcus. "But it would be more convincing if you knelt."

The man dropped to the road as if his ankles had been yanked out from under him. He clutched his hands in front of his face, fingers knit in supplication.

"Please, Marcus. I have a wife and children. I meant no disrespect. Have mercy."

As he spoke, the man's voice rose in pitch until it resembled a mosquito's whine. Revulsion filled Marcus's belly. What in god's name was he doing? He snapped the switchblade shut, mumbled something conciliatory—he wasn't sure exactly what—and slipped into the crowd.

26: A Focal Point of Hope

Thorin detested Juarez's alleys. It was here that his iron grip on the city was at its most tenuous, where slimy things could wriggle through his fingers and slip into the darkness, all teeth and malice and venom. The alleys had always been a world apart from the sunny *calles* and plazas that defined his realm, and now that he'd been crowned *Jefe* he felt almost like an ambassador in a hostile nation. He would've been more comfortable with a few *esbirros* backing him up, but even the most loyal men talked, and it would behoove him to keep this particular conversation as discreet as possible.

And for all their many faults, discretion was one thing the alleys did very, very well.

The man Thorin had come to see squatted on a dingy throne built of castoff wood and upholstered with old carpets. He was a round, toadish man, though his corpulence masked a hefty payload of muscle. As a member of the triumvirate, Thorin had heard rumors about this man that beggared belief. Yet a single look at him had made the worst of them seem all too plausible—and a few brief interactions during those heady years erased what little doubt remained. He fixed Thorin with a look that lacked the deference to which the Jefe had grown accustomed—that teetered, if he was being honest, just on the right side of amused contempt.

"Why *Jefe*, it's an honor to once again bask in your presence."

Thorin swallowed the invective that lunged instinctively to his lips at this slight. *This isn't your city,* he reminded himself. *It is your city's shadow. Tread carefully, for there are things lurking here you're best not to awaken.* He hoisted his lips into a smile.

"The pleasure is all mine, Krell. Though as you probably guessed, it's not pleasure that brings me into your abode, but business."

"Oh? And what business might that be?"

"I have a task for you. There's a certain individual who requires your attention."

"You're telling me there's someone the *Jefe* of Juarez can't handle on his own?"

Thorin kept his face taut and pretended not to notice the slight. "The situation is… delicate. Best if my hands aren't seen in the matter. Are you a follower of the fights in the Iron Circle?"

Krell buffed his nails against his linen vest. "I catch the odd bout here or there."

"Then perhaps you've noticed a young *marcada* making waves in the ring. Goes by the name of Selena."

"*Marcada,* hein? Who's her keeper?"

"Eric Todd."

Krell inhaled sharply through his teeth. "Todd's touchy about the way his girls get treated, and he's got quite a bit of muscle on his side. I mess with his goods, I could find myself in a bit of trouble."

"Here's the good news: Todd and the girl are on the outs. He's rescinded his protection of her."

"Right," Krell snorted. "I suppose he'll let me drop a load in his private latrine, too, since he's feeling so generous."

"It's true. Ask his body man if you don't believe me. Why do you think he's letting her fight in the Circle? She's a wild little bitch, more trouble than she's worth, so he's wringing what he can out of her and be damned with the rest. Meanwhile, she's got half the pea brains in this city thinking she's the second coming of *La Santa*. It's disruptive, it's dangerous, and I want it stopped. Now is that up your alley, or isn't it?"

Krell ran his tongue along the front of his teeth. "Yeah, I think I can accommodate you, *Jefe*. You leave everything to old Krell."

"I'm pleased to hear it. I've got your retainer here. I'll have a man bring the rest once the job is done." Thorin handed Krell a stack of *pesos*. Krell hefted it, setting the coins to clinking, and stuffed them it in his vest pocket.

"Pleasure doing business, *Jefe*. Don't you worry that kingly little head of yours. I'll see to it that everything's sorted."

Thorin resisted the urge to shudder until he was around the corner and out of view. He relented, submitting to the shiver that rose from tailbone to neck. Dealing with Krell left a gritty aftertaste, but it was a necessary discomfort. In a city like Juarez, no leader could ever rest assured in their ongoing power. Those who did soon lost it—and their heads as well, more often than not. Thorin had seen the deadly flaw in such complacency firsthand—It was, in fact, the reason he was sole *Jefe* now and not merely one of three—and he had no intention of succumbing to the same error. But while there were always factions to manage, resentments to quash, rivals to assuage or enslave or slaughter as nuance dictated, it was, more than anyone else, the *La Santa* cult that gave him pause. It festered in every corner of his city, a mold that no amount of bleach or sunlight could eradicate. He could smash its altars and execute its priestesses, but more would always appear in their place. It was a grass-roots movement, amorphous and leaderless, and that made a targeted strike against it all but impossible.

Except now, it seemed, a figurehead was emerging. A focal point of hope which, if snuffed out, would undermine the doctrine that gave life to the savage little tribe. Relinquishing Selena to Todd had started to seem like a terrible mistake, but now he wondered if it hadn't been a brilliant—if admittedly inadvertent—piece of strategy.

Thorin stepped out of the alley into the afternoon sunlight. He inhaled, taking in the mingling odor of horseshit and alkali dust, sweat, and frying *masa*—smells that were superficially nasty, but in their distinct combination formed a bouquet Thorin found quite pleasant. They pleased him because they were his, as everything in this world of light and frenetic order was his. And it would stay his for a long time to come. Krell would see to that.

Part IV: Sisterhood

27: Only Meat

The grate stank of offal. No rain had fallen for weeks, and the city's reservoirs had begun to show signs of drought. The flow of water that normally surged through the channel had become a sluggish trickle—too little to wash away the detritus of Marcus's grim craft, but enough to lend the leavings a soggy pungency. The resulting odor was half outhouse and half abattoir, a hideous alloy that had itself become a kind of torture preceding execution. Bad enough to die by an executioner's blade; worse still to do it atop a channel of filth.

Such thoughts occupied Marcus's mind as he went about the mechanical excision of life, the extraction of all that makes a man from the temple of meat that housed him. They were ugly and morbid thoughts, but they took him away from a place that was uglier still, and he'd grown better at following them farther and farther afield.

"Just one more today, Marcus," said Thorin.

"Yes, *Jefe.*" Even as he spoke, Marcus was already drifting away, his gaze darting through the bars on the abattoir's windows and into the city beyond. He hovered above the streets and alleys of his childhood, the dusty plazas where he gamboled with his friends while the *pensionados* sat beneath awnings on the boardwalk, their wrinkle-creased faces like maps to the forgotten cities of their youth.

A single word yanked him from his revery: "Marcus?"

He stood, epee in hand, and watched a pair of *esbirros* drag Emilio to the stone grate. Chains hung from manacles on each arm, the left clasped around his wrist, the right notched higher to avoid slipping free over the stump of his severed right hand. His eyes glowed a feverish red, the skin around them puffy and sore. A bruise spread from cheek to chin, the ghost of a giant fist visible in its discolorations.

"Emilio?" Marcus whispered. "What happened?"

"Caught thieving," answered Thorin, his voice dripping with mock gravity. "It is a difficult thing, to pickpocket with only one hand. But our Emilio is nothing if not ambitious. Is that not so, Emilio?"

Emilio turned his head toward Thorin. He didn't seem to make out the meaning of the *Jefe's* words, but merely followed the source of sound. The *esbirros* tugged on his chains, jerking him to attention. His gaze drifted about the room before settling on Marcus. Comprehension resurfaced.

Marcus took Emilio's remaining hand. His skin was damp and clammy.

"He needs a doctor, *Jefe*," Marcus pleaded. "He is not well. "Please, let me have him treated, and we can discuss the punishment for his crime."

"His punishment is already underway," said Thorin. "And he'll need no doctor in a few minutes' time."

The epee nearly slipped from Marcus's hand. His fingers fumbled for purchase and clasped tight around the pommel. The weapon felt suddenly foreign in his hands. He looked to Thorin, his face naked with pleading.

"I can't do this, *Jefe*. Please. Anyone else. Not him."

"You have to, Marcus," said Emilio. His words came out barely louder than a whisper, yet speaking them seemed to cause him pain. He grimaced, coughed, and spat a wad of bloody matter onto the tile floor. "Otherwise he'll make it worse. So much worse."

Marcus tightened his grip on the epee. His lungs burned with every exhaled breath. He locked eyes with Thorin and struck.

The blade sang a high silver note and clattered to the floor. Marcus dove forward and caught Emilio's head before it could touch the abattoir's filthy grate. It was the quickest blow he'd ever delivered. There was no time for fear, no time for pain. As a final gift, it was a sad and ugly one, but it was all he had to give. He clutched the head to his chest and felt the fading heat of his forehead, the dwindling thump of blood in his temples, the final butterfly flutterings of his eyelashes against his wrists. The stochastic firings of a nervous system in shutdown, mindless and empty, but he cherished every one of them. He found himself stroking Emilio's hair gently and stopped, thinking this disrespectful.

Not waiting to be dismissed, Marcus took Emilio's head and left the abattoir. He expected Thorin to shout him down, or perhaps even order the *esbirros* to thrash him for his impertinence. The *Jefe* did neither. He watched Marcus's slouching gait with wry amusement, though when Marcus turned to address him, he caught a flicker of fear behind Thorin's haughty mask.

"May I take the body, *Jefe*, to bury it with his people?" The words came out in flat affect, the way a child reads aloud from a book he doesn't understand. Thorin slipped his indifference back into place, smoothing out the cracks where unease had shown through.

"What difference is it to me what you do with it? It's only meat."

"As are we all," said Marcus.

Thorin smiled. "Not yet."

Marcus scooped up the body and carried it over one shoulder, cradling the head to his side with the opposite arm. He worked quickly, eager to leave the abattoir but also to escape from Thorin's sight before the Jefe noticed the incongruous smile playing on his own lips.

"No, *Jefe*," he whispered to himself. "Not yet."

28: A Powerful Charm

"You're crazy," said Mary.

"What makes you say that?" Selena replied. She tried glancing up at Mary's face to see if her expression matched her tone—flippant, but with a hard edge of sincerity underneath—but the angle was wrong, and she could see nothing but a vague flash of motion now and then when Mary worked the roots nearest her forehead.

The two of them sat in the women's barracks, Mary on her bed, Selena on the floor in front of her. Selena's hair had grown over the course of her captivity, and an off-hand complaint within Mary's hearing had spurred her on to unexpected fervor.

"Let me do a close braid," she'd pleaded. "I used to do 'em for the Montenegro girls. It's the perfect hair for a fighter. There'll be nothing left to grab onto."

Selena's solution had always been to chop it short with whatever sharp implement was handy, but Mary seemed eager, and it was as good an opportunity as any to ask for her help. Plus, she genuinely liked the girl—something in her loquacious banter fit a notch in Selena's personality.

She took up her position on the floor and waited as Mary's deft fingers wove her hair into flat rows. The occasional twinge would make her grimace as a rogue strand grew taut at the root, but the process was otherwise painless and actually oddly pleasant. They soon had the barracks to themselves, and Selena seized on the opportunity.

"I was wondering if you could do me a favor," she'd said.

"Shoot."

"I have to talk with Grace Delgado, and I need you to translate for me."

Mary's fingers stopped their acrobatics. "Why? What's she got to say that's worth hearing?"

With that, Selena told her the plan. Sharing it was a risk, but it was one she felt she needed to take. Mary's disdain for Grace was such that Selena needed a good reason to get her to act as intermediary— and with her in that role, she couldn't exactly keep her out of the loop anyway. Things would be different if she spoke *Mejise,* but the few phrases she'd learned were grossly insufficient, and in the end, she simply needed to trust her friend. Now, having laid things out plainly, Selena had to find a way to bring Mary around.

"You're talking about overthrowing the *Jefe*," Mary whispered. "Talk like that could get a person killed. And not in a quick clean way, either. That shit would be messy. Like bleach the cobbles and throw the remains to the pigs kind of messy. You know how they treat runaway *marcados*? Well, that's a slap on the wrist next to what you're looking at."

"I don't need anybody overthrown. I just need a couple days of chaos."

"I doubt he'll appreciate the difference if he catches you."

"It's a risk I need to take. As long as things stay static, I'm stuck here. Besides, the fault lines are already there. I'm just … deepening them a little bit."

Mary sighed. "What does it even matter what you're trying to do? It's not going to work in the first place anyway. Delgado was deposed. Sure, she was a visible member of *Los Hombres Sencillos*, but she's a *marcada* now. You really think she can help you?"

"We can help each other," she said, expressing more confidence than she felt. The fact was, she wouldn't know where Grace stood until she spoke with her, and she wouldn't be able to manage that unless Mary agreed to help her. "So will you do it?"

Mary shook her head. "Let's get a drink. I need to think about this some more." Her fingers made a final flourish and dropped from Selena's hair. "We're done here anyway. Check it out."

Rolling the kinks from her shoulders, Selena peered into the polished looking glass mounted to the wall near the room's communal wash basin. Her hair, previously frizzled, now clung to her skull in tidy rows running from her forehead to the nape of her neck, their procession marked by the tiny moguls raised by Mary's deft braid work. She gave an experimental tug at one row and found, even with her fingernails, she couldn't get purchase.

"I like it," she said, and was surprised to realize she was telling the truth. Mary threw her hands up in mock triumph. Selena grinned. She longed to get a definite answer about her plan, but Mary's jubilation was infectious. Besides, she knew better than to push too hard.

They left the barracks and headed for a nearby plaza, Mary leading the way. Selena suppressed the impulse to bring up her request on the walk, contenting herself to listen to Mary's rambling, desultory monologue—a soliloquy she had sustained, with interruptions, since the first time she and Selena met. Normally she found such verbosity irritating, but in Mary's case, it was oddly soothing. It reminded her of the radio serials her parents ostensibly listened to in Jericho— though actually playing to thwart the angel ears embedded behind the walls of their apartment, they maintained a comforting rhythm that drifted easily in and out of Selena's notice, a buffer of sound to be savored between more important tasks.

At the mouth of a plaza, they passed a fetish vendor, who beckoned them forward with fingers like twists of rawhide. Bones and pelts dangled from bits of wire suspended from an aluminum crossbeam. Stirred by the wind, they played a tuneless calliope as they clonked against one another. The vendor, an old woman with a profound hump and a sore by her left nostril, settled into easy banter with Mary, who fingered the merchandise and responded to the vendor's queries with arched eyebrows and quips of *Mejise*. Selena assumed Mary was simply humoring the lady, but after a minute's consideration she bought a string of snake skulls and affixed it to her wrist, where it hung alongside several other bands of assorted baubles.

The vendor turned her attention to Selena for the first time, likely hoping for another sale. Her eyes widened and the patter she'd prepared evaporated from her lips, unspoken. She bowed low and, murmuring something in *Mejise*, presented Selena with a pendant on a gossamer thread. Selena raised a hand, palm out, in a gesture of polite decline. Undeterred, the vendor hobbled around her stall and, extending her rumpled and meager height to the utmost, tied the string around Selena's neck. She tottered back and gave a satisfied nod, as if appraising a recently completed bit of craftsmanship.

"*Gracias,*" Selena mumbled, and left, unsure what else to say. Mary followed a few steps behind her.

Out of eyeshot from the vendor, Selena stopped to examine her gift. The string was fine and supple, its thin filament nearly translucent—not the coarse weave of hair or grass fiber she'd expected, but something almost like silk. The pendant it held was small but sumptuously detailed, a sunburst of ocher jags encircling a yellowish orb. Closer inspection revealed the fringe to be scorpions claws set in a bronze hub, at the center of which lay a mayfly suspended in amber. Mary whistled appreciatively.

"That's a powerful charm. You could move mountains with that thing, I bet. Bein' *La Santa's* envoy has its perks."

"I'm not anyone's envoy."

"Try telling that to the old lady."

"Maybe I would," Selena replied. "If I spoke any *Mejise.*" Though the truth was, she probably wouldn't. She hated exploiting anyone's faith, but if she was going to get out of this, she needed leverage, and their belief in her as some sort of divine representative was the only currency in which she was still solvent.

At its far end, the plaza branched into several smaller streets. Mary took the leftmost road and cut through an alley on her right. It was a familiar route, one that circumvented a long jaunt down *Calle Molinero* and brought them more directly to *Calle Rey*, where the best taverns were, according to Mary.

The alley represented a second Juarez, one easily missed in the crowds and commerce that frothed along its boardwalk-strafed thoroughfares. Out there in the open stood a metropolis, a great muscular heart pumping food and wealth and flesh through the myriad arteries that threaded the *pueblos* of the continent's vast southern desert.

A different sort of city dwelled in its alleys. In here, plazas and cobbled streets gave way to labyrinthine paths, all but subterranean if not for the filaments of open sky running between the roofs overhead. Cobbles mutated into a hodgepodge of gravel, boards, and dirt. The noise of the street fell away after only a few steps, swallowed by the alley's adobe mouth. The light itself seemed different, clothed in a grey-brown murk at once sultry and oppressive that settled over one's eyes until torn away by the starburst of an interior courtyard.

Kiosks, shanties, and other makeshift structures clung to the wider lanes—some were dwellings tenanted by an ever-morphing cast of down-and-out *blancos*, their unmarked skin the only possession of any value to their names; others were businesses run by only slightly less derelict proprietors, dealing fetishes, votive candles, cigarettes, and other more illicit fare.

Occasional gaps appeared in the alley walls, dead spaces between buildings that inevitably collected their own small assortment of dwellers, a pocket village springing up inside the city's stony abscess. Selena had spent no time in these squatter's hamlets, but she knew by reputation that they were among the fiercest bits of real estate in Juarez, crucibles in which the city's hardest outlaws were forged.

One such inlet appeared on their right. Its concave walls slumped into a curved and pockmarked floor, as if formed when some titan had thrust a colossal thumb into the still-drying adobe. A strip of canvas hung taut between two polls thrust into the building's outer wall, forming a crude awning that deepened the cavity's already sepulchral shadows.

The occupants of the hollow seemed well-accustomed to the gloom. They lounged on hillocks of landfill, nestled in depressions formed by the sustained indolence of a thousand loitering asses, their grubby fingers curled around bottles of smoky glass.

A stocky man with iron bands around each wrist made a bullhorn of his hands and hollered.

"¡*Oye chica! ¿A donde vas? Ven acá.*"

"*Vete a la mierda,*" cooed Mary.

A few men snickered at the exchange. The hollerer ignored Mary's reply, his gaze locked on Selena. A smile gleamed within a thicket of matted reddish hair. He made a cutting gesture with one finger, and a pair of his cronies shouldered in front of Selena and strafed the alley's bottleneck. Another two slipped in behind, cutting off any chance for retreat. Selena watched it all unfold, the rising tension not quite pushing her to action. There was a playfulness here that counterbalanced the threat, a gaudy jewel in the pommel of a dagger. It remained unclear which end they planned to show her.

The hollerer set his hands on the earthen bench and hoisted himself to his feet. He was a hunched, brawny hillock of a man, his arms and belly bulging in a queasy alloy of fat and muscle. His stride was lumbering and bowlegged, his squat thighs swiveling to accommodate his outsized upper half, yet there was a grace to his movements unique to the ill-proportioned, as if his body, in realizing it must invent a new grammar of motion in line with its strange dimensions, opted for an elegantly metered verse.

"¿Cuál es la prisa, bebé? Toma una bebida."

He held out the bottle and shook it invitingly. Selena stared at him blankly, her disinterest a parapet from behind which she surveyed the developing siege. What she saw wasn't encouraging.

"¿No hablas Mejise, hein? All good, baby, I speak the plains talk. Come, drink with us. We hear many stories about you."

Mary stepped forward and swatted the bottle aside. It struck the dirt and rolled off, a few glugs spilling from its neck.

"Piss off, Krell. She doesn't sell, even when the buyer's dick's not half rotted off."

Krell smiled, revealing teeth like the gates of a city sacked and burned centuries before—slanting ruins rising from ashen soil. "Ugly words from an ugly mouth. Could be I smack some respect into it, hein?"

Mary pointed to her cheek. "We've got the marks, fool. Mr. Todd doesn't like his investments mishandled. You fancy his *partidarios* giving you a talking to?"

Krell wagged a stubby finger back and forth. "For you, maybe yes. But her, not so. This girl disrespect Mr. Todd. Protection's gone. She on her own now."

"Bullshit," said Mary. She spoke with a voice like clashing steel, but her glance toward Selena betrayed doubt. Selena could do little to assuage it.

"Go on ahead, Mary," Selena said. "They won't stop you. Let's Krell and I have a chat."

"The hell I will. Don't listen to the asshole. He's off his head with cockrot. There's holes in his brain big enough to satisfy his deepest urges. Come on."

Mary took Selena's wrist and led her to the mouth of the alley. The two cronies who blocked her way made no sign of budging. She stepped into them as if expecting them to swing apart. They shoved her backward. Mary staggered, her left ankle catching her right shin, and nearly fell. Selena caught her shoulders and righted her.

"Easy," she whispered.

Mary took no heed. She charged at the two men. They turned as one and pressed their back flat against the alley walls. She brushed past, surprised, and beckoned for Selena to follow. As she raised her arm, the two men seized her as one: the first locking her arms behind her back, the second pressing her legs together. Mary writhed in their grip, but her frantic kicks and wild bucking barely budged them. She unleashed a torrent of verbal abuse at Krell, reverting to *Mejise* in her anger.

"*Se amable con ella,*" Krell said. "Todd like her still. One wonders why, *hein?*"

A dozen men closed in on Selena, forming a half circle against the alley wall. Some drew knives, others unlooped hatchets from their rawhide belts, still others wielded improvised cudgels with bent nails or tangles of wire abrading their tips. A quick scan revealed long odds of a clean escape; even if she took them by surprise, one slash could open her from neck to belly.

"This don't gotta hurt," Krell said, unfastening his belt. "We take it slow."

Selena flew at him. She hurled a fist at his nose, channeling force from her heels upward. His men would kill her soon enough, but she would go down fighting.

Krell's pudgy hand snapped up, viper quick, and seized her by the wrist. He pivoted, throwing his considerable weight into the motion. Her fist arced downward, trapped by its own momentum, and carried her down with it. He spun her round and tossed her against the wall.

Adobe cracked. Chips of ancient clay fluttered to the ground. Selena slid down the wall, found her feet, and met his charge with an uppercut. This one landed, but Krell barely reacted. He threw no punches of his own, but simply cowed her with his size. The semicircle of onlookers gave her no room to maneuver, and he soon had her in a crushing bear hug.

He forced her belly flat against the ground, arms trapped beneath his suffocating bulk. Her new charm bit into the skin between her breasts. A stink of sweat and sour wine oozed from Krell's pores. He pressed a clammy palm against the side of her head, forcing her face into the dirt. She tried to wriggle free, but it was like trying to burrow out from beneath a mountain.

When the pressure abated, it left so suddenly that she felt strangely weightless. She scrambled toward the wall, fists raised, and looked to see what had happened.

Krell stood with his back to her, holding his pants up with one hand. His semicircle had split apart and reformed in a cluster around their *caudillo*. Voices clashed in furious *Mejise*.

Selena could see little through the forest of legs. She felt a hand close on her shoulder and stopped herself half an instant before clobbering Mary, who had evidently freed herself from her captors and skittered over to drag Selena clear. Selena went willingly and took a defensive position near the alley mouth, which offered a better look at the source of the disturbance.

A clutch of *marcados* faced off against Krell's men. Though mostly unarmed, they seemed indifferent to their opponents' weapons, glaring down at the knives and hatchets with contempt. In the center of the group stood Paulo, Selena's first opponent in the Iron Circle. He glanced over at her and shot her a thin smile before fixing his gaze once more on Krell.

"La niña es una hermana del círculo de hierro," he said. *"Ella no será hostigada."*

Krell spat. He shrugged his shoulders as if bored with the whole affair. At this gesture, his cronies fell back, sheathing their weapons and dissolving into the shadows of the sunken annex. Paulo and the other *marcados* left the way Selena and Mary had come. Paulo caught Selena's eye, raised two fingers to his forehead, and gave a small salute.

"Cuídate, hermana."

Selena and Mary wasted no time leaving the annex. They walked briskly down the alley, taking a few unexpected byways to reduce the chance of being followed. Neither spoke until they emerged into the noise and bustle of *Calle Rey*, which closed around them like a mother's protective arms.

"I'll help you talk to Grace," Mary said.

Selena turned. "Yeah?"

Mary nodded. "Krell's not some ordinary gutter-dweller. He's Thorin's hatchet man. Todd may have thrown you to the wolves, but I'm not about to do the same. Paulo's not always gonna be around to call him off."

"I'm not even sure why he did it this time."

Mary shot her a strange look. "Didn't you hear him?" She smacked her forehead a second later. "Right, *Mejise*, I forgot."

"Why? What did he say?"

"The girl is a sister of the Iron Circle," said Mary. "She will not be harassed."

29: Terrible Gravity

The air in the mountain pass was thin and strangely intangible. Simon struggled to retain each breath, as if his lungs were hands and the oxygen an oily fluid constantly slipping through their clumsy fingers. He'd grown used to it inside the bunker, where his work provided ample distraction, but outside in the moonlight, he became more conscious of his breathing and the subtle inadequacy of each inhalation. Occasionally, he would edge toward panic, certain that he was slipping closer to some terminus of oxygen deprivation, each breath putting him deeper in deficit. But time would pass, and he'd grown no weaker, the air no thinner, and his heart would slow from gallop to trot.

An icy wind cut through the canyon. Simon shimmied deeper into the crevice of concrete that he'd claimed as a makeshift camp. He'd found a zippered blanket of slick, insulated fabric and cocooned himself inside of it, which kept out the worst of the cold. No doubt he'd be warmer inside the bunker, but he couldn't bring himself to sleep there. It felt too sepulchral without the clang and whirr of tools to drive away any restless spirits. Better to be up here among the ruins, which seemed less ominous if no less forlorn.

Simon enjoyed the sensation of cold air on his face, regardless of its aerobic deficiencies. A landscape of purple-black clouds drifted overhead. Occasionally, the moon shone through the gaps like a child peeking through knotholes in a fence, throwing glances of pale light across Simon's upturned face.

A distant sound cut through the steady sighing of the wind. Barely audible at first, it swelled in volume, a droning whirr atop the shuffle-crunch of wheels over crumbling pavement. Simon wriggled out of his sleeping bag and peered through the remnants of the building's front wall, his body laid flat. A figure wound its way along the compound's narrow road, wheels bumping over ridges of ruined asphalt. The vehicle alone was a pretty clear identifier, but the flutter of hair flowing behind her removed any doubt about who had arrived. Simon stood up and waved both arms overhead.

Emily brought the machine to a smooth halt next to Simon. She remained astride it, her left leg cocked over the seat. Simon grabbed the handlebar as if afraid she might drive off.

"Did you find her?"

"Sure. It was easy. She's made quite a name for herself."

"What do you mean? Is she okay?"

"Yeah, she's fine." Emily's eyes darted away and back. Simon's grip tightened on the handlebars.

"I need to know the truth, even if it's hard. Is she okay?"

"Yes, she's fine." Emily squirmed over her seat. "I mean, physically, she's not hurt or anything. It's just … she's a *marcado*."

"A what?"

"It means marked, branded. In Juarez, it's something they do to servants. It shows who belongs to who."

"You mean, like a slave?" Something cold and heavy landed in Simon's belly from a great height. He staggered, his grip on the handlebars the only thing keeping him from toppling over. Emily grabbed his arm to steady him. She got off the bike and lowered it gently to the ground, allowing her to lead Simon out of the road and back to his camp.

"It's more complicated than that, but yeah, basically. But it could be worse. The guy who bought her isn't a flesh trader or anything. As far as it goes, she's treated pretty well. No abuse, no chains, nothing nasty."

Simon took a moment to digest what he'd been told. "What did you mean, she's made a name for herself?"

"I had to ask around a little before I found her. I figured I'd get mostly blank stares. Turns out everyone's heard of the one-eared *Llanuresa*. She's a hero of the Iron Circle."

"What's the Iron Circle?" Simon asked, but even as the words left his mouth, he knew. If Selena was involved with it, what else could it be?

"The fighting ring," Emily confirmed. "She's been knocking out guys twice her size. Hasn't lost a match yet."

Simon nodded to himself. He rubbed his hands together, working the chill from his fingers. "Okay, so did you tell her my plan? Is she going to meet me north of the city, or…"

"There's a problem. *Marcados* don't have the right to leave Juarez. Anyone in a hundred miles who sees her is gonna know her for a runaway. And Juarez takes runaways seriously. There's big rewards for anyone who turns in an escaping *marcado*. The second she steps across city lines, there's gonna be half a hundred *cazadores* looking to drag her back and collect their finder's fee."

Simon slumped against a concrete pillar. He removed his glasses and rubbed his eyes with the thumb and forefinger of his free hand. Motes of color spangled the black canvas of his eyelids. The data stick in his pocket lurched west, extolling him with its terrible gravity. "So what do I do?"

"We talked about that. Right now, with Thorin in charge, things are running smoothly on the surface. Underneath, not so much. Her best bet for getting out of there would be right after a big upset. Something that threw the whole power structure into disarray."

Simon waited for her to continue. "Okay. So?"

Emily shrugged. "So we cause one."

30: Candle-lickers

Water dripped from the ceiling somewhere in the distance. Between that, the dim light, and the dank, clammy air, Thorin felt as if he'd ventured into a cavern miles under the earth. Even the sliver of sky peeking through gaps in the alley's plywood awnings couldn't dispel the image. It seemed fake, a clever illusion designed to lull him deeper into the abyss.

Thorin shook his head and dislodged these paranoid thoughts. Hidden or not, this was still Juarez, and he was still *Jefe*. He squared his shoulders to better suit the role and leveled Krell with the most withering look in his arsenal. The heavy man stared back, unimpressed.

"These things take time, *Jefe*."

"I hardly see what the holdup is. We're talking about one *marcada*. Are you so easily overpowered?"

"It's not just one *marcada*, though, is it? If it were, you wouldn't be staining your silk boots down here in the muck just to chat with me. She's got protection."

"Rabble," Thorin scoffed. "A few serfs and rag women who kiss her ring. Hardly the sort to stir fear in your breast, I would've thought."

"I don't mean the damn fetish vendors and candle-lickers. I'm talking about fighters."

"*Marcados*. So what? Put a little weight on their keepers, they'll fold sure enough."

"These aren't *marcados, Jefe*. These are the absolved. The Brothers of the Iron Circle. They've taken her into the fold."

Thorin pursed his lips. So the Brothers were protecting her now, were they? This was something else again. Though they inspired none of the suicidal devotion the *santanistas* had for their ridiculous death god, they were still well-respected—not to mention formidable fighters. If they had the girl's back, she would be difficult to take care of without a lot of fuss.

"Leave the Brothers to me. You just keep your eyes on the girl. I want her out of the way, and soon."

"Of course, *Jefe*."

Thorin wasted no time kicking the alley's dirt from his boots. Things were moving slower than he would've liked, but at least they were moving. Paulo and his crew could be dealt with, and Krell would be free to make his play. The fat oaf may have screwed up once, but he was ruthless. Thorin still trusted he had what it took.

And if he didn't? Well, there were more direct means at his

disposal. In fact, the more Thorin thought about it, an ancillary approach might be a good thing. Why stake your kingdom on a single shooter, when two at cross angles have twice the chance of finding their mark? He might get his own hands a little dirty in the process, but such was life. Leaders must make tough choices, after all. It was a particularly stupid truism that blood didn't wash off. Blood washed off just fine.

You simply had to scrub hard enough.

31: Two Good Hands

Cold moved fast in the south. Simon had sweated through the afternoon when the sun had cut neatly through the haze and set the hardpan to sizzling, but mere moments after it set the ground grew frigid, and a chill wind descended from the mountaintops.

He inched closer to the fire, fingers flirting with the orange flames. Heat licked his hands, its friendly tongue belying the set of burning teeth that would close upon him if he lowered his arms a few more inches.

Fire had always made Simon nervous, even as it fascinated him. There was strength and madness in its endless flickering dance, a power temporarily harnessed but never truly tamed. He preferred the cold obedience of electricity. It could be deadly too, but its reprisals invariably had a cause. Electricity punished incompetence; fire could strike at anybody.

Simon heard the puttering of the vehicle's engine before he could see it. His ears had grown accustomed to its pitch. Emily had made the run twice a week, give or take, hauling ears of corn and jugs of water in the vehicle's bulging sidesaddles. This schedule meant she was traveling nearly all the time, but she seemed not to mind the pace—indeed, she treated the machine the way one might a well-loved horse, her fingers caressing its chassis in quiet moments. Simon was grateful for the deliveries, and while he insisted she needn't trouble herself on his part, he couldn't really say no—without them, he wasn't sure how he'd manage to eat and drink.

The vehicle rounded a bend and came into view. Simon immediately sensed something off, but he couldn't say what until the figure crested the hill. The rider's features grew clearer in the waxing moonlight, their dimensions much too large and boxy to be Emily. Simon retreated behind a chevron of concrete that was once part of the building's foundation and watched the figure approach. Had Emily been waylaid on her latest trip back? He imagined a thin wire stretched taut between one of the narrow passes, its deadly length calibrated to neck height. A well-aimed carbine roaring from a distant mesa, its payload buried in the small of Emily's back. A pack of feral man-beasts descending on her camp, fingernails sharpened to deadly points.

He reached for his gun and realized he'd left it in the bunker with his other belongings. Not that it had any bullets, but at least he could've given the impression of being less than completely helpless.

The rider slowed, drifting along the narrow pass. The vehicle's wheels crunched over the cracked asphalt, rendered by time and temperature into hunks of blackish gravel. Its front wheel wobbled unsteadily—clearly, the rider was unpracticed and lacked Emily's innate grace with the machine.

Simon ducked lower behind the concrete protrusion. The rider pulled up twenty feet past it and cut the engine, the whirr of its dynamo more evident in its absence than it had been when running. He—it was definitely a he; at this distance, Simon could tell that much—brought his foot down and struggled to step free of the vehicle.

"Simon!" the man called. "Hey, Simon!"

It took Simon a moment to place the man's voice. When he did, he wasn't sure if it made him feel better or worse. He stepped from his hiding spot and waved.

"I'm right here!"

Otis returned the wave. He crunched his way along the road to the broken foundation where Simon stood. His face looked drawn with lack of sleep, its creases deeper than Simon remembered.

"Is everything okay?" Simon asked.

"It's fine," Otis replied. "Emily told me what you and her've been up to."

"Oh." Simon swallowed. He scuffed his shoe through the dirt.

"I'm not here to cause trouble with you about it. She knew how I felt and she made the decision she thought was best. I just came to say, I'd like to help you if I can."

"You would?"

Otis nodded. He pointed to the wedge of shiny tissue splitting his right cheek. "You know how I got this scar?"

Simon shook his head. In answer, Otis drew a hunting knife from his belt. It was a serious weapon, nine inches of steel tapering to a vicious point. He pressed the flat of the blade gently against his face. Its tip dimpled the loose skin of his lower eyelid. Simon winced. Otis laughed, a sound too dry to hold any real humor.

"Seems a fool thing to do to your face, huh? Can't say I much like how it looks, but I liked what was there before even less. A green star. Meant I was a field hand in the plantations of *Jefe* Thorin, he of the triumvirate—or the lone honcho now, Emily tells me. A *marcado*. Like your sister."

Otis sheathed his knife. He sat down on the concrete outcrop and looked up at the moon.

"I'd like to say I'm with you because it's the right thing to do. But I'm a father first, and fathers can't afford too much nobility." He scratched his chin. "Emily didn't know exactly what your plans were, but she said that you and your sister were headed somewhere in particular. Somewhere you could lay down roots. I'd like us to come with you, if we could."

Simon sat down next to him. "I could use all the help I can get, but I gotta tell you that there's no guarantee what's waiting for us. We're not way out here because we're chasing a better life. We're just finishing what our parents started. Right now, you've got the farm and your canyon. Is it really worth giving up?"

"I don't see as we've got a lot of choice. This has been a long time coming. Truth be told, I shoulda moved on years ago, but the roads around here are dangerous, 'specially for a runaway *marcado*. Staying put seemed the best bet, but it can't last. The irrigator goin' bust proved that. You saved this year's harvest, and I'm grateful for that. But what about next year? Or the year after that? Eventually, some other bit of machinery is gonna fail, or the water's gonna run out, or the soil's gonna dry up. I've got myself a leaky bucket, and I'm tryin' to bail out the tide. It ain't gonna keep working forever."

A fresh gale rolled down the mountain face and swept through the cleft where the town once stood, carrying with it a dusting of fine white snow. It settled over the stones and bricks and rubble, coloring the world a crystalline white. Otis brushed a few flecks from his pants and stood up.

"Could be we should take a look at what you've got so far. I'm no great shakes with gears and engines, but I've got two good hands and can follow instructions. Tell me what you need doing, I'll see it gets done."

Simon smiled. He appreciated the offer and the spirit with which it was given. But what he needed doing was more than any man could promise him.

In fact, he was starting to worry that it couldn't be done at all.

32: The Stones That Shifted Their Burden

The air in the tunnel smelled of death. The odor was distinct from the abattoir stench of blood and viscera and lacked the pungent reek of decomposition. In fact, there was nothing outwardly unpleasant about the smell at all—a faint dustiness, perhaps, and an earthy odor that recalled a decommissioned root cellar where winter preserves were once but no longer stored. Yet it was unquestionably death that Selena smelled, a distillation of its purest and most abstract properties.

Selena and Mary descended a dozen stone steps and entered a long narrow chamber with a bare dirt floor. Twin rows of pillars ran the length of the room, each of them capped with a candle burning feebly against the gloom. At the far end of the room, a skeletal figure perched on an antique throne, its body draped in robes of red and black. Its left hand rested on a scythe balanced across its thighs, while its right hand clutched a pewter globe. A corona of candles flickered around its feet, snagging glints of yellowish light from the coins and bones and bits of jewelry piled on its pedestal.

A crowd of worshippers knelt before the shrine, clutching their hands or pressing their foreheads to the ground in gestures of supplication. A few of them muttered catechisms, but most were silent.

As she proceeded toward the altar, Selena was conscious of the hollow slap of her feet, which seemed amplified by the very silence it broke. She expected the penitents to round on her or shoot her annoyed glances, but none of them seemed at all concerned by—or even aware of—her presence.

Mary, more familiar with the setting, moved with greater confidence. She stepped nimbly over the prostrate bodies and tapped a kneeling figure on the shoulder. Grace raised her head and regarded Mary with studied indifference. Mary whispered something to her in *Mejise*. Grace mouthed a reply and dropped her head, resuming her prayer. Mary tiptoed back to Selena.

"What'd she say?" Selena asked.

"She'll talk. She just has a few more things to say to *La Santa* first." Mary frowned at this last point, her disapproval apparent.

They moved away from the penitents and waited closer to the stairs. A haze of sunlight permeated the first few feet of the subterranean hall, allowing Selena to see deeper into the gloom that hung like inky drapery over the walls. Bones ran the length of the room, stacked in geometric patterns and dotted with blankly staring skulls. Selena wondered how many bodies were needed to furnish such a display. Hundreds, surely. Where had they all come from? The ones she could see bore the brittle yellow cast of relics. Perhaps they comprised the victims of the Last War or the plagues and famines that followed. Fresh bones were plentiful then—them and little else.

Grace rose from her ministrations and left the altar. She passed over the penitents with a light-limbed stride befitting her name. Her eyes flicked expectantly from Selena to Mary. For a moment Selena felt at a total loss for words. She looked to Mary for guidance, who seemed ready to translate but offered no suggestion of what to say. Her plan, held together at best by gossamer threads of intuition, seemed to unravel before her. She held the strands as tightly as she could and forced herself to meet Grace's eyes.

"Maybe we should go somewhere more private," she said.

Mary dutifully translated—or so Selena assumed, for Grace nodded and led them from the temple.

They emerged in the wan half-light of Juarez's tangled alleys. Selena had been reluctant to enter them after her encounter with Krell, but there was no other way to reach *Santa Muerte's* temple.

Grace strode through the winding paths to a blind alley, its arched doorway curtailed by a wall of large clay bricks. She pressed tight against the wall and shimmied to the left, disappearing into a narrow crevice invisible from the alley's mouth. Selena followed.

Darkness consumed her for a moment and spit her out into a tiny courtyard. Tufts of scrub grass burst from the hardpan. The courtyard's walls met at strange angles where competing buildings had grown into one another, leaving an angular scrap of negative space.

A statuette of a skeletal figure stood in the corner, her tiny shoulders draped in a flowing red robe. The remnants of a few candles rested at her feet, their colored lengths burned down to almost nothing. Grace genuflected to the figure before turning to Selena and speaking a few words of *Mejise*.

"She asks you to state your piece," explained Mary.

Selena looked from Grace to the tiny altar squatting in the dirt. The spirit of this strange ugly city stared from the empty sockets of its skull. It was a wild, creeping spirit, a frothing mist that would brook no containment would inevitably spill from whatever vessel attempted hopelessly to hold it.

Selena had been raised in a state religion, but not of it—A Seraphim and hence of the upper class, she studied the Gospels of the Final Testament as all New Canaanites did. She learned of its reverence for submission to higher authority, of the parable of the stones that shifted their burden and were thusly crushed beneath the mountain, of God's abhorrence of the sin of defiance above all things, but the unspoken assumption laid down by her teachers was that these rules didn't really apply to her kind. That the Salters bore the burden while the Seraphim stood at the pinnacle, with the middling Shepherds there to ensure the lowly Salters didn't spoil the view.

The truth of the gospels was never openly questioned in her house—for even in the quietest corners it was suicide to deny the brief return of the savior during the Last War and his establishment of the new Canaanite Order as a bulwark against the encroaching chaos, with the Archbishop serving as his earthly mouthpiece—but nor were its teachings revered or even referenced. There seemed no fervency of belief among Seraphim or Salter, but simply an acceptance of the Testament's rules as an extension of natural laws, as immutable as gravity. Religion was the state, and the state was religion. Knowing the cult of *Santa Meurte* could exist not just outside of the state, but in open defiance of it, fascinated Selena. More than that, it formed the crux of her plan.

"I'm leaving Juarez in two weeks," she said. Mary echoed her words in *Mejise*. The two found an easy rhythm and soon Selena ceased to notice the translation at all. "I've been told how rare it is to escape. I've seen what happens to those who try. I don't care. There's something expected of me, and I intend to do it or die in the attempt.

"I don't know much about you, other than that your brother was killed and your birthright was taken away from you. Maybe you don't want it back. Maybe you've made peace with your situation or decided that there's no changing it. But if you do want it back and are willing to try to take it, with all the risk that comes with that, I see a way how we might be able to help each other.

"You're a *marcada*, like me. But you're also a Delgado. This isn't my town, but from what I've heard that name carries some weight. And from my own experience, being a *marcada* doesn't stop people respecting you. But respect for a fighter isn't respect for a leader. So my question is this: if Thorin looks like he might topple, will your brother's former men support you? Can a woman and a *marcada* be a *Jefe* in Juarez?"

Grace knelt down before the shrine of *Santa Meurte*. She

scratched a scab of dirt from one of the nubs of candle, lit a match, and touched its flame to the wick. She held it there a moment as the fire performed its embryotic doubling, then shook out the match and tossed it aside. Smoke rose from the candle, filling the tiny courtyard with the scent of lavender. Grace stood and gave Selena her answer. It required no translation:

"*Si.*"

33: Flickering Orange Semaphore

Marcus could feel the sickhouse breathing on him. Wet air lapped at the back of his neck, dampened his palms with its relentless condensation. That his own sweat was the actual cause of this moisture made no difference to him. He adjusted his serape to hide the wedge of exposed skin between hair and collar and wiped his hands on the front of his pants.

He had always hated sickhouses, hated them with the bone-deep loathing that can only gestate in fear. It was not the sight of injury that frightened him—Marcus had seen the insides of too many men to fear the exposure of such anatomy, and had performed dozens of feats of ad hoc surgery in conditions far from sterile. Nor did the promise of death, mixed into the very mortar of every *enfermeria* and *hospicio* ever built, give him pause.

It was simply that sickhouses reminded him of his father. His presence filled every bed, rode every gurney, dribbled from every corner. To cross their threshold was to shed inches and years, husking away his defenses until only a trembling kernel of boyhood remained.

He recalled those final visits with absolute clarity as some unknown malady—nameless but for the nebulous and shifting phrases that fumbled to catch and classify his symptoms: *la viruela, la palidez gris, el demonio sudoroso*—prodded his father mercilessly along on his slow march toward death. He remembered the way his father's eyes sank deeper and deeper into their sockets, leaving him to peer through cranial tunnels at the world receding around him. The funk of his sickness, sour at first and by the very end strangely sweet. The moan, weak but constant, a reedy pathetic timbre so unlike his real voice, as if from a lost and frightened child weeping in the caverns of his throat. The slow implosion of his body as the germs dissolved his flesh and chipped away his muscle, leaving behind a sagging tent of skin and bone.

The twitch of his mother's finger brushed the recollection from his mind. He patted her hand and waited as her eyes fluttered open, their brown irises growing wan and cloudy behind a skein of milky tissue. A Grey Sister appeared at her side, bony fingers proffering a tin cup of cool water. She brought the cup to his mother's puckered lips and held it steady as she drank. The muscles in her neck twitched and shuddered with the effort of swallowing. She broke off with a contented sigh. The Grey Sister disappeared as quickly as she'd come, her legs mere hypotheses beneath the whicker of her floor-length dress.

"Are you awake, *madre?*" he asked. "It's Marcus."

His mother's eyes fluttered open.

"Marcito. It's—" Her words dissolved into a cough. It folded her inward, wasted muscle showing in tight cords beneath her tissue paper skin.

"Please, mother. Don't strain." He smoothed out her blanket and hiked it up to cover her shoulders. "I need to speak with you about something. It is no easy thing, but I promise to heed your words, whatever they may be."

His mother closed her eyes. Her breath resumed a gentle rise and fall that could signal sleep, or perhaps simply rest. She nodded, once, a barely perceptible jostle of her head.

"I'm afraid, mother. Afraid that I may do something terrible, something that will hurt our family. I'm afraid because so far, I've chosen not to do this thing, but that choice becomes harder every day. I don't know how much longer I can hold on.

"I've hurt so many people already. I'm very good at hurting people. I used to take pride in that, and to me, that's the most shameful thing of all. I didn't realize that if you cause enough pain, it starts to stick to you. And soon it stains everything you touch.

"What should I do? I can't stay here, I can't run. Every move I can make brings more blood, more pain, more death. I'm so lost, mother."

Marcus watched the slow smoothing of the creases on his mother's face. Pockets of loose flesh formed at the corners of her mouth, her thin chest worked its creaky bellows beneath the cotton blanket. She was getting farther and farther away, coming back less and less often.

Perhaps he'd left it too long.

He gave her hand a final squeeze and rose to leave, the rustle of his serape nearly obscuring the whisper that passed her lips.

"Ask *La Santa*, Marcito. She will know."

Marcus rubbed his face. *Always with La Santa. Don't I know enough about death that I can do without counsel from her foolish saint?* With an inward sigh, he knelt before the shrine, his eyes level with *La Santa's* empty sockets. He drew a *peso* coin from his pocket and set it at the icon's feet. His devotion made, he took a match from the pile, struck it alight with his thumbnail, and touched the flame to a candle. He couldn't bring himself to speak to the shrine aloud, but he set the thought at the front of his mind: *okay, saint. I've long been your servant, however little I believe. Show me the way forward.*

He watched the flame perform its endless pirouette, searching for messages signaled in flickering orange semaphore or jotted in arabesques of smoke. The flame answered only with enigma, or more likely didn't answer at all. Its reflection burned in his pupils, and he closed his eyes against it. He licked his thumb and forefinger and pinched out the candle. The flame died with an indignant hiss. He and *La Santa*, it seemed, had nothing to say to each other.

As he turned from the shrine, he saw a *marcada* standing over his mother's bed. Slashes of blue marked her cheek and forehead. Her hair, its flaxen tint darkened by weeks without washing, clung in tight cornrows to her scalp. Marcus nearly didn't recognize her and took half a step backward when he did.

"Selena," he said.

Selena sat down on the chair next to the bed. "Is this your mom?"

"*Sí*," he replied, *Mejise* rising unbidden to his lips. It was remarkable how quickly his mind had reverted to its mother tongue. Hadn't it felt like a foreign language to him just a few weeks before? He shifted his thoughts back to *Llanures*—a task that took a moment's effort, as if forcing a wheel from one rut to a second one running in parallel.

"Is she okay?"

"She is as one can expect. She sleeps much, and is often in pain. But the Grey Sisters treat her kindly, and her thoughts are sometimes clear."

"That's good." She watched his mother for a moment. Something large and hungry stirred beneath the still waters of her face.

"I've heard much of your exploits in the Iron Circle. It seems like many have taken notice."

Selena's eyes flicked to the shrine of *La Santa*. "Something like that."

"Such attention comes with risks, of course. It is, how you say, a double-edged sword. I've overheard Thorin speaking unfavorably of you."

"Well, I'm not much of a fan of his, either, if we're being honest."

"I am being serious, 'Lena. Thorin's interest is rarely of a healthy sort. You would be wise to fade from view for a time. To do otherwise puts you in danger."

Selena chuckled at that. Marcus didn't get the joke. For a girl so often dour, she showed flashes of humor at the strangest times.

"I'm sorry, 'Lena. For all that has happened. My folly was not yours to bear, and you should have paid no price for it."

"Don't," she spat, her voice spiky with sudden anger. "Don't splash your guilt around like that. It's not your fault Thorin's an asshole, and it's not your fault he managed to grab power."

"Perhaps. But I could have told you not to come with me. I could have left you at the nearest *pueblo* until my business was done."

"Yeah, and you could've bailed on your debt and used the money to fund our trip west. Or you could've never gone into debt in the first place. In every shit thing that happens, there's always a way to blame yourself. Something you did, something you missed, something left unsaid. But you know who never blame themselves? Fucks like Thorin, or the Mayor, or the Archbishop of New Canaan. Those guys never misstep. Every choice they make is the right one, every problem is someone else's fault." Selena pointed to her brand. "You know who I blame for this? The guy who gave it to me. Everything else is happenstance."

The room fell silent apart from the distant ablutions of the Grey Sisters and the rattle-wheeze of Marcus's mother's breath. Selena looked at the old woman with an expression close to longing. When she spoke again, her voice sounded at half its previous volume but somehow struck Marcus's ears with greater clarity.

"I'm not here for an apology. I just want to tell you about something that's happening in two weeks' time. Maybe you can help me with it. Maybe it can help you."

Marcus listened.

34: ¿Quien Lo Hizo?

Selena's knuckles ached. She shook her hands until the sensation receded and resumed her flurry of punches. They struck a muffled tattoo against their burlap target, rendering an ever-deeper concavity into the slurry of dirt and leather that comprised its innards. Flecks of red dotted the grey-brown fabric, bloody stamps imprinted from the fissures in her chafed and stinging knuckles. She noted their concentration in a few key regions—belly-height, liver-height, face-height—and made these her targets. The dots grew thicker, nebulae condensing into crimson stars.

A crowd gathered at the mouth of the courtyard where Selena had set up her makeshift gym. She would've preferred somewhere private, but apart from the barracks she had no space to call her own, and she doubted the girls would appreciate the noise and mess imposed by her training.

Mary stood amongst the other onlookers and studied Selena's

progress, her expression teetering between impressed and appalled.

"Shouldn't you save a little for the fight?"

"It's days away yet," said Selena. "I need to keep fresh." She continued punching as she spoke and noted with satisfaction that her voice betrayed no signs of fatigue.

"You know best, I guess, though it seems to me that your hands shouldn't be bleeding."

"If your hands aren't bleeding, you're not working hard enough."

"I can live with that," Mary said, and withdrew into the crowd. She chatted with a few women—it was mostly women watching, Selena noticed, most of them middle-aged or older though some were as young as her—and reluctantly collected a few gifts, which she stored in a growing pile nearby. Neither Selena nor Mary was entirely comfortable with these offerings, but the women who gave them brooked no refusal, and in the end, it was easier to just take them. At least they were objects of little concrete value; Selena would've felt a lot worse if her patrons were bequeathing *pesos* or food, neither of which they could much afford to part with.

She hurled a final few punches and stepped back, noting with satisfaction the bruised concavities that formed around her targets. The bag vibrated for a few moments as it absorbed its final volley of abuse. A trio of guy wires held it tight to the ground while a hempen rope suspended from a rafter bore its weight. Selena continually expected some passer-by to pillage the setup for these materials—purchased with the dwindling remnants of her cancelled stipend—but so far no one had. She unwound the strips of cloth from her hands and rubbed the feeling back into her fingers.

The crowd dispersed, though not before half a dozen women approached Selena to proffer their own trinkets personally, which she would accept with a small nod of thanks. A few of them offered a small blessing or encouragement in *Mejise*. Selena grasped no more than the odd word and so could only smile stiffly and mumble *gracias*, but the speakers seemed aware of her limited comprehension and expected no greater reply. Perhaps that's why they spoke in the first place; it was almost like a prayer to *La Santa Meurte*, hopes tossed into a grinning visage where they would sink or float by a judgment beyond their knowing.

Gradually the alley cleared, leaving Mary and Selena alone.

"You've become quite the storied individual," Mary said. "You should hear some of the things you've done. Rode with the harriers down to Zapata. Plundered Mad Hector's hidden treasures and escaped from his oubliette. Crossed the Delta Sea on a raft you built from the bones of your enemies."

"That last one's only half true," Selena corrected.

"The latest rumor is about your ear. Some of the women are saying it was bitten off by a scorned lover."

Selena wrinkled her nose. "Ugh. Couldn't I have lost it in a battle or something? Maybe wrestled a mountain lion?"

"Don't worry, they're saying you got even with the guy in the end."

"What, by biting off *his* ear?"

"No," grinned Mary. "Not his ear."

The two women retreated to a nearby tavern, where Mary ordered two ceramic cups of *te de poleo*, one of which she thrust on Selena despite her earnest but knowingly pointless refusal. They'd been through this ritual many times, and Selena had yet to successfully ward off Mary's proffered drink. She told herself it was because to refuse outright would be unkind, though in all honesty she'd begun to crave the brisk tingle the liquid left on her throat.

"So," Mary said. "You're still planning to go through with this?"

Selena glanced around the room. Most of Juarez spoke little to no *Llanures*, but that didn't make it prudent to blab about her plans in the middle of a tavern. She gave a curt nod. "Of course I am. I told you. It's too late to change my mind anyway."

The two women looked out the window at the horizontal strip of sky between the lintel and the roof of the building opposite. The moon hung just barely visible in the top-left corner, its gibbous belly waxing with each passing day.

"How soon 'til it's full, you think?" Selena asked.

Mary considered it, head tilted. She held her hand up and pinched its image between thumb and forefinger. "Three, four days. It's easier to tell once it gets there."

Selena nodded. Four days. It seemed an impossible stretch of time, the sort of centuries-long fabrications that she used to read about in her pre-War history classes and dissect with whispers at her parents' table that night—the rise of Christian Rome under Julius Caesar to its collapse before the godless barbarians; the death of the flawed but orderly *Drittesreich* to the cancerous spread of Secular

Globalism. An insurmountable span of days, and yet at the same moment not nearly long enough.

She thought about Simon and the girl who'd contacted her on his behalf—Emily, Selena was pretty sure. God, her whole plan rested on the girl's tiny shoulders, and she wasn't even certain she remembered the kid's name! Still, there was nothing she could do but hold up her end, and hope that, when it came down to it, Simon could hold up his. It was beyond risky, but slim odds of success were better than certain failure, and the thought of her inaction resulting in New Canaan's conquest of the Republic of California—knowing her parents' crucifixion had been, atop its irrefutable cruelty, pointless—was worse than any punishment Thorin could dream up.

They finished their *poleo* in companionable silence and returned to the barracks, where Selena intended to spend the rest of the morning soaking her chapped knuckles in the washbasin. As they approached, she noticed her fellow *marcadas* gathered in a cluster by the front door, chattering in frantic *Mejise*. Selena couldn't catch the meaning, but she recognized the tone: the giddy anxiety of a crowd witnessing a tragedy at arm's length. She pushed through the crowd, murmuring *disculpe*, and made her way into the barracks.

A coppery stink hit her nose, followed by the cloying stench of meat going bad. A halo of flies circled her bed, their buzzing inordinately loud in the otherwise still room. She pulled back the covers.

Paulo's severed head gazed up at her, his waxen flesh settled into an expression of peculiar calm. On his cheek, just below the red X that denoted his freedom, someone had carved a star.

The flies descended on the exposed stump of his neck. Selena waved them off and returned the blanket to its original position. She gathered the linens into a ball with the head at the center and carried them from the room. The girls stepped away from her, hands raised, as if she were brandishing a large and deadly weapon.

She and Mary took the head to the Iron Circle. A network of catacombs spread under the arena, their earthen walls carved into crude dormitories where the seasoned fighters stayed. Selena went inside and found some men she recognized.

"*Lo siento,*" she said, and handed the bundle to them. The man who took it from her had broad shoulders and skin the color of fallow soil. A red circle and X atop his former brand marked him as a Brother of the Iron Circle. He unwrapped the blanket, eyebrows jumping as its contents grew visible. He inhaled sharply through his teeth. The other men crowded in behind him.

"*¿Quien lo hizo? ¿Qiuen?*"

Selena turned to Mary. "What are they saying?"

"They want to know who did it."

Selena turned back to the men, watched the molten anger flow across their faces and cool into unyielding stone. Saw the power, untapped, still coursing beneath the surface. She spoke her answer before she was even fully aware of it.

"*Jefe Thorin.*"

Part V: The Judgment of la Santa Meurte

35: Phantom Fireworks

The moon hung over Simon's head. He studied its bulging roundness, hoping to convince himself that the haze was playing tricks on his eyes.

"Do you think it's full?" he asked.

"It's full," said Emily, not looking up. She tended to the twin pots hanging over the cooking fire. Beans boiled slowly in the first, while a thick cornmeal paste sizzled in the second, its bottom crisping with oil. She took a taste with a wooden spoon, nodded, and continued stirring. Otis nodded his approval.

"Full," he agreed. "Tomorrow's the day."

Simon looked up at the moon, hoping to spot something that might refute their assessment. But it was no use. It was a perfect sphere, a pale egg in which some cruel monster finalized its gestation. Come sunrise the shell would crack, and the creature would be free. Simon wasn't sure what it looked like, but he knew it was vicious, and he knew it was hungry.

A hand rested on Simon's shoulder, squeezed. Emily gave him a reassuring shake. "Hey. It's gonna be fine. We got stuff on our side those goons've never even dreamed of."

Simon closed his eyes and shook his head. "But what if they don't work?"

"Of course they work. We got them out here, didn't we?" She motioned to the notch in the western wall of the gully where they'd camped. Inside its shadowy recesses lay the dormant engines of Simon's last hope. He'd fixated over their tiniest detail, studying every joint and seam and mechanism. But despite his preparation there was so much left untested, so many variables left unknown.

"There's more to it than that," he said hopelessly, aware that this statement couldn't convey one one-millionth of his true concern. Its inadequacy was laughable; it was like calling the ocean wet.

"You're right to feel nervous," Otis said. "What we're doing has its dangers, sure. But there's danger in all things out here. You live in this wasteland, you face peril. It's in the food you eat—when it's even there for you to eat it—and the air you breathe. You've just gotta get used to it, else it'll chew you up from the inside."

"I don't see how I could ever get used to it," said Simon. "But I can live with it, I guess."

"Well then, that'll have to do. Come on, we should fill our bellies and get some sleep."

Simon managed the former—the cornmeal was savory despite its simplicity, and went nicely with the beans—but the latter was beyond his grasp. His eyes remained open long after Emily and Otis had gone to asleep, their slow breaths settling into a companionable rhythm, one rising as the other fell.

Doubts crowded his mind, shouldering past one another and shouting in fierce competition to be heard. *What if the batteries lost their charge in the night? What if one of those old bits of machinery gives way? What if the electrical components—that you'd had no way to adequately test, by the way—fizzle out? What if you screw something up the way you always do? What if that screw-up gets someone killed? What if that someone is Otis? Or Emily? Or Selena?*

What if she's dead already? What if that guy who bought her went and sold her to someone even worse? What if you can't find her? What if the people who took her find you too? What if they find the data stick? What if they've tortured Selena until she told them everything? What if they've contacted New Canaan?

The thoughts kept coming, pressing in tighter and tighter, the stink of their bodies filling his lungs, choking him.

Stop it, said a voice. Though it spoke calmly where the others shouted, it cut them off mid-word as if bellowing through a bullhorn. The silence that followed throbbed in Simon's ears.

You know what you're doing, Simon, the voice continued. *You were the smartest kid at St. Barnabas. You could rewire anything the lectors threw at you. And you don't slack off when there's work to be done. If we fail, we fail, but it won't be on you. This is our best shot, and we can't take it if you're too busy beating yourself up with self-pity. Now get some sleep. Tomorrow we carry off a coup.*

Simon opened his eyes. Phantom fireworks burst across his field of vision. He rubbed his face until they faded, waited for the murmur of the old voices to return. They never did. Neither did the last one, though he could recall it much more clearly than the others. It had come as if spoken inches from his ear, yet its owner lay twenty miles to the south, handling her own doubts with the steely resolve that had always stirred in him love and terror in equal measure.

"Thanks, Selena," he whispered.

And as he drifted asleep, he could almost believe that she heard him.

36: ¡La Santa Viene!

Mary put a hand on Selena's arm and squeezed.

"You okay?"

Selena nodded. She spat onto the hardpan and scuffed a bit of dirt over the damp spot. Strings of mucus formed a shifting lattice between the roof of her mouth and her tongue. The surge of anxiety troubled her. She'd never felt nervous before a fight in the past, and indeed it wasn't the fight itself that made her nervous now, but rather the tasks that went along with it. Her fingers crawled to the small of her back, where a narrow tube was secreted beneath the billowing hem of her shirt. She touched it, still half-surprised to find it was actually there.

Since her meeting with Emily several weeks before, her every action suggested a bedrock presumption that the girl would live up to her end of their plan. They'd hashed it out over half a dozen cups of *te de poleo*, sketching phantom maps with their fingers and debating strategy as if they were wizened mercenaries on a job and not a couple of kids playing at war, and Selena had carried the role on her shoulders ever since.

But that didn't change the fact that her partner in all this was a girl no older than her brother, and that her story was all but unverifiable in its details. She trusted that the girl had met Simon and won his confidence—how else could she know what she knew?—but everything beyond that had to be taken on faith.

So when the girl reappeared that morning outside the barracks, her face drawn and lined with a poor night's sleep, her presence seemed almost otherworldly. The feeling passed quickly, flushed away by a flood of relief. Muscles she didn't even know she'd been tensing suddenly relaxed, tingling with reprieve. A thousand things could still go wrong—she'd be astounded if nothing did—but the way forward remained clear to its first step.

Selena slipped out as discreetly as she could manage. She led Emily to a quiet spot nearby, forcing herself to remain silent until she was out of earshot from the street. When she allowed herself to speak, the words burst out of her in a hoarse bark.

"Did it work? Is he here?"

"It worked," she answered, her voice pitched twenty decibels below Selena's. "We're just outside town. There's an arroyo we're using for cover. When's the fight?"

"They start at noon. I'd give it an hour from there before I'm on. I can't be more exact than that."

"That's fine. Here." She handed Selena the metal tube. "Simon's idea. Smoke signal. Turn the base 'til it clicks, point the other end up and wait three seconds. We'll get as close as we can beforehand so you're not stuck waiting long."

"Right." Selena tapped the tube against her thigh. There were so many things she wanted to ask, but wasn't sure how. Fists clenched, she inhaled deeply and took a stab at it.

"I just wondered … Simon. He's okay?"

"He's fine. He wanted to come see you. We told him it was too risky."

"You were right. It is." She swallowed. "Thanks."

Shaking the recollection aside, Selena took out the signal tube and handed it to Mary.

"I need you to do something for me."

Mary looked at the tube skeptically. "What is it, a bomb?

"No, nothing like that. It's a signal. Once I've won the fight and started my announcement, find a clear spot outside, turn the knob, and drop it."

"What if you don't win the fight?"

Selena considered the question. "Use your judgment."

"Great. Really banking on my strong suit." She motioned to the alcove. "I think you're on."

"Right. I'll see you once it's over."

"Yeah, let's hope."

Selena stepped into the Iron Circle. Her eyes skimmed the crowd, tallying rows of spectators. They easily numbered in the hundreds, maybe even thousands. Their myriad voices slurred into a single meaningless burble, low and constant as the sound of a distant waterfall. She knew the acoustics of the amphitheater favored her position over theirs, but even so, could such a heaving mass be swayed by a single voice? She rolled her opening words around in her mouth, prodding their alien contours and shaping their syllables with her lips and tongue. She had no need of them yet, but when the time came, she wanted them to be ready.

She spotted Grace Delgado, who sat near the center of the arena's longest row. It was a spot chosen deliberately, for it was easy for many spectators to see but hard to reach from the aisles. Grace met her gaze and gave her the tiniest of nods. Though the gesture was meaningless to anyone but the two of them, Selena dropped her eyes from it anyway, flushed with anxiety at their conspiracy being uncovered. She cast her eyes about randomly for several seconds, miming a casual survey of the crowd, before allowing herself a glance at the alcove where the Brothers of the Iron Circle congregated during fights. They were out in force this afternoon, which Selena took for a good sign. Her conversation with them had been terse, and they made no formal plans, but their presence comforted her all the same. She couldn't' say to what extent they were for her, but after seeing their reaction when presented with Paulo's head and the terrible desecration enacted on its cheek—for a *Hermano*, a sacrilege almost worse than the beheading itself—she knew without a doubt that they were very against Thorin.

Her opponent arrived, cutting her contemplation short. He leaped over the Iron Circle and approached with long, cocky strides.

A compact man with a narrow waist and wide shoulders, he moved with a leonine bearing that was more hunter than fighter. An ornate pattern darkened his cheeks in blue-black arabesques, fanning down to his neck and curling in two symmetrical tendrils around his eyes. It was the most expansive tattoo Selena had ever seen on a *marcado*. He looked to Selena like a revenant dredged from some purgatorial abyss, an uneasy spirit seeking atonement through combat. She shook these thoughts from her mind and made herself see him as a man. No good ever came from mythologizing your opponent.

As he closed the final fifty feet between them, his motions tightened, and he shifted from his easy gait into a fighter's stance. It was an unusual one, the fingers of his right hand hanging loose, as if reluctant to make a fist.

The fight began. Selena tested him with a few jabs and crosses and found him more cautious than she'd expected. He made no effort to fire back, merely bobbed away from the heavier blows and rolled the lighter ones across his raised wrists. Such caution in attack would usually be matched by the fighter' footwork, but her opponent made no effort to shy back. In fact, he seemed eager to carve away the distance between them, inching past her outer range and into the field of heavier blows.

What is this guy doing? sneered a voice in Selena's head. But while his strategy seemed amateurish in its inconsistency, his fundamentals were solid: he could take a punch without flinching, and his feint and parries were deft.

Overhead a momentary flash of sunlight broke through the

yellow-grey haze, its fleeting glow reflected in the polished bend of the Iron Circle. A sister ember flickered in the hollow of her opponent's loose left hand. A klaxon in her head sounded a warning. She dismissed it as jitters—the shine could've been anything—but the klaxon blared on.

Selena kept pushing, raising a few welts and blackening an eye, and finally, the man looked poised to strike. He chambered a cross with his left hand and swatted with his right. It was a superficially obvious ploy, an attempted hijacking of the reflexes—trick your opponent into deflecting the tap while the heavy punch soars through unopposed. A seasoned fighter would simply absorb the tepid blow and throw his effort into blocking the real attack. Selena had done it hundreds of times. But the klaxon still rang in her ears, and before she knew what she was even doing, she snatched his right arm by the wrist and twisted it until it presented palm up.

The device was so small it could be easily mistaken for a bit of jewelry: a steel band with a raised segment along its length. The tip of a needle peeked from a tiny hole in its center. Though barely wider than a hair, it stood out in the frenzy of Selena's seeing as if magnified a hundredfold.

The man's arm went rigid. It snapped down, open-palmed, and made to slap against Selena's wrist. She let go at the last second, and the hand swiped only air. It continued down, driven by an outsized force robbed of its expected resistance. Selena guided it along its arc and drove it, palm-first, into the man's thigh.

She heard the tight snap of a triggered spring. The man gasped as if stung. He recoiled, eyes bulging, and stared at Selena in horror and incredulity. His face turned first pale, then blue. Foam poured from his mouth. A high wheeze whistled through his sputtering lips, ascending in pitch until it disappeared. He grabbed his throat and scratched at it, dragging deep gashes in his skin in his desperate tunneling for air. Black stains dappled his fingers. For a moment Selena thought this to be another symptom of the poison, but she soon realized that what she'd taken for a tattoo was actually a charcoal ink applied before the fight. Behind it lay the hairless cheeks of a young and frightened man, unmarked save for a green star beneath his right eye.

Thorin's mark.

A hush settled over the crowd. In its wake Selena heard the long low sigh of wind coming over the amphitheater walls, carrying with it the mingled odors of the streets beyond. She went to speak and found her jaw immobile. Her words, so carefully aligned, tumbled backward down her throat, choking her. In the front rows, onlookers began glancing at one another, confused by the inaction.

Selena looked past her opponent to a spot in the crowd. Her eyes locked on a woman not much older than her. She had a long face with a thin nose and a smooth, rounded chin. A fringe of black hair lay over her forehead at a slight slant. Selena didn't know the woman, but her words needed a target, so she opened her mouth and spoke to her.

Her voice rang through the arena. The word's she'd prepared lined up neatly at her lips, leaping from their perch like a platoon of paratroopers. Taken one by one, Selena could only guess their meaning, but she'd rehearsed them well with Mary's coaching and understood their overall message as if she were a native speaker of *Mejise*:

"Citizens of Juarez! I have come as a messenger of *Santa Muerte*, who has found disfavor in the sacrilege of your leader! Our lady demands you right this wrong, or she will exact a terrible vengeance. I forswear my allegiance to her chosen sovereign, and will fight only at her pleasure."

As her words diffused outward to the distant seats on a current of incredulous whispers, Selena snapped her heels and straightened her back. Moving with the stiff-limbed precision of a military drill, she swiveled counterclockwise, dropped to one knee, and raised her right fist in salute.

"To Grace Delgado, emissary of *Santa Muerte!*"

The murmuring increased. The name of Delgado rang in their memory, causing heads to turn instinctively in Grace's direction before the former *Senador's* sister had even fully stood.

She did so slowly, her narrow shoulders covered by a simple black serape. Her hair sat at the nape of her neck, long strands woven into a spiraling braid. Unarmed and unadorned, she nevertheless exuded a regal bearing that the marks of her ownership couldn't deface. She was a queen laid low, but unquestionably a queen, and the crowd fell all but silent the moment she first spoke.

Her voice thrummed with authority, each syllable crisp and magnified. Selena caught only a scant few words but knew the overall message by heart: that Thorin had overreached, that his presence was a humiliation of the men and women who'd served Delgado and Evangelista, that he sullied *La Santa Meurte* with his cowardice and broke her altars out of fear. That *La Santa* was displeased and would wreak a terrible vengeance on those who did not rise up in her name, and that her blessings would guide the hands of those who did.

The crowd's reaction gave Selena no reason to doubt the accuracy of her interpretation. Eyes widened. Mouths hung agape. Citizens hid their faces or raised their fists and cheered.

Sensing the growing disquiet, a group of Thorin's *esbirros* spilled into the arena, burly men with cudgels clutched in their meaty fists. They made their way into the stands and waded through the crowd. Some stood aside for them, but others blocked their path, moving with deliberate sluggishness or thrusting out their chests to act as shields.

Six of them stepped into the Iron Circle and headed for Selena. She rose from her knees but held her ground. The men raised their clubs. Behind them a pillar of green-grey smoke threaded its way skyward, listing west on the prevailing winds. How high did it need to get before Simon saw it? And how long would it take him to act when he did? Seconds passed, Grace kept speaking, and the enforcers inched their way toward her.

One of the *esbirros* lunged forward, swinging his club like a broadsword. Selena ducked under it and delivered a haymaker to his liver. A second man closed in and brought his club straight down. Selena had no time to dodge and parried instead, sweeping the blow aside with the back of one wrist. The club skidded along her forearm with enough force to rattle bone, slid past her elbow, and thudded into the dirt by her feet. Selena loosened the man's teeth with a few rabbit punches but lacked the stance for a knockout blow. He clenched his jaw through the onslaught and rammed the butt of his club into Selena's belly.

Selena tensed for the strike at the last second but was knocked back all the same, giving the man time to wind up another swing. Blood ran from his nose, dying the lower half of his face red. A savage grin split his jaw, bearing twin rows of red-flecked teeth. Selena raised her arms in a last-ditch effort to block a blow that never came. Instead one of the Brothers of the Iron Circle slammed his fist into the *esbirro*'s temple. The club flew from his hand mid-swing and stuck into the dry earth like a javelin. The fighter spat on the fallen *esbirro* and kicked him twice in the side.

By then, the first *esbirro* was finding his feet. Selena chambered her leg and kicked him in the side of the knee, sending him sprawling back to earth. She jumped on his back and slammed his head into the ground until his body went slack. The Brothers charged past her, driving the remaining *esbirros* from the field.

In the stands, Grace's oration continued. The *esbirros* had nearly reached her. A clutch of partisans stood firm, but in their frustration Thorin's men had taken harsher measures, their efforts to brush past or sidestep replaced by punches and shoving. She carried on undaunted, her voice straining to cut through the noise of the struggle inching ever closer. Selena looked over her head to the column of smoke. Where the hell was Simon?

One of the *esbirros* fought past the last of Grace's defenders and seized her by the shoulders. Grace slammed an elbow into his mouth and kept speaking. Hands closed around her arms, grabbed her hair, wormed their way toward her neck. Her head snapped back. Words rasped from her throat, their meaning lost in the growing chaos.

A distant rumble shook the arena. A few heads in the crowd turned in search of its source, but most ignored it in favor of the more immediate action unfurling before them. Smoke plumed over the arena wall, drawing more gazes away from the melee. Worried chatter swirled atop the tumult, its spin rising to cyclone force as the stadium's northern wall exploded.

The crowd erupted into a flurry of fists and feet and screams. The *esbirros*, blindsided, turned their attention from Grace long enough for her to slip away and several of her compatriots to bludgeon them senseless. A tsunami of smoke and rubble washed over the Iron Circle. The stink of ash and cordite filled Selena's nostrils. Through smoke-stinging eyes she saw Grace leap onto the banister dividing audience and theater, arms raised in exultation. The churning chaos seemed to part as she opened her mouth, clearing a path for her words.

"*¡La Santa! ¡La Santa viene!*"

37: Mask of Dust and Dirt

The vehicle's cab was too big for Simon. The seat was nearly as long as his legs, forcing his ankles to cantilever over the edge if he tried to sit flush against the backrest. His other option was to perch on the lip of the seat, but then the steering wheel eclipsed the lower half of his vision. In the end, he tucked his feet beneath his bottom and knelt, a position that boosted his head sufficiently far above the dashboard to see. It left the pedals totally inaccessible, but he wasn't driving anyway.

A gust of wind blew through the vehicle's open windows. Dust stung Simon's eyes and lined his nostrils with a desiccating coating that itched and ached by turns. He scratched a spot on his septum. The brittle membrane tore. A thread of blood trickled over his philtrum and beaded on his upper lip. He wiped it away and pinched the bridge of his nose until the bleeding stopped.

A haze of sand and grit collected on the vehicle's windshield, leading the outside world a sepia tinge. Simon thought about cleaning it but decided not to bother. Even with the dirt, his sightline was plenty clear. Emily had scouted the location days before the arrival of their tiny convoy, and he had to admit she'd chosen well. The mesa formed a slanted table atop the plains, its southern end cresting a cliff face some thirty feet high while its northern flank receded at a gentle angle the vehicle's chunky puncture-proof wheels could easily navigate. A frieze of tarwort and yucca provided ample cover, allowing them to creep the truck to the very edge with only minimal risk of being seen. Juarez sprawled across the valley below, a cluster of hub-and-spoke neighborhoods centered around a large earthwork structure. The city was too tightly-packed and tangled to offer much enticement for bandits in search of an easy raid, but it arose in a primitive era and had made no provisions for an attack from above. Why would it? Nothing with that sort of capability existed within a thousand miles of this place. Or so they likely thought.

Emily had been the first person in a very long time to stumble upon the cache in the mountains. But others had found it at some point between her discovery and the moment it was first abandoned. Simon could never know for sure who those people were, but he'd pored over every inch of the place and seen what they'd taken and what they hadn't, and it gave him a pretty good idea. They were fierce but frightened, a band of thieves or partisans who'd watched the world crumble around them, denizens of a sandcastle half-swallowed by the tide. The wares they unearthed had sat untouched long enough for the fuel cells and batteries to die, and they lacked the arcane knowledge necessary to oversee their resurrection. They were scavengers on a fresh corpse, and it made them cagey but not totally desperate—there'd been no effort to strip the place bare, and Simon even found the rusted shells of unopened canned goods in some forgotten cubbies, their insides long since moldered to inedible mush.

They'd ignored the tools and screws and other supplies geared to rebuilding; their interest lay in more destructive pursuits. Firearms, grenades, antipersonnel mines, they plucked them all with abandon, leaving nothing but vacant shelves labeled with the yellowing names of their plundered wares. In this effort, they'd been thorough, though their sights were narrower than they could've been. If they'd been more technically acute, they may have investigated the cargo bay more closely. They probably fumbled with the bigger vehicles in the hopes of getting them moving, but lacked the technical knowledge to do anything beyond press a few buttons.

Simon figured this was why they failed to note the significance of the roof-mounted mortars, and consequently overlooked the crate of incendiary rockets stashed amongst the spare tires and engine parts.

The rockets were the one thing Simon hadn't quite dared to test. He had too few of them to spare and too little an understanding of their precise capabilities. This decision had seemed prudent at the time, but its downsides emerged with sickening clarity as the moment of his attack arrived. What if the rockets were duds? Far from inciting city-wide chaos, the entire fusillade would do little more than dent a few walls or maybe crack an unlucky bystander's skull.

And that's assuming they fired at all—they could easily fizzle out and do nothing, or worse, explode inside the barrel. Simon imagined the flash of light, the shriek of buckling metal, the instant of incredulity and fear as the flames escaped their bondage and rendered his body into so much ash and tallow.

And what if they worked? A single twitch of his index finger would turn some segment of a quiet city into hell. So what if that city championed slavery and boasted rulers who found their seats by slitting throats and orphaning children? The bombs didn't care who they burned. Simon had pulled a trigger once before to save his sister, but the target had been valid and the danger imminent. This was a different matter altogether. This wasn't justice or self-defense; this was an act of war.

But he and Selena were at war, weren't they? And they weren't the ones who'd started it. But Juarez didn't start it either.

Simon positioned the mortar with a few taps of a joystick. His finger caressed the trigger protruding from its tip. Pressure mounted on its spring ounce by sluggish ounce. He felt the first yield as the button descended into its housing, the play of muscle against metal in uneasy equilibrium. The spring was light, calibrated to a few pounds of pressure at most. A toddler could manage it.

Otis and Emily stood outside the vehicle. Emily dragged her foot along the ridge of the mesa, chipping stones loose from the dirt and sending them skittering down the cliff face. Otis stared at the squat adobe huts that described the city's border, his body still and rigid. He seemed less a man than a man-shaped outcrop of artfully weathered stone. He turned his head to glance at the vehicle, spoiling the effect.

"It's time, I think," he said.

Simon nodded. He adjusted his grip on the joystick, made a few minor adjustments to the mortar. Gears whined, and hydraulics wheezed. He pictured the cannon perched above him, a hollow, black eye gazing into the city's apocalyptic future. Sweat dampened the joystick's rubberized grip. He rubbed his eyes, hiking his glasses onto his forehead, and slid from the seat. Otis cocked his head, curious and concerned. Simon set his glasses on the bridge of his nose and sniffed.

"I can't do it." The words came out as a sob, choked and damp with misery. His breath hitched, clambering up a windpipe slick with mucus.

Otis took the boy in his arms and patted his shoulder. "This is a hard thing you're doing," he said. "It's not something that should be up to children. It's not right."

"But I need to!"

Otis shook his head. "You don't need to do it. But it needs to be done."

Simon blinked, for a moment not understanding. Otis stepped past and climbed into the vehicle's cab. Far from a giant's den, the front seat looked positively cramped when accommodating his lanky frame. He took the joystick with his right hand and squeezed the trigger. *Phthuff!* The missile was airborne before Simon even had a chance to panic. He watched the arc of its trajectory, his stomach lurching as if it were him being launched through the air.

The rocket landed with an orange flash. A crackling rumble followed. Smoke rose from the point of impact, dark clouds lit from below by the flaming wreckage. Otis stared, transfixed, at the carnage. He tweaked the joystick and fired again. This time he hit an enormous structure in the center of town. A sustained rumble echoed over the plains as the wall collapsed.

The shots came faster, their targets random at first, but soon concentrated on a crescent of land to the south. The streets here were wider, the buildings larger and built from a broader range of materials. Their grandeur meant nothing to the bombs, whose flames found if anything a heartier meal. Otis continued bombing the rubble, his lips folding into a snarl. A thin whine escaped from the back of his throat, swelling throughout the onslaught into a scream. He kept screaming and firing after the last rockets were spent and the mortar clicked drily overhead.

Emily climbed into the seat beside her father and pried his fingers from the joystick. When the last of them was free, she took his hand and clutched it in both her own. The screaming subsided. Otis closed his eyes. Tears leaked from their corners and down his chin, spreading like cracks in the mask of dust and dirt that the desert had made for him.

38: Forfeit

There were few veterans among New Canaan's Seraphim. Generals and colonels hailed from Selena's class, and the Templars occasionally held a paramilitary role, but actual blood-and-guts, on the ground fighting was a Salter affair. As such, Selena had never had much more than an abstract notion of war, apart from the bombastic and almost surely apocryphal stories of New Canaan's righteous insurrection against the globalist non-believers in the wake of the Last War.

To her knowledge, she'd only met one true veteran in all her years in New Canaan. It had been at a soiree hosted by some under-Cardinal or other. The Seraphim delighted in such parties almost as much as Selena loathed them, but as she'd left childhood behind, her participation had gone from strongly encouraged to mandatory. Support for the regime was essential for long-term survival, and as double agents for the hated Republic of California, her parents had more to lose than most.

Understanding this made the events no less palatable, but it did ensure her attendance, begrudging though it might have been.

The veteran was a shy boy no more than a few years her senior, his receding chin partially masked by a band of fuzzy brown stubble. His posture was unlike that of most Seraphim men, who sprawled with loose-limbed confidence over any surface on which they sat, stood, or leaned, asserting hegemony over their square yard of space. He sat in the corner of a red velvet divan with his knees pressed together and his hands in his lap, long fingers curled around a tall glass of amber liquid from which he drew occasional sips. He'd looked as miserable and out of place as she felt, and it was perhaps this quality—coupled with the knowledge that she needed to socialize with someone or else face her parents' pointed disapproval—that led her to approach him.

"Can I sit?" she asked, motioning to the space beside him. His head swiveled toward her, nodded, and resumed its original position. The rest of him hadn't moved an inch.

They sat in silence for a while, nursing their drinks and gazing off in separate directions. The venue was exempted from power rationing for the event by edict of the Diocese of Light and spent its privilege lavishly. Bands of color-shifting LEDs twined around support columns, and snatches of baroque music burbled from speakers in the corners. Selena was content to lounge in silence, but her parents had stressed how important it was to converse and not to look sulky. She fumbled for something to say and noticed a bronze medal pinned to the boy's lapel, its face embossed with a lion's head roaring in profile.

"Is that a Heart of Daniel?"

The boy tugged his shirt from his chest to get a better look at the medal. He observed it with mild distaste, as if it were a small and unobtrusive stain he'd only just noticed. "Yeah."

"Where'd you serve?"

"The Outer Baronies, mostly."

"That's where you got the medal?"

"Yeah."

"I guess you were in a battle then, huh?"

"Yeah."

Selena bit her lower lip. The boy's discomfort was palpable. It figured the one person she wanted to talk to—a first at one of these events, she believed—was also the most tight-lipped. Normally, some under-Bishop's whelp latched onto her and spent the evening fawning over his own meager and doubtless inflated accomplishments, all while worming his fingers over as much covered flesh as he could get away with. But now here she was, speaking with an honest-to-god veteran—a Heart of Daniel recipient, no less—and it was as if every word required deliberate extraction, a tooth pulled without anesthetic.

"What's it like? Being in a battle, I mean."

Selena cringed even as the words were leaving her lips. *God, what a stupid question.* She opened her mouth to apologize but stopped when she saw the look on the boy's face. His eyes rose from their meandering at his feet and fixed on some unseen point in the distance. His hands unclasped and gestured as he spoke, etching patterns in the air.

"It's pretty much just chaos. It's loud, and you're either scared or angry, usually both. But there are moments sometimes where everything seems totally still. The battle keeps going on all around you, but it seems far away, or like it's happening behind glass. Then all of a sudden, the glass breaks and it all pours back in on you. But for those few moments, it's actually sort of beautiful."

They'd said little else to one another after that, though the boy's words had stuck with Selena. She recalled them now, watching as pandemonium closed around the arena's throat, choking it with smoke and fists and fire, while her patch of earth remained untouched. It was very much as the boy described. Not beautiful, exactly, but hypnotic.

Mary's voice, hurled from the alcove, broke the spell: "C'mon, already! Let's get out of here!"

They waded through a tide of fleeing bodies, going with the current where possible and fighting it where necessary. Melees erupted here and there, but most of the people around her seemed more interested in seeking shelter than combat. Fire smoldered in the guts of crumbled buildings, tentacles of smoke squiggling through the debris.

A packhorse bolted down the road, trailing an unmanned wagon. The wheel hit a rut, and the wagon toppled. Bushels of squash and cornmeal spilled onto the cobbles. The horse continued undaunted, dragging the wagon on its side until the wood splintered and the wheel broke off. An old woman whipped a kerchief from her head and began filling it with handfuls of cornmeal. Others followed, and soon scavengers blackened the street from boardwalk to boardwalk.

Selena recalled the sacking of Fallowfield, dead Shepherds and farmers piled in the road like driftwood on a dried-up riverbed. *Is this sort of thing gonna keep happening wherever I go?* Her entire trip was supposed to avert a war, but it seemed wherever she went, she ended up causing one. She reached reflexively for the data stick and remembered that Simon had it. Her fingers twitched in discomfort at its absence. It was a talisman of sorts, a reminder that the path she walked hadn't been of her choosing, and that the blood on her hands wouldn't wash clean if she strayed; it would drown her, and the world with it. She was only doing what had to be done.

Sure, but I bet Thorin and The Mayor would tell you the exact same thing.

They came to a strip of adobe storefronts running east-west. Beyond it, the city's core loosened into wider residential streets, which gradually flowed away to a loose cluster of mud huts and scrubland. Somewhere north of those fields jutted a lone outcrop of granite that Emily had set as their meetup spot. It wasn't far, maybe an hour by foot. The thought that she could leave Juarez behind so quickly was difficult to grasp. She looked back at the chaos she'd sown. She hoped whatever bloomed in its wake was better than the swamp that came before. But she couldn't be sure. Her hand went once more to the small blank spot by her hip, felt the stick's absence, and climbed instead to the bronze and amber pendant hanging around her neck. She ran her thumb along its edge, its texture alternating smooth and jagged.

They cut through a narrow gap between buildings. Selena traced her fingers along the wall's pitted length, reading an illegible history in its bumps and creases. They reached a gap in the wall where a narrow tributary met their wider alley. Canvas and corrugated metal formed a patchwork awning and draped the gap in darkness. Selena let her hand drop to her hip.

A large and looming shape exploded from the darkness and slammed into Selena. She managed to raise her arms to her chest before the crushing weight bashed her into the opposite wall. Flakes of dried earth fluttered onto her hair, her shoulders. A sickle of teeth cut the darkness like a crescent moon on its back. Eyes like polished onyx gleamed overhead.

"Well now, here is some luck for Old Krell," said Krell. "I no thought I'd see you back in my alleys, girl. Where your boyfriend? I guess he not so tough now that he a foot shorter, *hein?*"

Other men oozed through the crack and into the alley, thwarting Selena's attempts to break free. Mary reached past the throng and clawed at Krell's forearm.

"Cut it out, asshole. Let her go."

Krell watched her scrabbling with amusement. Her nails left white trails on his forearm, even drew blood in a few places, but by his expression, you'd think he were being accosted by a newborn kitten. One of his men put a hand on her shoulder. She swatted it away, earning more cackles from the crowd, which parted just long enough to swallow her.

Playful shoves grew sharper, meant to bruise and block instead of taunt. Mary threw a few punches before a broad-shouldered man with crudely shorn stubble pinned her arms behind her back. She looked from one face to the next, her indignation softened with the first markings of fear.

"You'd better tell your goons to let me go, Krell. I don't care what bullshit rumors are swirling around with your dirtbag friends, but Selena and I still got Todd's marks. You guys mess with us, you're gonna wake up one morning with your balls mashed to *masa*."

Krell's smile sharpened at the edges. He released Selena from his grip. Three men flowed in to take his place, quick as liquid from a poisoned cup. She wriggled for a moment but could find no foothold for escape. A rabbit punch to the cheek encouraged her to hold still.

Krell sauntered over to where Mary stood. He squared his stance before her, feet planted a shoulder's-breadth apart and ran a finger down her face. It charted a slow, deliberate curve, extending the fringe of her brand along its implied trajectory: down her cheek, along her jaw, into the slight cleft of delicate skin between the tendons of her neck. There it paused, pressing a slight dimple into her skin. "I no think so, girl. I tell you already, her mark is forfeit. ¿Y *tuyo?*"

His hand dove to his belt and in a single smooth motion drew a knife and plunged it into Mary's belly. The men loosened their grip, and she slid from their arms like a load of soggy sheets and struck the ground with a dull thwack.

"Mary!" Selena burst free of the arms that held her and rushed to her friend's side. An elbow plunged into her belly, but she barely felt it. She crouched down next to Mary, cradling the wounded girl's head in her hands. Mary's mouth worked silent syllables into the air.

Selena held her, urging her to speak, as if her words were a balm with which she could heal herself. But no words came. The hands that had held Selena resumed their grip, and this time she lacked the strength to break away.

Krell stooped to clean the blade on the hem of Mary's shirt, sheathed it, and moved back to Selena, his steps resuming their slow swagger.

"Mouthy thing, *hein?* Never mind, pet. I no got the same treat for you. *Al menos no todavía.*"

The other men laughed at this supposed witticism. Selena tried to meet it with a withering smirk, but her face couldn't force even the sourest smile. There was simply nothing left to offer.

39: A Trio of Refugees

Simon stared into the setting sun. Though dulled by the band of haze armoring the horizon, its rays remained sharp enough to sting. Simon blinked against the pain but held his vigil. In some half-thought-out way, it seemed as if hope hung high above him, its feathered appendages frail and flightless, and his continued glare was the only thing keeping it aloft. To drop his gaze was to acknowledge the path the sun had forged across the sky since Otis launched his barrage on the city, to accept a passage of time far longer than Selena should have needed.

"She should be here by now," he said.

Emily looked to Otis, who shifted uncomfortably. It was the first thing any of them had said in the better part of an hour.

"Hard to say. It's a good distance 'tween us and the Iron Circle. Could be two hours on foot."

"It's been three," Simon countered. "At least."

"Maybe the roads out of town are all clogged," Emily offered. "It's bound to be pretty messy in there right now."

Simon shook his head. They'd seen others fleeing the city. They poured out of the main roads or dribbled through the outer fringe of houses, fanning out across the plains. A few had even passed within a dozen feet of Simon, their possessions wrapped in ratty blankets and clutched to their chests. The youngest of them, a girl no older than Simon, regarded him with a solemn look. The parents paid him no attention at all. Otis had stowed the truck in a nearby gulley and the two-wheeled vehicle in a tuft of cactus and scrub grass, and so the three of them probably seemed like no more than a trio of refugees resting before resuming their exodus.

If these people—many of them old or infirm or stunned by calamity into a lumbering, aimless flight into the wilderness—could make the trek, why hadn't Selena managed it yet?

Because she's dead, that's why. Dead or dying.

Simon closed his eyes against the statement, as if his eyelids could bar the words from entering his skull. They hacked their way in regardless.

Or maybe she's just captured. They take slaves there, don't they? What better opportunity than a riot to bump up your stock a little. They probably pay people to do just that sort of thing. Sister catchers! Fifty pesos a pop! Half price if they're damaged, but don't stress too much about it. A couple fingers or toes missing, what's the harm?

Simon felt as if his body were in the process of demolishing itself. His teeth ground through enamel with hacksaw steadiness, his every breath raked talons up his windpipe, a gallon of acid burbled in his belly. He wanted to move, to storm the town, to scour its streets until he found his sister, but a voice inside him sneered at the suggestion. *Yeah, and what are you gonna do? If someone really has done something to Selena, and she couldn't stop them, what chance on earth do you have?*

The answer was none. No chance whatsoever.

The sob he swallowed tasted of bile. He held it down as best he could, choked, and spewed a cord of stringy yellow vomit over the desert hardpan. He hunkered on the balls of his feet, hands pressed to the ground, and retched out a final teaspoon of sour fluid. A line of fire singed him from chin to belly. He wiped his lips with the back of his hand and, with a convulsion of disgust at the chunky film that clung to it, dragged his knuckles through the dirt until they came away dry.

A hand came to rest on his shoulder. Emily's face dropped into the periphery of his vision, her mouth pinched into a thin line. She rubbed his back gently until his breath no longer hitched.

"It's gonna be okay," she said. "It's bound to be pretty messy down there right now. But we can wait. We'll stay here as long as we have to until she comes out."

"She's not gonna come out," he hissed, startled at the venom in his voice. He chewed his lower lip and drew a few slow breaths. "I know you're trying to help. But something's wrong. And unless I go in there and do something, it's not gonna get any better."

Emily glanced over at Otis. He stood a dozen feet back, his eyes resting on the city in the distance. He seemed deep in thought, though Simon guessed he might be simply doing his best to give him and Emily a moment's privacy. Emily leaned closer to Simon.

"Then we go in there and do something," she said.

Simon smiled. It was a weak one, but sincere. "That's exactly what she'd tell me not to do. How are we supposed to find her? Where would we look? And even if we stumbled across her by some miracle, what are we going to do about it? It's not like she's just napping. She's either badly hurt or being held prisoner somehow." *Or dead*, chimed the voice in his head. *Don't forget that one.*

"That's why we've got to try."

"Your dad'll never let you go. And he's right not to. We'll just have to wait."

Emily withdrew. Simon let her go, not looking, not listening. His eyes saw only the patch of dirt in front of him, his ears heard only the distant hiss and rumble of Juarez in the throes of a riot. It was a hushed, sibilant sound, almost peaceful in its way, undulating in volume like the swell and crash of waves on an empty beach. He listened to it until another sound peaked over the din. It was a higher-pitched tone, constant against the city's flux. It swelled in volume but not pitch, cresting as the sleek vehicle zipped between Simon and Otis. He had little more than a second to mark the familiar flutter of her black hair before she was gone, bouncing down the hillside toward the town.

Otis reacted first, but his response was just as ineffectual as Simon's. He ran after her, his voicing cracking with strain as he called at her to come back.

"Emily! Emily!"

A clod of loose earth crumbled beneath his foot and spilled him down the hillside. He fell to one knee and skidded to a halt, scraping the skin from his shin and the heels of both hands. He hurled himself upright and kept running, but Emily had already cleared the hill and crossed the valley's rocky basin. She rounded onto the northern trader's road and zipped past the huts and out of sight.

Though momentarily stunned by Emily's sudden departure, Simon shook free of his stupor and ran down the hill after Otis. He moved quickly but without the fevered desperation of a frightened parent, and managed to keep his footing even when the gravel-shod hardpan slipped and crunched beneath him.

He caught up to Otis a few hundred feet later. The older man bent forward, hands resting on thighs, breath heaving. He watched Emily's disappearing form with a look of utter despair.

"What do we do now?" Simon cried.

Otis muscled the look of anguish from his features like a man shifting a heavy burden. The look that replaced it was stronger but no less worrying: a stony-browed resolve that would brook no excuses.

"We go after her."

"But how? We'll never catch up to her."

"Not on foot, no."

He jogged back the way they'd come, feet slipping on loose gravel, until he reached the mortar truck. He leaped inside, and Simon followed.

"Do you know how to drive this thing?"

"I got us out here, didn't I?"

Simon didn't reply. It was true, Otis had driven the truck onto the mesa, and from there to the arroyo where they bivouacked. But there was a difference between driving a vehicle along an empty plane and racing it through crowded streets in the middle of a riot. Simon would have preferred a driver who'd done more than the former before lunging head-first into the latter.

If you've got another driver on hand, you let us know, said the ever-familiar voice. *For now, it's Otis or nothing, so unless you plan on leaving Selena and Emily to their fates, you'd best just deal with it.*

For once, Simon and the voice agreed. He fastened the strap around his waist and grabbed onto the seat as the transmission screamed into gear, flinging them forward like a slug from a slingshot.

40: Twelve

Before the blasts, before the fires, before the refugees and rioters surged with white-water fury through the streets, Marcus knew something was about to change.

His foresight wasn't perfect, for Selena had told him of her plan the week before, and he'd dismissed it as the fantasies of a strong but beaten girl. He knew from firsthand experience that she was not to be underestimated, but Thorin's rise to power had jarred the peculiar mechanism that had always allowed him to sense the rising and falling fortunes of those around him. Her plan was farfetched, yes—but the Battle of Fallowfield had been farfetched too, and he'd had sense enough to peek beneath its superficially poor odds at the iron core of the girl driving it. Under Thorin's yoke, cowed and beaten, such an assessment was beyond his powers. He lacked the strength for hope, and so indulged in cynicism—a heady drug despite its bitter taste.

He stood as he did every day lately, hands folded behind his back, awaiting the arrival of his first client—a term Thorin often used, its true meaning evident not in the name itself, but in the smirk that accompanied it.

Some days a dozen men would die by his hand, other days none at all. Some would be acquaintances, others strangers. They were young and old, men and women, *marcado* and *blanco*, field serfs in rags and merchants in silken finery. Marcus dispatched them all with cold efficiency, adjusting his technique only to the disposition of the subjects—the merchants quivered and begged and struggled, necessitating a quick jab to the belly, while the peasants and *marcado* usually met their deaths stoically, allowing Marcus to aim for the heart, a neater and more honorable end.

A few of those he had killed were friends, though whether Thorin knew them to be such was an open question. Perhaps they were a test of Marcus's loyalty, or an unspoken punishment for his initial insubordination. Or maybe they were just unlucky saps who'd met with Thorin's displeasure for one reason or another. Marcus said nothing to any of them, and none tried to dissuade him, though he looked every one of them in the eyes as he delivered the blow.

The morning had been quiet so far, without a client in sight. The usual gaggle of courtiers and sycophants milled about, their numbers bolstered by a few *esbirros* acting as bodyguards. Manuel was among them, but the others were strangers, more or less—he knew their faces and had caught a few names over the weeks, but had spoken with none of them.

Marcus counted them, an instinctive act he hadn't bothered with for some time. This alone should have alerted him to the change in the air, but his mind was elsewhere, and he tallied thirteen, including Thorin, and logged the number without even realizing it. The sum rose unbidden a few minutes later, supplemented with the positions of each man and the weapons at their disposal.

Thorin shifted in his throne. He spun his rings one by one, tugged at the silver brooch that held his cloak in place. A stout carving knife rested on a table eighteen inches from his right hand. He slouched, forcing his elbow to bear some of his weight, slowing a potential draw by at least half a second. Next to him stood two *esbirros* with clubs hanging from their belts. The taller of the two had a pistol in a holster on his left hip, and one of the courtiers wore a rifle on a strap around his back—an affectation more than a practical tool, judging by its antiquity and the way it hung, which favored visibility over draw time. There were no other firearms in sight, though three men wore robes that could obscure small arms. He watched the shift and rustle of their garments as they walked and deemed two certainly unarmed and the third unlikely.

These details and a thousand others flashed through his mind in the span of a single breath, cross-checked and filed for future use. They receded only to make room for appraisal of the *fthoom-crash* of heavy impact somewhere in the distance.

Thorin sat up and turned his head in the direction of the sound. "What was that?"

Without further instruction, a pair of lackeys scuttled to the door, racing each other for the honor of being first to report. In their brief absence, Thorin seemed to forget the sound altogether, returning to his idle amusements. Following this unspoken directive, the room returned to its chatter as if nothing had happened. On the surface, Marcus did likewise, but beneath his placid mask, his brain scrawled frantic calculations on the walls of his skull. The time for action was now—unless it wasn't, in which case a hasty twitch of the wrist could paint a trail of blood from his feet to the farthest outposts of his lineage. His heart, which even in the heat of battle rarely roused itself above fifty beats a minute, rattled like a timpani in a swelling crescendo. Sweat prickled his forehead.

Yes or no? Yes or no?

The messengers returned. Their former haste was gone; neither seemed keen to be the first in the room. They engaged in a silent struggle for as long as they dared until the loser stepped forward and, tongue circling dry lips, spoke.

"There's been a fire, *Jefe*."

"A fire? Where?"

The boy's tongue made another circuit of his lips, leaving them no damper than it found them. "Many places, *Jefe*. It seems they've come from the sky."

"From the sky? Have we offended any gods you'd care to mention? Talk sense, boy!"

"It's *La Santa*. That's what they're saying. *La Santa* has come. And she's angry."

Thorin brooded over this remark, his frustration at these opaque announcements tempered by uncertainty. Marcus faced no such dilemma. He locked eyes with Manuel, who seemed likewise to sense the tectonic shift occurring beneath their feet, and motioned to the far corner of the room.

"Go," he mouthed.

Manuel's face went pale. He tiptoed back from the crowd and made his way in the direction Marcus had indicated. Marcus recalibrated for his absence, charting the position of the room's remaining bodies. A single word rose to the forefront of his mind, and it told him exactly what he needed to do.

Twelve.

No one noticed him as he shuffled from his post. The boy's pronouncement caused enough confusion that the wanderings of a lowly *verdugo* were easy to ignore. Moving with deliberate nonchalance, he drifted sideways in a wide arc, putting himself between Thorin and the door. The two messengers hovered ten feet behind his left shoulder and could be glanced in his periphery. The room's other occupants were clear in his line of sight. Time to begin.

The sword was in the *esbirro's* chest before anyone, but Marcus had seen it move. It struck at a forty-five-degree angle, cleaving muscle and collarbone before catching on a nexus of rib and spine.

Eleven.

He'd picked the unarmed *esbirro* for his target, allowing the second man time to draw his pistol, which he did the instant he realized what was happening. Marcus smiled gratefully. Strapped to a dead man's leg, such a weapon could be plundered at any moment and used when his back was turned. Better to have it out in the open and accounted for. A backhand strike severed the gunman's hand before the finger had a chance to fire. It cartwheeled upward, still clutching the gun.

Marcus left the man to contemplate his diminished stature and plunged the sword through the belly of the courtier with the rifle, who seemed in his panic to have entirely forgotten that he was armed. A stew of blood and shit burbled from the wound. Marcus kicked him backward, hoping his corpse would be heavy enough to make retrieving the gun cumbersome.

Ten.

The pistol landed with a plop. Two men went for it at once. Marcus worked the sword in a figure-eight motion, severing first one head—

Nine.

—then another.

Eight.

He stomped on the hand until its grip gave way and kicked the pistol into the abattoir's gutter. It clattered down the grate and out of reach.

By now even the room's less battle-seasoned occupants had registered the attack and shaken free of panic's paralysis. The messengers turned on their heels, tripping over one another in their effort to flee.

Marcus disliked killing men with their backs turned, but he had no desire to see them crying murder in the streets. Twelve was enough for him. He ducked beneath a wooden club swung by a shirtless *marcado*, kicked a courtier in the side of the knee hard enough to crack the bone, and whirled to the door. The first messenger died when the sword stabbed through his neck.

Seven.

The second died slower from a slash to the belly, a fact Marcus lamented but couldn't afford to brood over.

Six.

With the runners dead and the gun out of play, the melee found a moment's pause. Marcus sized up his opponents. He was halfway done by raw numbers, but knew the second round would be harder than the first. He'd hacked through the chaff, now it was time to crack the wheat.

Thorin remained on his throne, back rigid, face pale and expressionless. The knife on the table beside him had been knocked to the floor in the tumult, and Thorin had made no move to grab it. The *esbirro* rolled on the ground at his feet, clutching the trunk of gore where his hand had been.

The remaining four men stood around them in a protective semi-circle. Two were *esbirros,* one young and gangly with a knife in each hand, the other stout and middle-aged, meaty fist wrapped around a hatchet. The next was a merchant by the look of him, with fine clothes and skin unruddied by labor, who wielded a curved blade the length of his forearm in a stance that implied surprising competence. Tension pulled the expression from their faces, but Marcus sensed in them only modest fear and no panic.

Last was the shirtless *marcado.* An indentured Iron Circle fighter, he was hairless from head to toe, his bald head spackled with tattoos. A line of silver rings pierced the flesh beneath each eye, pulling his cheeks into a permanent smile. His muscular chest glittered in ornate patterns sewn into his skin with golden thread. While no less collected than the others, his demeanor suggested none of their reluctance. If anything, it radiated glee. He twirled his narrow club with a juggler's economic grace, hands betraying no unnecessary movement.

Marcus shifted his grip on the sword and tried it one-handed. It felt steady enough, though his swings would have less power. In a slow, fluid motion, he reached his free hand into his serape and drew his switchblade. His thumb settled on the trigger. It pressed down, and the blade sprung from the handle. *Schwick!* Thus armed, he closed on the foursome, moving in a bishop's diagonal, face flush with his opponents.

Part of him hoped that the bravest among them would strike out solo, but no such luck. They came at him as one, a wall of steel and iron and polished hardwood. He feinted backward, coiled his calves, and charged. His switchblade sank into the merchant's thigh while his sword ran through the younger *esbirro's* belly and tore its way through his side. Steel rasped against bone. Blood misted the air, rank and humid.

Five.

A twinge of pain alit on Marcus's shoulder. Ignoring it, he twirled and brought the sword down. The blade cleaved the merchant's face in two from the nose up before stopping against the thick ridge of his sinus. He tried to tug the blade free, found it caught, and abandoned it.

Four.

The *marcado* aimed a two-handed blow at Marcus's head. Marcus dodged it by inches, shoved the *esbirro* off-balance before he could strike out with his hatchet, and closed in for a killing blow. The effort nearly earned him a broken leg; the *marcado*, seemingly over-balanced from his swing, dropped the illusion and delivered a sharp backhanded strike toward Marcus's knees. Marcus caught the deception too late to dodge and chose instead to close on the blow, letting the club hit his thigh a few inches above its grip and robbing the swing of most of its power. Most was not all, though—he winced at the damp thwack of bursting blood vessels and the ripple of impact up his leg. He retaliated with a jab that found only air. The *marcado* slithered to his side and worked the club like a lance, stabbing his chest and belly with remarkable force.

Aware of his overreach, Marcus sprung back. His injured leg had gone numb below the knee, and the lack of sensation nearly caused him to topple. He righted himself at the last instant and swiveled out of range of the *marcado's* merciless club.

The *esbirro,* emboldened by his partner's success, charged in from the left with hatchet raised as the *marcado* pounced from the right. Marcus caught his wrist and pulled him in close as if to dance. They performed a quick pivot, making the *esbirro* an unwitting shield against the marcado, who pulled his strike before it rendered the *esbirro's* skull into so much broken crockery. The save was artful but scarcely mattered—Marcus had already bisected the man's heart with a single surgical stroke.

Three.

Marcus nudged the *esbirro* forward, toppling him against the *marcado*. The *marcado* wriggled free of the dead man's weight, but not before Marcus carved a shallow red culvert up his side, the tip of his blade jouncing over ribs. Most men pulled back from such strikes, but the *marcado* leaned *into* the cut, worsening his injury but also catching Marcus off-guard. He rammed an elbow into Marcus's nose.

The blow dyed the room a blurry red. Biting down on the pain, Marcus followed his adversary's example and fought the need to recoil. It was a prescient move, for the *marcado's* club hammered down through the space where Marcus's head would have been. It struck the ground hard enough to chip stone. Marcus stomped on the club, knocking it from the *marcado's* grip. He jabbed downward, expecting the *marcado* to reach for his weapon. Instead, the man wrapped his hands around Marcus's neck and squeezed.

In his many years as a fighter, Marcus had suffered nearly every bodily injury he could name. He'd been shot, stabbed, slashed, and bludgeoned. He'd been kicked, punched, bitten, and clawed. He'd taken bottles to the head and rocks to the belly, dodged missiles of every size and weight, parried swords and axes and shovels with edges honed to deadly keenness. He'd wriggled free of every possible hold and tackle. But as the *marcado's* fingers closed like steel cables around his windpipe, it occurred to him that he'd never been choked. Not truly, anyway—there'd been moments in melees where he found it hard to breathe, forearms pressed to his neck or knees weighing on his chest, but he could always gulp in a lungful of air after a few uncomfortable seconds.

The *marcado's* attack was different. His thumbs bypassed muscle and sinew and rammed hard against his larynx. Marcus's lungs spasmed, his diaphragm heaved, but not the faintest wisp of air got through. Drawing breath was like trying to slip coarse thread through a needle's eye.

With a grunt of effort, Marcus steadied his feet and jabbed his knife into the *marcado's* belly. He twisted the blade; sure the man's grip would slacken. It tightened instead. He stabbed again, aiming higher this time. Still, the *marcado* squeezed. His cheeks rose higher, revealing acres of yellow-black teeth.

Shadows whorled across the edges of Marcus's vision. A distant roar filled his ears. Numbness chilled his fingertips, creeping from knuckle to knuckle until it had conquered his hands. He could feel the switchblade slipping through his sweat-greased fingers. Leaden shackles dragged his arms to his sides. Fighting their weight with his last frisson of energy, he windmilled his arm and stabbed the blade hilt-deep into the *marcado's* eye.

The *marcado's* hands clenched tighter, and for a moment Marcus wondered if they would retain their grip in death, paying out posthumous retribution like a bee's stinger. The fingers loosened, and the *marcado* fell, his dead face frozen in a rictus of lunatic glee.

Two.

Marcus gasped with relief. His first breath seemed full of ash and splinters, but the cool air soon worked its way into the battered tissues of his throat. He fought the urge to double over and simply breathe, aware that his task was not yet complete.

During the chaos, the one-handed *esbirro* had wormed his way over to the courtier's corpse and was frantically trying to unstrap the rifle from the dead man. He continued his struggle as Marcus stood over him, drew his chin upward with his index and middle fingers, and cut his throat.

He looked up at Manuel. Delgado's former *teniente* was familiar with violence—even among Juarezians, who were rumored among outsiders to bathe in the blood of their enemies, Manuel was a seasoned veteran—but the slaughter in Thorin's abattoir had been something else altogether. He stared like a child witnessing his first public execution, arms hanging limp, eyes wide and blank, as if in attempting to see too much they saw nothing at all.

"Manuel," said Marcus. "Go."

Marcus didn't watch to see if Manuel followed his direction. The patter of footsteps followed by a slamming door told him as much. He turned to Thorin, still seated on his throne.

One.

41: A Razor's Edge

Mary-Katherine Montenegro was well acquainted with pain. She'd spent many years with palms red from scouring and purple-black stripes up her legs and back, an ever-shifting map of her many disobediences as a plantation ward. A different sort of pain followed, punishments unlinked to any crimes and enacted far from the parlor-room stage of her public reprimands, in closets and cellars, fingers that squeezed too tight and wormed into unwelcome places. And through it all, the aches of household labor: overtaxed muscles, slivers from rotting rake handles, fingertips nicked by the slip of a paring knife. Juarez was a rough town from top to bottom, and Mary had started in a low place and, with an inexorable downward trajectory usually reserved for liquids, managed to seep her way through the narrowest cracks into one even lower.

But her hurts, though plentiful, had been invariably shallow—the kind her body could manage on its own with no more assistance than a bandage and a bit of antiseptic. The wound Krell dealt her was something different. It was deep and puckered, idiot lips disgorging a stream of blood. She pressed against it with the heel of her hand, slowing the flood but not stopping it. Blood leaked through her fingers and out the seam where her palm met her belly. She held her fingers up to her face to get a better look at the stuff leaking out of her, decided she'd just as soon not know more about it, and let them drop again.

With herculean effort, she dragged herself from the alley and into the main road, her brain flicking frantically through plans for rescue and vengeance. But now that she'd arrived, her energy spent, it seemed like no better a place to die than the alley had been. She took a final staggering step and collapsed against a wall. The adobe felt warm and pleasant against her skin.

Her legs outstretched, she gazed between her feet at a swath of *Calle Roya*. Her eyes, losing focus, drifted upward until all they saw was the sky, an unblemished canvas of grey. She was dimly aware of voices and a nearby frenzy of motion, but the details were sketchy, and she found herself unconcerned by them. Better to let the chaos, exhaustion, and pain wash over her, to stop fighting the current and float instead, hoping it would carry her somewhere better. She closed her eyes and set herself adrift.

Hands seized her beneath the armpits and hoisted her upright. Annoyed, she made her limbs go slack, hoping to slide from her interloper's grip. But the hands only tightened, hoisting her up and scooting her back until her tailbone lay flush with the wall. Petulantly, she kept her eyes shut, refusing to give whoever was accosting her the satisfaction of acknowledgment. Let them rob her if they wanted. It's not like she had anything worth taking.

An arc of cool ceramic pressed against her lower lip. The container tipped forward, pouring water into her mouth. She drank reflexively, her thirst too deep to be overridden by petty defiance.

"Where is she?"

It was the voice, familiar yet changed, that got her eyes open. It rang with effortless authority, the sort that carried without shouting across a crowded room. Grace Delgado stood over her, the afternoon sun at her back, wreathing her face in a reddish silhouette. Several men stood to her either side, imperfect eclipses dividing their faces into hemispheres of light and shadow.

Mary blinked several times. The figures remained, so she figured she wasn't hallucinating. "Where is who?" she asked.

"Selena. She left the Iron Circle with you, didn't she?"

Mary looked from Grace to the men surrounding her. She could see enough of them to tell they were *marcados*. Tough ones, too, by the look of them. She noted the common pattern on their cheeks: a green star, Thorin's mark, its emerald brand unfaded by time. Understanding clicked into place. These were Delgado's men, held in thrall after Thorin pissed all over *la paz inquieta*. *Blancos* made *marcados*, throwing off their shackles and marching under a *marcada* queen.

It was at that moment that she realized the scope of what Selena had done—what she, Mary, had helped do. The act itself had been fairly minor—more a nudge than a hammer-blow, given the scale of violence Juarez was accustomed to—but it only takes a slight shove to get a boulder rolling, if said boulder is balanced precariously enough. And Juarez had teetered on a razor's edge since Thorin took power. Now it was in free fall, and who could say where it would land, or who would be crushed when it did?

Pain sank deeper into Mary's belly. She bit down on a scream, grinding it between molars until it lay still. Grace may be her ally, but she wasn't her friend, and she had no intention of showing this haughty woman the depths of her current suffering. She drew a long but shallow breath, holding her diaphragm steady to avoid the agonizing extension of her stomach muscles.

"Yeah," she answered. The effort needed to talk was immense, greater than she could have imagined. Each word felt like another drop of life ruthlessly squeezed out of her—and given how she felt, it wouldn't take more than a few sentences to wring her dry. "Krell got her. Me too. They took off." She flapped her hand in the direction of the alley.

Grace turned to the man on her right, his angular chin darkened with stubble. Though by the look of him only a few years her senior, he bore the scars of a long and hard-fought lifetime. A particularly gruesome mark bisected his face in a swooping diagonal. It ran from just below his left eye to the right corner of his mouth, swallowing on its path most of his left nostril.

"Do you know this Krell, Andrio?"

"Yes, *Jefe*. But we haven't time to track him down. The *esbirros* are regrouping. They want to put a lid on this thing, and if we don't act fast, they're gonna manage it. We can't let ourselves get distracted, chasing through the alleys after some girl."

"She is not just some girl," called a voice from outside their huddle. Mary looked past the *marcados* to an old woman, her wrinkled face peering out from beneath the broad brim of a straw sunhat. "You're speaking of the emissary, are you not? The one sent by *La Santa*?"

Others entered the crowd, drawn by the invocation of *La Santa's* envoy. They murmured one to another, a susurrus of rumor spreading outward in a wave. Grace put truth to the old woman's words.

"We are. She has been taken by a *pandillero* in Thorin's employ. We fear it is his intention to harm her."

The crowd's voice swelled with anger. It distilled itself through the prism of the old woman, who glowered beneath her straw hat.

"Lead us to this man."

Grace looked to her lieutenant. "Tell me where to find him. Then take the others and check Thorin's men."

"I am not a Delgado, *Jefe*. When the people see you, they also see your brother and remember the kind and sure hand of his leadership. When they see me, all they see is a *marcado*."

"You're not the only one who bears a brand, Andrio. You will speak with my voice in this matter. The others here know it and will vouchsafe. I am needed elsewhere." She glanced down at Mary. "Is there anyone here who can tend to my sister? She has been badly hurt?"

Mary looked around, wondering what sister Grace was talking about, before realizing the ex-*Senador's* sister was referring to her.

A woman tottered from the crowd. She made the lady in the

sunhat seem young. A squat, wizened stump of a woman, nearly as wide as she was tall, she scuttled over to Mary and lowered herself onto her haunches—an act that Mary feared might cause the woman to topple over, but which she handled with a dancer's ease—and ran a hand along her forehead. Her fingers were bent and brown as tree roots, but her touch was soft.

"Stay fearless, child. I've some fieldcraft in my day, and know a few girls nearby with more. We'll set you to rights and get something for the pain."

Mary mumbled her thanks, but her attention was on Grace, who stood at the alley's mouth. Despite her brand and tattered clothes, she didn't look the least bit like *a marcada,* or even a cozened *Senador's* sister. She looked like a field marshal surveying enemy troops, aware of but undeterred by their greater numbers.

"Grace," she wheezed. The effort of it nearly split her in two.

Grace returned and hunkered down next to her. Their eyes met. Mary searched them for anger, contempt, sour joy at her predicament—feelings that Mary, to her shame, thought she might experience if their situations were reversed. She found none of these. Her eyes dropped to her lap.

"I'm sorry. For how we treated you. For how *I* treated you. You just had so much once, and we had so little…"

Grace touched her arm. "I understand. I'm sorry too. Sorry I couldn't see your hurt until I felt it myself."

For want of a response, Mary nodded. "Good luck, *Jefe.*"

Grace smiled.

42: Heroic Acts

For one awful moment, Simon felt as if he'd been yanked backward through time. A fishhook pierced his belly and reeled him across the weeks and miles to Fallowfield at the moment of its battle, dropped him flopping amongst its smoke and gunfire and cordite stink. Could he die in a moment he'd previously survived, or was he inoculated against such an occurrence, doomed instead to trudge once more through the southern wastes, to lose his sister a second time? He wasn't sure which case scared him more.

Before he could decide, the world righted itself, and he realized with a bitter sort of relief that he was still in the present, and the conflagration into which he charged was different from the one he'd endured before. This wasn't Fallowfield, and there were no Shepherds to flee or sympathetic farmers to seek out for aid. In fact, the situation seemed less a battle than a riot. There was fighting, yes, but of an aimless, desultory sort, as private scuffles flared up and sputtered out with the dazzling speed of fireworks. If there were factions at war, Simon struggled to tell them apart.

Juarez was a much bigger city than Fallowfield, and as such, there was a lot more of it to wreck. The townsfolk shouldered this challenge gamely. While most of them seemed intent on fleeing above all else, there were plenty left who spotted a brief window of opportunity and wasted no time in smashing through the glass and grabbing everything they could from the other side.

Simon watched the chaos unfold with a curious detachment—born, he assumed, by the fact he was viewing it from a raised perch behind half an inch of shatterproof glass. The sounds that filtered into the truck's cab were muted, robbed of the shrill urgency that would raise his hackles under normal circumstances. It was easy to pretend that the events occurring on the other side of the glass were happening somewhere else, to a different set of people.

The illusion held until the first flaming bottle struck the vehicle's hood. Blue flames skated over the green-brown metal, blazing a trail of blackened, bubbling paint. Other missiles followed, rocks and cobblestones pelting the doors and rattling across the roof. The windshield juddered in its frame with every blow, but the glass, true to its name, refused to crack.

The cluster of people outside thinned into a line, fanning out in a V shape to bar the vehicle's progress down the city's north-south thoroughfare. Otis swerved around people as best he could, but they were spaced too close together for the bulky vehicle to slip through. With a huff of frustration, Otis cut the speed and nosed to the right, muscling past the crowd. He could've plowed through them easily, but Simon could see he didn't want to do that, and was glad. He didn't relish the thought of what a truck this big would do to a body at speed.

The crowd converged around the vehicle, but as Otis predicted, none were quite insane enough to stand in its direct path. They broke to either side, clinging to the doors and hammering on the windows with sticks and fists and rocks. Otis gunned the engine the moment they passed the human barricade. Many of the assailants dove for cover or tumbled from their perches, but several latched onto the side of the truck, shrieking faces pressed to the glass.

"What do they want?" Simon cried.

"What we're drivin'," replied Otis, teeth bared. He worked the wheel back and forth, trying to shake off the last few climbers. His eyes roved about the street as he drove, sweeping for signs of Emily. Simon forced down his fear and looked as well. The sooner they found her, the sooner they could end this lunatic tour of Juarez's combusting core.

The crowds passed by in a blur of beige and brown and red. How could he possibly make out any one person amid this tumult? It was like trying to spot one pebble among thousands at the bottom of a murky river.

The vehicle's tires jounced over a boardwalk, tilting the cab at a dizzy angle. Otis apparently shared some of his daughter's innate dexterity and talent for vehicles—he'd picked up the basics of maneuvering this behemoth easily enough, as Emily had with the two-wheeler—but he still struggled with corners and occasionally fishtailed in a queasy slalom before wrenching the wheels back to true.

A wooden cart exploded against the vehicle's front end. Emaciated ears of corn flew from the wreckage and rained down over the hood. Horses screamed and bolted for cover. Simon didn't know horses could scream. It was a remarkably human sound, and it echoed in his mind as a fresh wave of rioters battered the window next to Otis's head.

Otis gunned the engine and swerved around a stone fountain at the center of a plaza. Simon felt the truck lean to the left, its right wheels losing their grip on the cobbles. For an instant, he felt certain the vehicle would roll, but Otis cut the turn short, and the wheels plopped down with an anguished squeal of overtaxed suspension. Simon closed his eyes. How much longer before they hit something that wouldn't break or dive out of the way? Something was sure to stop them eventually, and the vehicle's momentum was its only weapon. The mortar remained mounted to the back, but it was out of ammo.

The truck rounded a corner and nearly ran over the two-wheeled vehicle sprawled across the dirt road. A man with a harelip was fiddling with the handlebars, trying to get the engine started. Thin arms blotched with scabs burst through the tatters of a greyish shirt. A tattoo depicting a silver eye glared at Simon from one cheek. The face's other eyes noticed him a second later.

Otis braked hard enough to hurl Simon against the dashboard. He caught himself just in time, avoiding a broken nose and possibly a cracked skull, earning instead an ugly jolt up his forearms.

As he righted himself and worked his hands over opposite wrists in search of damage, he saw Emily pulled off to the side, pinned to the ground by another man, this one marked with a crescent moon. Blood trickled from her nostrils. Her left eye had swollen to a squint, the angry flesh already fading to the blotchy purple-black of a thundercloud.

Otis slammed the gearshift into park and leaped from the truck.

"Wait," Simon cried. "Don't open the door!"

But Otis was already gone, the door was open, and eager rioters poured into the cab. They skittered over every surface—pawing dials, jabbing buttons, and snatching anything loose enough to yank free.

Simon scooted back until his shoulders touched the passenger door. A rough mass pressed against his tailbone. He reached for it and found the unloaded gun Selena had given him several eons before. He pointed it at the would-be carjackers. "All of you get out of here! I'll shoot!"

One of them, his torn but well-tailored clothes pegging him as a merchant type, took the hint and scarpered. The others carried on as if Simon had done nothing. One man, his face disfigured by open sores, grabbed the steering wheel and tried to press it into the dashboard as if it were a single enormous button.

Simon paused, unsure how to proceed. Did the guy know the gun was unloaded? Or did he simply think Simon lacked the guts to fire it? *Maybe he doesn't even know what a gun is.* A warning shot would make the point pretty clearly, but of course for that Simon needed bullets. With a cry of frustration, he hurled the gun at the man's head.

It was a good throw. The gun spun once in the air before its barrel struck the man square on the temple. He slumped sideways, dazed, and tumbled out of the cab, landing on an incoming rioter and sending him sprawling to the ground. The other rioters, now aware of Simon as something more than a cowering child to be ignored, grabbed him by the shirt and tried to haul him out of the cab.

"Hey, let go!" Simon's hands scrabbled about the cab for purchase. They found a metal protrusion beneath the passenger seat—a lever for height adjustment, noted the tiny pedantic engineer that four years at St. Barnabas' Engineering Academy had implanted in his brain—and locked onto it. His joints screamed in their sockets as the mob tried to dislocate them. He kicked wildly. His foot connected with something hard and brittle—a nose, maybe—and made it crunch. Twin bolts of pain pierced his right ankle. Someone was *biting* him. He kicked harder, pulling his leg free, and retched at the damp patch of mingling spit and blood that trickled down his heel.

The tension in his shoulders was growing unbearable. He felt like a wishbone being torn in two. His fingers slackened their grip, unable to ignore the rising shriek of his joints begging them to relent. He curled his legs toward his belly and pistoned like a swimmer pushing off from the side of a pool. His heels struck a man in the forehead and knocked him back, but another soon took his place. Simon wondered what they'd do to him when they got him out of the truck—whether they'd be content to toss him aside, or if they had something darker in mind. He begged his failing fingers to hold on a little longer.

Otis rose up like a wave and crashed over the rioters. He held Emily under one arm and wielded a short length of steel pipe with the other. He worked the pipe like some strange cross between a knife and a hammer, jabbing and swinging and gauging in a mad flurry of his free limb. Emily bawled in his grip, her good eye squinting as tight as its injured partner.

He let Emily go once he'd gained a foothold on the truck. She curled up on the floor of the cab, hands knitted protectively around the back of her head. With both hands free, Otis's ferocity seemed to double. He fought less like a man than a lion, a predator blooded and cornered and pitiless with mammalian rage. A patch of dark red bloomed on the front of his shirt. It grew as he fought his way into the truck, its bottom border distending into crimson rivulets that beaded through the soaked cotton.

The rioters fought back, but soon fathomed the depth of Otis's anger and fled before it, reasoning that a wheeled contraption wasn't worth their lives—especially when they didn't know how to drive it anyway. Simon slammed the door behind them and engaged the lock.

Otis collapsed over the bench seat. He tucked his legs beneath his belly and began hoisting himself upright. He made it to hands and knees before the effort wrung a deep, hacking cough from him. Flecks of blood sprayed the upholstery. His limbs trembled and gave out, spilling him into his own sick.

"Dad!" Emily cried. She scrambled onto the seat and cradled Otis's head. Otis raised one unsteady hand and touched her cheek. A greyish haze rolled across his eyes, but his smile was oddly content.

"Got you," he said and coughed a gasp of blood into his closed fist.

Together, Simon and Emily managed to move Otis to the passenger seat. He groaned as he slumped against the backrest. The red patch on his chest spread laterally, widening with a fresh spurt of blood. Simon didn't know how much blood there was in a person, but Otis had clearly lost a lot already; it was unlikely that he had much more to spare.

A fresh crowd gathered around the truck and tried to get inside. They rattled the door handles and banged the windows. Simon heard the kettle drum clatter of feet on the roof, kicking and stomping. The mortar swiveled on its axis as the rioters batted it back and forth. The vehicle was built for combat and not easy to damage without heavy equipment, but it was far from invulnerable. Simon didn't want to stick around to observe what innovations in carnage the blood-simple crowd might concoct. He turned to Emily, who was stroking her father's forehead with one hand. Her fingers shone with sweat—whether hers or her father's Simon couldn't tell.

"Can you drive this thing?" he asked.

Emily ignored him. Her fingers continued their slow loop: tracing his hairline, sliding down the ridge of bone beside his temple, skirting each eyebrow, and returning to where they started.

"Look, I don't want to be a jerk, but we really need to get out of here. The doors and windows on this thing are pretty strong, but they're not gonna hold off the crowd forever."

Gently, Otis plucked Emily's hand from its track and folded it in his own. "He's right, Em. We gotta go."

Emily sniffed, wiped her nose, nodded. She shimmied into the driver's seat and grabbed the steering wheel. Her legs strained to reach the pedals, while her forehead barely peeked over the dashboard.

"I can't reach," she said. "I need someone to work the lever-things."

Simon looked at her. "You mean me?"

"Unless you'd rather steer."

Swallowing, Simon climbed into the recess beneath the dashboard. Two pedals rose from the rubberized floor, their tops flattened to better match the driver's feet. He reached for one of them, paused, bit his lip. He'd *fixed* this stupid thing, he should know which pedal did what, but the knowledge was gone, pilfered like a wallet by some talented pickpocket.

"Which one makes it go?" Simon cried.

"The one on the right. Hurry!"

Bodies pressed against the windows, battering the glass and eclipsing the afternoon light. It was like being buried in a slow landslide of human flesh. Simon shoved the pedal down with both hands. He was unsure how much counter-pressure the bar would exert, and was surprised at how easily it moved.

The truck bounded forward, transmission squealing as it flitted through gears with the rat-a-tat speed of a cardsharp riffling a deck. Simon's stomach lurched with each swerve of the wheel. He craned his neck over the seat, trying to catch a glimpse through the passenger window and seeing nothing but Otis's pale forehead and beyond it a wedge of grayish sky. He closed his eyes, pressed harder on the pedal, and braced for inevitable impact—hoping that whatever they hit would be lighter and smaller than the truck.

Over time—how much Simon had no idea; seconds stood for ages before toppling—the quality of the road changed, from the drumroll thunder of cobbles to the axle-busting jostle of a poorly-tended dirt road, which gave way to the long, loping undulations of the plains. Emily reached down and tapped Simon on the shoulder.

"You can slow down," she said.

Nodding, Simon obliged. The two developed a crude and wordless symbiosis, through which Emily's toe applied varying pressure to Simon shoulder, and Simon mirrored the force against the pedal. She gave him a final tap signaling him to brake and put the truck into park. It had barely stopped moving before she was back at Otis's side.

They laid him out on the bench seat. The position made tending to him awkward, but the two of them together still lacked the strength to move him. Emily shimmied between the seat and the dash and unbuttoned his shirt. The fabric made a wet tearing sound is it pulled free of skin, revealing a wound far deeper than Simon had thought.

A blackish hole puckered two inches above Otis's navel, curling up to the left in a sardonic half-smile. Blood burbled through the gash, a fresh spout of it with every exhaled breath. There were other wounds too, sneering from his chest and shoulders. But the one in his belly was the worst. Simon groaned at the sight of it, swallowing the sound as best he could to limit Emily's dismay—a futile effort since she couldn't be much more dismayed than she was already.

"Oh, Dad," she moaned, hands pressed to her mouth. She fished a snatch of cloth from her pocket, its brown fibers stained with dirt and oil, and pressed it to the wound. She compressed it with both hands

"Oh, Dad," she repeated. She seemed unable to say anything else. And what else *could* you say when your father lay gut-stabbed and dying in the cab of a truck after he'd charged straight into a riot to rescue you?

And why was she in that riot, chimed a voice in Simon's head. *It was for* you, *right buddy? Another brave fool dead simply because he was dumb enough to try and clean up your mess.*

He's not dead yet, Simon countered, but even in his head, the voice lacked conviction. He'd never seen anyone die up close before, but Otis looked pretty much how he imagined it. His eyes had taken on a glassy marble cast, pupils pinned to an arbitrary spot on the ceiling, and his face had paled and softened into a waxwork of itself. Each breath came with the damp, ugly sound of a wet rag torn in two.

Otis reached out to Emily with one trembling hand. She took it, and he led her close. His eyes rolled toward her—Simon could almost hear the sticky sound they made in their sockets—and fixed her with a steady gaze. He smiled. The gesture pumped life back into his waxen features.

"I guess you see why I never wanted you goin' to Juarez," he breathed.

Emily's breath hitched. "I'm sorry, Dad! I'm so sorry! I didn't mean—"

Otis pressed a finger to her lips. His smile warmed further. "You did right. It doesn't matter if it went wrong. You won't be blamin' yourself for this, Em, you hear me? If you love me, you won't do that."

Wiping her eyes, Emily nodded. "Okay," she said. She did her best to mean it, but Simon could hear the doubt behind the words. Otis must have heard it too, for he folded his hands over hers and shook his head.

"I've been away from that place a long time. Seein' it burn might've cost my body plenty, but it did my soul a world of good. Something good can come out of this yet. You tell this Selena when you see her. Only so much you can do to change a building when it's standing. You knock it down, you can build it back up however you like. Juarez was a prison. Whatever stands up in the rubble don't have to be."

Otis brought his daughter's fingers to his lips and kissed them. His head dropped back a moment later, the last of his energy spent.

Simon expected the breath that followed to be his last, but he held on for another twenty minutes, oscillating between frantic, shallow-chested gasps and the long slow breaths of a man in deep meditation. *Death is tidier in stories,* Simon thought, recalling the heroic acts described in The Last Testament, where sainted knights, victorious but dying atop the corpse of some fell beast, delivered orations on the evils of secular worship, elegantly expiring as the last word of their perorations escaped their lips.

When it came, Simon and Emily nearly missed it, their attention flagging from their prolonged stillness and worry over things to come. A high, wheezing sound whistled from deep in his throat, shrill and quiet as a kettle in another room. His hands shook, fingers clutching at phantom objects, balled into fists, and slackened. Emily touched his cheeks with her fingertips and looked into his eyes. They found her gaze for an instant and widened, as if something huge and fundamental were trying to escape through their narrow apertures. The last gust of air left his lungs, and his eyes rolled back, the whites like gibbous moons in a twilight sky.

43: Death In Combat

Sound is a funny thing, thought Marcus. The tumult outside was far from inaudible. It bled through the walls of the abattoir like grease through fine paper. Shouts, crashes, cries of pain and rage, the shrill ululation of anarchic joy; whinnying horses, splintering wood, shattering glass, the piff of distant gunshots, and the crackle of flames—Marcus could hear all of these things, if he chose to listen for them. Yet his impression of that moment was one of absolute stillness, the sort of silence skies proffer in the minutes before a storm. He looked at the *Jefe*, awash in silence, and the *Jefe* looked back at him.

Thorin remained seated. He hadn't stood once since the fighting began. It was the shock of it that pinned him in place, Marcus figured. That and the sheer speed at which events unfolded. It was hard to say how long the whole thing had taken. Ten seconds? Maybe fifteen? His mind had gone to its familiar place where time lost its momentum, where instants crystalized into discrete objects to be measured and weighed at length.

"How quickly things change," Marcus mused. He studied the knife in his hand as if for the first time, delighting in the simple geometry of its blade, thumbing the sultry roughness of its grip.

Thorin's fingers twiddled against the armrests of his throne. He slathered a smile across his face and slouched back in a gesture of exaggerated calm. It was an impressive performance, under the circumstances; Marcus had forgotten the depth of Thorin's wiles.

"I suppose you expect quivering? There is no need. You've been mistreated. A just ruler is a hard ruler, and sometimes that weight comes down unfairly on one man's shoulders. You've overstepped, as have I, so let's discuss what we can do to make things right. We will start in the most obvious place: your debt. Consider it paid. As for further recompense, you'll find me a very generous man."

"I can absolve my debt on my own," replied Marcus, wiggling his knife. "As for payment, there's only one currency I want from you, and it's in your veins."

"Then you are a fool." The oily bonhomie was gone, cast aside like a tool found ill-suited to the task at hand. "You think such slaughter will go unpunished? I'm the *Jefe* of Juarez, last survivor of the Triumvirate. Touch me and you're doomed the moment you walk out that door."

"That may very well be. Assuming that, when I step out that door, you are still the *Jefe* of Juarez. And that, I'm afraid, seems very much in doubt." He motioned to the chaos, now plainly audible beyond the building's walls. "Do you hear that? It's the sound of your dynasty collapsing. Your reign is over. It was short, but eventful."

"You dog. You think some fires and a riot can break my rule?"

"In truth? No, I don't. Not on their own. I think it will be an upset, but your loyalists will not be wiped out altogether, and when the streets fall quiet you can reclaim what's yours. That it, if you live. But it's the 'if' that always gets us in the end, isn't it, *Jefe?*" Marcus chewed the last word like a piece of taffy, savoring its syllables. It had tasted so bitter before, but time and circumstance had sweetened it considerably.

The first glint of true fear shone in Thorin's eyes. The negotiator had fallen to the tyrant, and now the tyrant vanished just as quickly. Behind his was the true man, not *Jefe* but simply Thorin, a shivering weakling in an outsized crown. His red eyes welled with tears.

"So it's come to this, has it? You're to murder me in cold blood? Will that fill the hole inside you, Marcus? Will that lessen the ache?"

"It might. It just might. But no. I'm not going to kill you in cold blood, *Jefe.*"

Marcus bent down and took a knife from an *esbirro's* belt— poor fool didn't even get the chance to draw it—and tossed it to the ground at Thorin's feet.

"I am a man of honor. And a man of honor doesn't kill an unarmed opponent." He looked at the carnage around him. "Where possible, of course."

Thorin stared at the knife as if it were a particularly repulsive insect. He glared at Marcus with arms crossed, his fear partially buried beneath a wall of sulky insolence. Marcus tutted.

"Death in combat is usually quick, *Jefe*. But if a man doesn't fight, it can come slow indeed."

Thorin stood up like an old man, one hand braced against the small of his back, the other inching toward the handle of the knife. His eyes stayed locked on Marcus's switchblade. He looked to Marcus like a squirrel taking food from a suspiciously outstretched hand, all fits and starts and coiled-spring nerves.

His hand closed the final six inches in a single clumsy snatch, fumbling the knife and nearly dropping it in his crouching retreat. Marcus watched the whole thing with amusement.

"Very good. Now, *Jefe,* show me how a conqueror fights."

It wasn't a fight, really. Marcus slid into range with his knife at his side, making no effort to strike. Thorin tried a top-heavy swing that nearly pulled him off his feet. Marcus side-stepped it easily. His ever-thrumming street fighter's brain noted half a dozen motions that could have killed Thorin outright, and another dozen that would have crippled him. He acted on none of them, preferring to observe to clumsy puppetry of Thorin's attacks.

The *Jefe* wielded his weapon as if it were the leash of a large and poorly-trained dog. It scented blood and darted, dragging Thorin two steps behind. Marcus watched the spectacle with a mixture of amusement and pity. Growing bored, he reached out during one of Thorin's lunges and slashed a culvert diagonally down his wrist.

The *Jefe*'s fingers went slack, tendons severed, and the knife clattered to the floor. Thorin followed it a second later. He dropped to his knees, his ruined forearm cradled to his chest, and fell into his side, where he curled into a ball and whimpered.

Marcus's smile flattened into a thin, pinched line. The drop of pity he'd felt for this creature evaporated, and his amusement soured into contempt. He thought of Emilio at the moment when his hand had been lopped off, that look of almost child-like disbelief and hurt. Of the relentless infections that slow-cooked him in the days that followed. Of that final moment in the abattoir before he died by Marcus's blade, his eyes brimming with neither hate nor sorrow, but simple understanding.

These thoughts and a thousand more broke free of the vault where he'd stored them. They entered his knife hand and guided it to Thorin's back, where they split his jacket at the seam and flayed a strip of skin from hip to shoulder. Blood bubbled in the newly exposed tissue, less a spurt than a slow seeping of groundwater from an aquifer. Thorin shrieked, hands flying to the debased flesh. Marcus caught them and pared the tissue from their fingers, one after another.

Thorin's screams grew louder. The sound grated on Marcus's ears. He stuck the blade in Thorin's mouth and, with a deft scooping motion, sliced through the root of his tongue. The screams grew no quieter, but took on a liquid, gurgling quality.

At that moment, Marcus saw himself as he looked from outside: a mad beast with a foam-flecked snout laughing as he mutilated his prey. It was an act of debasement so grotesque it scarred the subject and object alike—an onanist molesting his own dark reflection. He staggered back, repulsed. Thorin writhed on the concrete, mewling nonsense with a half-severed tongue. He was a spider with seven legs torn off, a broken thing clinging pointlessly to life. Marcus stabbed him in the chest once, twice, a dozen times. He lunged without elegance, thoughtlessly, with a clumsiness he hadn't known since infancy.

When he'd finished, he knelt by the body and wept.

44: Gracias

Selena hadn't realized how deep the alleys of Juarez went. She and Mary had used them as shortcuts in the past, and these journeys had shown her the alleys were big—big enough to count as streets in their own right, replete with enough beggars, vendors, and pedestrians to rival all but the largest *calles*. But it wasn't until Krell dragged her into his lair that she began to understand the true scope of their byzantine depths. The alleys weren't a mere supplement to the city's outer roads, auxiliary channels catching *Calle de Jefes*'s spillover when the flow was high. They were a parallel urban ecosystem, with their own flora, fauna, and food chain.

And their apex predator had Selena by the wrist, and he wasn't about to let her go.

The alleys twined and bent and bulged and narrowed, tracing a route that seemed to double back on itself endlessly yet never cross its own path. Gradually the ground sloped downward, and the slice of sky overhead thinned into a greyish wedge. The wedge vanished, and they were underground, the cool earth carrying a smell of must and minerals.

"Why are you doing this?" Selena asked. "Thorin's probably dead by now, and even if he isn't, his reign is over. You won't get a dime for this he hasn't paid you already. So why bother?"

Selena didn't expect an answer beyond "shut up!" or a clout around the head, but asking the question gave her the chance to feign breathlessness. Krell surprised her.

"Because I am the hunter, girl," he said. "And you are my prey."

During their voyage through the labyrinth, Selena made no effort to break free of Krell's grip. She gave a few phony tugs, hapless and clumsy, playing the weak little girl that men like Krell so easily saw in her, but that was all. A serious attempt would have been pointless— even if she managed to slip his grasp and evade the dozen men behind him, where would she go? The path was so tangled, and the light so dim, she couldn't even begin to retrace her steps. There was a time to buck and a time to simply watch, and their passage through the alley had been the latter. Her energy was better spent searching for opportunities. So she played the docile captive and bided her time.

Then they reached the room, and she saw the chair, and everything changed.

The room was a crude circle hewn into the dirt and plastered with red-black clay. Its walls tapered inward at neck height, forming a dome fifteen feet high at its center, from which an electric lamp hung suspended. The sight of electricity felt anachronistic in this place—

she'd encountered little of it outside of Todd's *hacienda*—and gave her a renewed sense of Krell's power. If *Jefe* Thorin got by with corn oil lamps, how did this crevice-dwelling ghoul get electric light?

Below the lamp, floating atop the yellow island of its glow, was a large metal chair. Coal black where it wasn't flecked with rust, it had the cobbled-together look of Last War salvage. Bolts as thick as Selena's thumbs secured it to the ground. Manacles yawped atop its armrests like hungry mouths. A second set, large enough to accommodate ankles, grinned from crossbeams between the chair's front legs. Hinges connected its joints, allowing its captive to be bent into all sorts of inventive and uncomfortable shapes.

As she studied the chair, her strategy of watch and wait vanished. It had been the best play with a poor hand, but now the game had changed altogether. It was time to fight. That it was a fight she couldn't win was irrelevant. She was outnumbered, out-armed, and trapped in the nexus of a labyrinth that her opponents knew intimately, and she knew not at all. To fight back was laughable, futile.

But letting Krell put her in that chair was worse. Perhaps she'd live a bit longer if she did, but it wouldn't be good living. Nothing pleasant happened in a chair like that. Whatever happened in its confines would be horrible, and she could do nothing about it but beg for mercy.

And Selena was not one for begging.

If she was going to die today, then she could at least make sure she died on her feet.

Her arm snapped free of Krell's grip. The ragdoll weakness she'd played at earlier was gone; she struck like coiled steel and Krell's fingers, expecting no more than a bit of wriggling, parted easily. She chambered a kick and rocketed her foot into Krell's knee. The blow knocked him down, but fat and muscle sheathed the bone, and the blow lacked the brittle crack of a shattered patella or dislocated fibula—something to put him out of action early. She brought her heel down on his tailbone and vaulted over him, putting his prostrate body between her and the other men.

Krell's men fanned out across the room. She'd hoped they might rush her, giving her a chance to skirt the horde and make for the door, but they were too clever for that. Several planted themselves in the doorway while the rest closed in as a single constricting line. Selena backed up, scanning the room for weapons, exits, points of tactical advantage. There were none. The room was a featureless egg, smooth-walled and barren save for that hideous chair.

Her target was a slight man about her height. His face jangled with piercings beneath a frieze of pointed black hair. Threads of muscle ran along his skinny arms, but he was small enough to bowl over, and that was all Selena needed.

She charged the line, aiming for a beefy man with a spider tattooed across his face standing two bodies to the right of her real target. There was a tiny gap to his right, and she made for it, broadcasting her intentions before springing on the wiry man and driving her forehead into his nose.

Cartilage cracked. Winkles of metal lacerated her cheek, but the piercings weren't weapons, and they did more damage to his skin than hers. The wiry man toppled, and Selena leapfrogged over him. Hands grabbed for her, and she dodged them all, landing mid-sprint and dashing for the doorway. The men stationed there were bigger than the guy she'd tackled, but they also hadn't expected her to break through the cordon so quickly. She spied a gap in the lower left of the doorway and dove for it.

She almost made it.

The guards caught her around the waist and hurled her back into the room. She landed awkwardly, torquing her right ankle until it squealed and falling to one knee. The line closed in, became a circle of flesh three men deep, and pummeled her into submission. She threw punches against the onslaught, but it was like fighting the tide, and every split lip or busted nose was replaced with a fresh one before the blow had even fully landed.

The circle grabbed her with its myriad hands and dragged her toward the chair. She fought with all she had, but the current was too strong.

"*Déjala ir, Krell.*"

The words struck the crowd like a whip crack. Selena craned her neck to catch a glimpse of the doorway, where Grace Delgado stood with arms crossed. She stepped into the room. Behind her trailed a phalanx of women armed with bits of refuse—broom handle bow staves, table leg cudgels, knives pilfered from kitchens or fashioned from bits of pointy metal. They wore kerchiefs and homespun dresses and dirt-streaked dungarees. Selena recognized a few of Todd's girls, but most were older, *blanca* and *marcada* alike.

Krell stepped out of the crowd and looked the lot of them up and down. He grinned, a huge toothy fissure dividing his face into two unequal hemispheres. He said something in *Mejise*, spat, and cackled.

For a moment, the two groups held each other in stasis, a malevolent cord pulled taut between two banks of staring, somber faces. The break was short, but Selena had no intention of wasting time. She swatted free the hands that held her and dove between a pair of legs, driving her fleeing heel upward into its crotch as she went. Her action snapped whatever force had hung between the men and women, and the room collapsed into pandemonium.

Clubs swung, knives jabbed, missiles flew. Blood greased the floor and tinted the air with its bright coppery stink. Selena slugged a man in the jaw, drove her elbow into another's belly, and ducked a haymaker thrown by a third. A fourth managed to sock her in the shoulder. It was a hard blow and spun her around. She salvaged the momentum into a right hook that knocked him flat.

The urge to reach the door and safety burned away, swallowed by a roiling tide of molten fury. Blood pounded in her ears at a jungle drum tempo. Her fists hardened into granite, her legs became pistons of spring and steel.

A knife skated across her ribcage, carving a shallow gash that stained her shirt a vibrant red. She barely felt it. Her knuckles struck a nose, and the nose exploded, blood showering from cracks in the ruined cartilage. She stomped on the man's neck as soon as he fell, grabbed another man's ears, and drove his face into her forehead. Wet, warm fluid broke across her cheeks like summer rain. Later, its presence would repulse her, but at the moment, she was elated. A lunatic's cackle ripped through the room. Selena released it was coming from her. Knowing this made her laugh harder.

A huge pair of arms closed around her from behind. They threw her to the ground, driven by a terrible weight. She whirled onto her back and saw Krell's face hovering over her, fat and pitted as a harvest moon. His grin had broadened further, but the mocking humor in it had curdled into rage.

"You think a *marcada* bitch and some withered old *brujas* can save you?"

She kicked and writhed and hammered with her fists, but he outweighed her, and without leverage, her blows lacked heft. There were certain positions where raw meat counted more than anything else, and Krell, through instinct or guile, was a master of edging his opponents into them. His fingers crawled like slugs over her chest and up her neck.

His thumbs settled against her eyes and pushed. The pain was excruciating. She whipped her head to the left, and his thumbs slipped free. He smashed her face with the bottom of a closed fist and tried again.

The pressure resumed, intensified. It felt like an inverted mountain balanced on her corneas. She slashed out, blind and frantic, snatching for the lever that would relieve this unsupportable load. Her hands found something sharp, closed on it, and thrust upward.

A jet of hot blood splashed across her chest. The thumbs fell away, allowing her to see Krell, his look of triumph drifting into confusion. Her fetish medallion erupted from his neck, barbed shells sinking into wattled flesh. He clawed at the object, trying to pull it from his skin. Before he could manage it, Selena rammed the heel of her fist against the amulet.

"When you see *Santa Meurte,* tell her I say thanks."

The fetish had sharp points at every angle, and its barbs sank nasty divots into her palm before the bone stopped their progress. Facing no such impediment at its other end, it burrowed into Krell's neck like an enormous and ravenous chigger. He opened his mouth, but no sound came out. Bloody spittle stretched over his lips in a fine membrane. It swelled with his final exhaled breath and burst.

His body collapsed over her, enveloping her in momentary darkness. She wriggled her upper body free in time to see Grace and the other women forming a protective circle around her. The men, rudderless at the loss of their leader, pulled back, unleashing invective in *Mejise* as they fled.

The women bent down and rolled Krell's body off Selena. Grace extended a hand and Selena took it. She stood and looked at each woman in turn. They looked back at her, faces smooth with wonder— at her, at what they'd done, at the changes convulsing the city above them. Selena saw it all and had no idea how to respond. She lacked the words even in her own language, which she assumed none of these women spoke. There was only one thing she could think to say.

"*Gracias.*"

45: Someone Else's Turn

The *haciendas* had escaped the worst of the fighting, but it was still clear by looking at them that something had changed. The fields, normally buzzing with the labor of *blancos* and *marcados* alike, stood empty. Implements of farming lay strewn about the pastures over which sheep and cattle wandered, oblivious to their newfound lack of oversight.

Nearer the houses, the porches where guardsmen held watch were also mostly vacant. A few embattled figures stayed on, crouched behind makeshift parapets with weapons clung to their chests, but they were a minority. And at Mr. Todd's *hacienda*, there were no guards left at all.

"It's a damn ghost town out here," said Mary.

She rested her hand on the bandage wrapped around her stomach. Her fingers skirted the spot where the wound lay beneath several layers of gauze without actually touching it. It was an unconscious gesture she'd picked up in her recovery, a flirtation between fascination and pain.

"You face one lousy uprising, and all your indentured servants go and quit on you. How's that for gratitude?"

"Shameful," Selena agreed. In truth, she was a little surprised. Juarezians weren't unacquainted with political instability—they'd weathered a shift from a triumvirate pseudo-democracy to a dictatorship not long ago. Surely, they must have had plans to combat unrest of some kind.

"I guess when your boss's ex-slave becomes heir apparent to the entire government, you start to think about earning your pay elsewhere."

"I thought 'slave' was an offensive term."

Mary shrugged. "Yeah, well, times change. And we *were* slaves, if you get right down to it."

"True. We were."

They climbed onto the porch, which sagged slightly under the weight of their party. Todd's girls were all accounted for, along with two dozen Delgado men loyal to Grace. Their presence seemed prudent in the fading anarchy of Juarez proper, but out here it felt a bit ridiculous. Selena had expected some token resistance at least, but it seemed they could walk into Mr. Todd's manor without facing any opposition at all.

This, she soon learned, was only partially true, for there remained one guard too loyal—*or too stupid,* Selena mused—to desert in times of trouble, and he faced her in the hallway with rifle in hand.

"Hi, Trejo," Selena said.

Mr. Todd's enforcer looked even uglier than usual, his bald head rumpled with wrinkles. He snarled down the barrel, which was pointed squarely at Selena's chest. His left eye narrowed to a squint while the right one stayed wide, its dead pupil floating faintly in its sac of yellow-white fluid.

"You have a lot of nerve coming here after what you've done, girl."

"I could say the same thing about you, pal." She glanced down at the gun. "I think you're gonna need more bullets."

A voice called through the doorway to Trejo's right. "God's sake, Trejo, put the damn shooter away. This ain't the Alamo."

Trejo lowered the gun. One of Grace's men snatched it from him.

Todd sat in his usual chair, a glass in one hand and a bottle in the other. He filled the glass with amber liquid and set the bottle down on the floor next to him. Motes of firelight from the hearth danced along the glass, edges jiggling as he swirled it in a practiced clockwise motion. He sipped, grimaced, swallowed.

"Have a seat."

Selena sat. "What's the Alamo?"

"A bit of ancient history. One I don't intend to be repeating." He took another sip from his glass. "Funny to see you in the hot seat. I thought Miss Delgado was our new *Jefe*. You her ambassador or some such?"

"She prefers *Alcalde,* actually, but no. I'm just here to ask a favor." She unfolded a strip of parchment, over which scrawled several sentences of ornately-lettered *Mejise*. "This is a writ surrendering your hold on me and rendering my brand invalid. I'd like you to sign it."

Todd raised an eyebrow. "That's some favor. You cost me an awful lot of *pesos*. I'm supposed to just give up property I bought and paid for?"

"Your property's gone either way. The *marcado* trade is done. This is just for the outlying wranglers while the word is still spreading."

"And you think a piece of paper's gonna convince a *cazadore* to give up his livelihood?"

"The smart ones, yes. It'll prove I'm not worth the trouble. As for the others, I've got other tools to persuade them." She drew a knife from her belt.

"Well, well, abolition, easy as that huh?" Mr. Todd signed the paper and handed it back to Selena. "Welcome to freedom, kid. But I'd wait a spell before pinnin' any medals to your chest about it. It's easy to tear something down, you don't like it. Puttin' up something in its place is another matter. You ever think about how all these ex-*marcados* are gonna feed themselves? What'll they do for work? Where are they gonna live? A lotta people are gonna be hurtin' before long."

"A lot of people are hurting already, Todd. And they've been hurting a long time. Maybe it's someone else's turn."

Selena stood. The knife in her hand glinted in the firelight. For the first time, Todd's mask of sardonic composure slipped. His tongue circled his lips.

"C'mon now, be reasonable, girl. I signed your paper. I never touched you wrong or pulled anything untoward. Think of where you coulda ended up if I didn't step in. Compared to that, I was pretty damn good to you all."

"You could've been better," Selena said, and brought the knife down. It sank into the headrest half an inch from Mr. Todd's right ear. "But you could've been worse, too."

She straightened up, folded the paper in half, and tucked it away. "I've got my writ, so you and I are square. But that's just me. The rest of these women have their own minds to make up about you. Better limber your wrist up some. I suspect you're gonna be signing a lot of paper."

46: The Sisters of the Iron Circle

Simon and Emily gathered stones from a nearby arroyo.

The ground was rocky, and hunks of stone weren't hard to come by. Some peeked through the hardpan and had to be dug out by hand. Others lay strewn atop the dirt, abandoned by the vanished waters that had sculpted them to egg-like smoothness. Occasionally, one of them would spot a particularly good stone and point it out to the other, but for the most part, they worked in silence.

They set the stones around Otis's body, forming an outline at first and working inward. Soon he was encased in a sarcophagus of red-grey rock, his face the only part of him still visible. Emily knelt next to his head, licked the ball of her thumb, and scrubbed a bit of dirt from a crease next to his eye. She whispered something in his ear, stood, and laid the final rock in place. As she did, a dusting of snow fell from the haze-grey sky. It settled on the cairn like a thousand petals from some tiny forgotten flower.

"Simon!"

Simon whirled. He saw Selena in the distance, limping slightly but unquestionably alive. A dark-skinned woman walked beside her, a hand pressed to her belly.

Simon's heart battered his ribs like an animal in a cage. Building the cairn had distracted him from the looming question of Selena's whereabouts, allowing him to avoid, at least partially, his growing assumption that she was gone. Now she was here, running toward him in a stiff-legged stride, and the assumption simultaneously emerged and dissolved. It was a disorienting sensation, a push-pull of impulses and emotions, and it rendered him paralyzed. He could only stand there, mouth flapping, as she closed the final distance between them.

First, she hugged him. It was a big hug, and it lasted a long time. When she finished, she took him by the shoulders.

"Do you still have it?"

The question triggered something inside him, allowing him control of his body again. Nodding, he took out the data stick and handed it to Selena, who studied it a moment before putting it in her pocket. He didn't ask if she wanted it and she didn't ask if she could have it.

She looked from the cairn to Emily. "Shit. What happened?"

Simon told the story while Emily stood over the cairn. He tiptoed around her running off and making him and Otis give chase, but otherwise gave a full account. Selena filled him in on her side, blushing at the look of naked sympathy with which he regarded her tattoo. He touched it as if inspecting the sight of a particularly nasty infection.

"Does it hurt?"

"No. It itches sometimes, but that's it."

She approached Emily and put a hand on the younger girl's shoulder. "I'm sorry about your dad."

Emily nodded in recognition, though her eyes remained fixed on the stone covering her father's face.

"We're heading west soon. I've got a couple things to sort out in town first, but it shouldn't be long."

"You're going back in there?" Simon asked. "Is that really a good idea?"

"Things have calmed down. Once Thorin's men found out he was dead, their whole side just sort of collapsed. He didn't have a successor, and no one wanted to be the last man standing in a headless army." She turned back to Emily. "You should come with us. I can't say it'll be easy or safe, but it's the best I have to offer."

Emily looked up, wiped her eyes. "That's what he wanted."

"Well, at least I can give him that much. What about you. Mary? Had enough of Juarez?"

"It ain't the land of milk and honey, but I think I'll stay all the same. This is home, good or bad." Her eyes flicked to the side. "Grace invited all of Todd's girls into the fold. Looks like I'm a made woman."

Selena smirked. "You're telling me you can really live under the reign of a *marcada*?"

"*Marcadas* are a thing of the past, girl. You know that."

"I guess you'll need something else to show you're an *Hombre.*"

Mary rolled her eyes "You really are out of touch, northy. *Los Hombres Sencillos* are as dead as Thorin. New name for a new era."

"Oh? So what are you?"

"Can't you guess? We're *Las Hermanas del Círculo de Hierro.* The Sisters of the Iron Circle."

47: A Promise

As he held his mother's hand, Marcus couldn't tell which one of them was trembling. The tremors were slight but constant, a subcutaneous roiling of nerves at the end of their endurance. He raised his other arm and watched for movement. There was none. He exhaled a sibilant stream of relief, though guilt soured his next breath. *It's always about you, isn't it, Marcito?* Chided a voice.

No, his own voice replied. *Too often, perhaps. But not always.*

Sighing, he stroked his mother's hand. Her fingers squeezed— an almost imperceptible gesture, but it sparked elation somewhere inside him. A short sensation, birthing no flame, but welcome.

"I've done more evil work, *madre*," he said, his voice now firmly settled into the comfortable rhythms of *Mejise*. "But it was for a good purpose. I believe I've made you safer, and that counts for much. *La Santa* will hold me to account, and I think she'll judge me kindly."

He heard footsteps but didn't bother to look in their direction.

There was no need; he knew who was coming.

"How is she?" Selena asked.

"Much the same. And you?"

"Better. Sorry for messing up your hometown."

Marcus smiled. "Nothing it did not deserve. But perhaps California should fear your coming, yes? It seems wherever you go, revolution tends to follow."

"It runs in the family." Selena studied her shoes. She toed a bit of grout that had come loose from the tile floor, batting it back and forth before it went astray and skittered under the bed. "Look, I know this is shitty of me, but winter's almost here, and I'd hoped to reach the Republic weeks ago …"

Marcus raised a hand in a soothing gesture. "Peace, 'Lena. I remember my promise. The Grey Sisters have done more for my mother than I ever could, and they will do so as long as needed. With my debt absolved, I have paid them better than I could ever have hoped, and I trust the money will find its way into my mother's care. There is nothing left for me here. I am simply saying goodbye."

"Right. I'll be outside." She began leaving, paused, turned. "I'm sorry. About your mom. And your cousin. And just, everything."

"And I, 'Lena, More than you can imagine."

"I don't know about that. But thanks."

Alone in their tiny corner of the room, Marcus kissed his mother's forehead. He set her hand on her chest, patted it, and let it go. "I must go again, *madre*. I made a promise, and it is taking me farther than those I made before. I may never return. But if I do, it will be as a better man." He closed his eyes.

"This I promise," he added. Whether it was a promise to his mother, or himself, or someone else altogether, Marcus didn't say. In the end, he supposed it didn't really matter.

As long as he kept it.

Acknowledgements

The road to publication for *Iron Circle* was much shorter than it was for *Yellow Locust*, but I still had a whole lot of help along the way.

Thanks first of all to the Month 9 Books team for their support throughout the publication process: Georgia McBride, Tara Creel, Emily Midkiff, Jennifer Million, Christine Hogge, and everyone else who helped out behind the scenes.

To the folks at the Ottawa Public Library, who ensure that great local books (I hope mine counts!) get onto their shelves and into the hands of readers: Christine Chevalier and Jessica Halsall.

To Alec Shane, my agent and foremost editor, who always sees the forest for the trees—and the best path to the clearing on the other side.

To my friends and family, who support me in ways too numerous to list here.

Most of all, to Chantal, my wife and partner of 17 years, and my three children, two of whom currently have names: Lavender and Hannela. Baby 3, whoever you are: I dedicate this book to you.

Justin Joschko

Justin Joschko is an author from Niagara Falls, Ontario. His writing has appeared in newspapers and literary journals across Canada. His first novel, *Yellow Locust*, was published by Month9Books in 2018. He currently lives in Ottawa with his wife and three children.

OTHER MONTH9BOOKS TITLES YOU MIGHT LIKE

YELLOW LOCUST

Find more books like this at http://www.Month9Books.com

Connect with Month9Books online:
Facebook: www.Facebook.com/Month9Books
Instagram: https://instagram.com/month9books
Twitter: https://twitter.com/Month9Books
Tumblr: http://month9books.tumblr.com/
YouTube: www.youtube.com/user/Month9Books
Georgia McBride Media Group: www.georgiamcbride.com

Neither quick fists nor nimble feet can save Selena Flood, a fighter of preternatural talent, from the forces of New Canaan, the most ruthless and powerful of the despotic kingdoms around.

YELLOW LOCUST

JUSTIN JOSCHKO